ALL OF ME

Visit us at www.boldstrokesbooks.com

By the Author

Searching for Forever

Same Time Next Week

After the Fire

All of Me

ALL OF ME

by

Emily Smith

2018

ALL OF ME

ISBN 13: 978-1-63555-321-5

This Trade Paperback Original Is Published By
Bold Strokes Books, Inc.
P.O. Box 249
Valley Falls, NY 12185

First Edition: November 2018

CREDITS

EDITOR: SHELLEY THRASHER
PRODUCTION DESIGN: SUSAN RAMUNDO
COVER DESIGN BY TAMMY SEIDICK

Dedication

To those who tried their best to teach me.
Mr. Clark, for always cutting out my first paragraph
immediately. Professor Schofield, for encouraging me
to never be afraid to tell my story. And to all the
strong, smart, queer women writers who came
before me and paved the way.

PROLOGUE

"Oh good, you're still here." Teddy Thompkins, the second-year surgical resident at Boston City Hospital, barreled through the door of the doctors' lounge and into the open chair next to Dr. Galen Burgess.

"Where else would I be?" Galen didn't look up from her computer screen. It was already seven thirty pm, and she had at least another couple of hours' worth of notes to catch up on before she even thought about going home. She paid little mind when the door opened again, even when a chorus of voices sang from behind her. The residents' lounge was like a turnstile for young doctors in any and all state of mind and body. Singing was hardly unusual.

"For she's a jolly good fellow..." Galen finally spun her chair around to see what the ruckus was all about, only to find three of the other residents on her team standing expectantly in front of her holding a mammoth cake with even bigger smiles on their faces.

"Congratulations, Chief," Teddy gushed, filling in the silence left by the decrescendo of their off-key melody.

Congratulations? For the life of her, Galen couldn't come up with anything she or her friends had to celebrate.

"What are you jerks all worked up about now?" she asked.

"You haven't heard yet?" Carly, the sweet, mousy Intern with the world's curliest hair, asked.

"Heard what?"

"Of course she hasn't," Teddy said. "Too busy saving lives all day."

"You're such an ass-kisser." Carly stuck out her tongue at him.

"I really have no idea what you guys are talking about. I was in a whipple all day with Mueler and just finished an add-on lap chole that wasn't supposed to go to the OR until tomorrow. Now, if someone wouldn't mind filling me in..."

"You're chief resident!" Teddy nearly exploded, seemingly eager to be the first to share the news with his best friend of the last couple of years.

Chief resident? The words sounded jumbled and foreign, and Galen struggled to make sense of them with a mind surviving on two hours of sleep and too busy sorting out antibiotic choices for an abdominal abscess on the floor upstairs.

"I am?" she whispered.

"Have you practiced sounding surprised?" Carly was teasing her.

"I forgot they were announcing it today..."

"Come on, cut your cake. We spent a lot of money on this thing," Teddy said. "And then, we're going out for drinks. Lots and lots of drinks."

Galen smiled, just a little at first, and then more and more until her grin felt like it might actually take over her entire face. "Anyone have a knife?"

The group looked at each other blankly and then began patting down the pockets of their white coats.

"A whole room full of surgeons, and not a single one has a knife?" Galen couldn't resist badgering them.

"Here! I've got a ten-blade!" Teddy pulled a scalpel out of his locker.

"Good enough." They laughed as Galen tried to slice the cake with the same precision she used in the OR and dropped the ragged pieces onto a brown paper towel. "And you all better keep your traps shut about these cuts."

Once they'd finished licking the frosting from their fingers, Galen kicked her feet up on the table and folded her arms behind her head. "That was great. Thanks, guys." She smiled at them. "Now all of you get out of here so I can finish my notes. Go home. It's eight thirty."

Teddy got up first, and the others followed. "Hey, you're the chief."

Chief, Galen thought as she looked around the now-empty lounge. I could get used to that.

Chapter One

Nine Months Later

Statistics have shown that more hospital complications happen in July than in any other month. Galen never let that thought get too far away from her when that time came every year.

July 1—the day medical students suddenly become doctors. There's no good way to transition what are usually essentially children from a position of observer to caretaker, decision maker...lifesaver. But that's what Galen would be there for. The chief resident is expected to guide the fledgling physicians into the world of medicine with as few casualties as possible. She only hoped she would be up to the task.

"Can you smell that?" Teddy said, pushing his mound of home fries and bacon to the register of the hospital cafeteria.

Galen took a small sip from the steaming cup of coffee in her hand, not caring that it was hot enough to scald the inside of her mouth. She'd been on call all last night and hadn't dozed off for more than five minutes before the trauma pager went off. A little soft-tissue burn might wake her up some. "What? Your impending heart attack?"

"No. That." Teddy turned his nose up to the air and sniffed dramatically. "Fresh blood. New interns."

"Is it July already?" Galen tried her best to sound nonchalant as she handed the cashier a five and walked off with Teddy trailing behind.

"Oh, don't pretend you've forgotten. This is the biggest day of your chiefdom. The time for you to flex your muscles."

"Thanks, Ted. I was doing a good job not worrying about it too." Galen hit the button for the elevator, too fatigued to imagine her legs carrying her up the four flights of stairs to the lounge. She loved her job, but it had been a long night with hours spent in the OR trying to repair the lacerated liver of a thirty-year-old woman who'd been hit by a drunk driver on the way home from an AA meeting.

The elevator doors glided open onto the fifth floor, where a strikingly tall man with silver hair and a stern brow stood waiting.

"Good morning, Dr. Burgess," Galen said coldly. From the first days of her Internship, her father had insisted she call him Dr. Burgess at the hospital. Not that she minded. Henry Burgess was more of an attending to her than he was a parent, anyway. The brief eye contact flooded her with awkwardness, and she quickly snagged her pager off her scrub pants. "I'm sorry. I have to take care of this."

"Of course. See you in the operating room. And don't forget, it's July first." As if summoned from the bowels of the hospital, the elevator swung back and opened its doors for her father's always-grand departure.

"How long do you think that fake page trick is going to work on him?" Teddy asked once they'd started walking again.

"Oh, it doesn't work. Dr. Burg...my father is many things, but stupid is not one of them. He knows as well as I do that there's no page. But it gets us both out of having to talk to each other any longer."

"I don't know how you manage to stand across an OR table from him for hours at a time if you can't even make small talk in the hallway." Teddy shook his head.

"That's different. There's no small talk in the OR. He does his thing, and I do mine."

"And what happens when you screw up and he has to tell you what to do? He is your attending, after all."

"That's easy," Galen said, pushing open the door to the lounge. "I never screw up."

❖

Galen loved everything about being in the OR. She loved the smell of the powder from her sterile gloves. She loved the constant blips from the monitors that meant her patient was doing well under her knife. She loved the pace her pulse increased to when she made that first incision. Even operating with her father couldn't taint that sensation. In fact, operating was about the only time she liked her father.

"Jen, I'll take a number-eleven blade, please." Galen let her gaze linger on the petite scrub nurse at the foot of the OR bed just long enough to bring out the crimson around her brow. They were covered with surgical masks and caps, but Galen didn't need more than her eyes to flirt.

"Eleven blade, Dr. Burgess." Jen handed the scalpel to her and glanced at the floor coyly.

Galen's father cleared his throat. "Are you quite ready to start, then?"

"Yes, sir." Henry Burgess was more than likely very aware of Galen's flings. Everyone at Boston City was.

Galen didn't have to go far to find women. Plenty right there in the hospital were interested in getting to know her better. Jen had been the nurse on a handful of her cases when she asked Galen to get a drink across the street at the bar inside the Hilton one night. She hadn't made it halfway through her first glass of rosé before whisking Galen upstairs to a room for the rest of the evening. Nights on call can be long, and if the pager remains quiet, there isn't always a lot to pass the time. Galen never had a hard time finding company, whether it be Jen or someone else. She wasn't after more than that, and everyone knew it.

"Have you met the interns yet?" Galen's father never expressed much in the way of emotion. Unless, of course, that emotion was disappointment. He was an expert at disappointment, his favorite target for which, of course, was his daughter.

"Not yet." Galen didn't look up from the monitors in front of her as she watched her laparoscopic instruments maneuver gracefully through her patient's abdominal cavity.

"And why not? As chief resident, it's your job now." For just a micro-second, Galen glanced over to meet her father's cold glare. *Damn it.* She corrected herself quickly, but it was already too late. "Dr. Burgess. What is the first rule of laparoscopy?"

"I'm sorry, sir." Galen kicked herself under the operating table.

"That's not what I asked. What is the first rule, Dr. Burgess?"

"The first rule," she said, careful not to so much as blink, "is don't ever take your eyes off the monitors."

"Correct. And what did I just see you do?"

"I took my eyes off the monitors." Galen knew arguing with her father was like sparking nuclear war. You simply weren't going to win.

"You're a fifth-year now, Doctor. Chief resident. You should be setting an example as a surgeon, and as a leader. I expect better from you."

"Yes, sir."

They completed the rest of the procedure in near silence. *So much for never screwing up.*

Rowan Duncan had been waiting for this day as long as she could remember. Or, at least since March 15. Match Day—the day that fourth-year medical students across the country learn where they'll spend the next three to seven years of their lives. She was a solid student who managed to graduate toward the top third of her class, but residencies are competitive. Especially surgical residencies. And Rowan wanted nothing more than to be a surgeon.

She walked down the seemingly endless hallways of Boston City Hospital like an Amish tourist in downtown Manhattan, still in disbelief that she was actually a doctor, never mind a doctor at one of the best hospitals in the country. The novelty was wearing off quickly, though, as she glanced at her watch and realized she would be late if she didn't figure out where the hell she was going. She had to ask someone.

"Excuse me?" The next person to cross her path was a tall, young doctor with stern eyes and short, golden-blond hair poking out from underneath her scrub cap.

"Yeah?"

"I'm looking for the North Elevators. Can you just..."

The woman's face softened a little, and she pointed to a sign directly above their heads.

"North Elevators...Right..." Rowan's face burned. "Of course they're right there..."

Without a word, the woman smiled and continued down the hall, and Rowan followed the signs to the elevator bank only a few short steps away.

❖

"Don't you have a meeting to be at, Chief?"

Galen was trying to catch up on her morning's worth of charting when Teddy found her in her new office. "Not until two pm."

"It is two pm."

Galen glanced at the clock on the wall, one of the few decorations she had up so far, and leapt to her feet. "Shit. Thanks, Teddy."

Her first day with the fledglings and she couldn't even be at her own meeting on time. No. She could work with this. Attendings are always late. In fact, no one important was ever on time for anything. Galen could just tell them she was in surgery... an emergency surgery. As she raced down the hall, she thought of the coolest possible procedures she could—a ruptured aortic aneurysm? No, how about a massive spleen laceration from a car wreck? Hell, why not make it a multi-systems trauma? The interns won't know the truth…

"Dr. Burgess." The interns wouldn't know. But her father would. Why was it such a surprise to her that the man who so badly wanted to see her fail would be there, watching, scrutinizing her every move? "You're late."

"I'm sorry, everyone. I was…" The shoebox conference room was wall-to-wall with white-coat-donning, doe-eyed new doctors, but she could only stare at the heartless battle-axe who'd helped create her. "Charting. Paperwork sucks. Get used to it now. Which brings me to my first point." She shifted her gaze away from her father and back to the room. "Surgery is not sexy. It's consults, and turfing, and long, grueling hours on your feet. This is not *Grey's Anatomy*. You want sexy, go to plastics. You want to work? You're in the right place."

She scanned the faces in the crowd, soaking in the look of horror and possible regret that was all but a rite of passage to a new surgeon, until she stopped at one she recognized. Elevator Girl… She was cute, with that long, straight brown hair and those smart little glasses. She perked up a little but then stopped. *No. You can't fuck the interns, Galen.* Satisfied she'd scared the shit out of her new protégés, she looked back at her father, who was staring back at her with the subtlest of approving grins. He nodded once, got up, and left the room.

"Rounds start at five thirty am. That means you better be here at four thirty to review your labs, ins and outs, events, everything. When you show up on my rounds in the morning, you better be familiar with everything about your patient. I want to know what he ate for breakfast. I want to know what his last four white counts are. I want to know what shade of yellow his pee is." A soft chuckle broke out from the back row. "That's not a joke. Know everything, or find yourself in clinic." Silence. "Any questions?" After a brief pause, all ten hands in the room shot up. Galen once again found herself drawn to the shy one with the bad sense of direction. "You. Elevator Girl."

She liked the color the girl's cheeks turned, and she found herself picturing her naked, flushed body sprawled out across her own bed. *No. Stop that, damn it.* "Rowan. Rowan Duncan. Dr. Duncan, now…I guess," the girl said.

"Do you have a question, Duncan?"

"I do, actually." Galen's belly warmed a little at Rowan's seemingly shifting confidence. "When do we get started?"

❖

"So, that's our chief." A tall, redheaded woman wearing an expensive-looking pencil skirt under her white coat had moved to Rowan's side.

"I guess so."

"She's a piece of work, huh?"

Rowan nodded but hadn't quite figured out what to think about her new boss. She certainly seemed tough, but Rowan had expected that. What chief resident wasn't tough? But there was something else about her. Something Rowan couldn't look away from. Dr. Burgess could be as mean as she wanted to be—Rowan could only hope to be half the surgeon she was someday.

"I'm Makayla, by the way." The redhead smiled at her kindly.

"Rowan. Nice to meet you."

"Nice to meet you too. I'm sorry the rest of our group is too busy ass-kissing to introduce themselves to us," Makayla said.

"Ass-kissing isn't my thing."

"Mine either." They laughed, and Rowan's anxiety deflated.

"You want to get a coffee?" Rowan asked.

"Love to."

CHAPTER TWO

The fact was, Rowan had already been told an enormous amount about her new chief resident. Maybe Galen had forgotten, or maybe she just didn't care, but it almost seemed a rite of passage for the outgoing interns to dump all the department gossip on the incoming ones. And Dr. Galen Burgess seemed to be prime gossip material. Everyone in general surgery knew she could sew better than most attendings. But they also knew she jumped into bed with half the hospital—the other half was men. That was the rumor, at least. Rowan didn't know how much truth there was to this, and really, she didn't care.

Her hometown of Euless, Texas, just outside of Arlington, wasn't so crazy about lesbians, but she wasn't like all the other conservative Southerners she knew. And that included her family. Who Galen slept with really didn't matter at all to Rowan. Besides, she was happy with Brian.

Rowan's boyfriend, Brian, still lived back in Texas. They knew that when she began applying for residencies, she'd be living in some other part of the country. Brian had a good job with a software company in Austin, and besides, Rowan figured she probably wouldn't have a lot of attention left to give him over the next six years anyway. She knew they'd probably get married eventually. She loved him, after all. He was good to her. He let her be a surgeon.

"What's the deal with Dr. Burgess anyway?" Makayla blew the steam from the top of her coffee as they walked back up the stairs to the residents' lounge. "Galen? Can we call her Galen? Or do we have to call her Dr. Burgess?"

"What do you mean?"

"I mean, obviously she's gay. Look at her, am I right? Don't get me wrong. I'm fine with that. If she were a guy, I'd probably be all up on that…"

For some reason, Rowan's skin crawled a little. "Yeah."

"Well, I heard she, you know, gets around. Nurses mostly. Apparently she doesn't touch other surgeons."

Rowan wanted her to stop. "I just want to see her operate. I heard she was doing whipples in her second year, almost completely unassisted."

"Is that true?" Makayla opened the door.

"It's true." A warm, unfamiliar hand landed on Rowan's shoulder, and she turned around slowly.

"Dr. Burgess…"

"Galen is fine. Really." Galen smiled softly at her, and a trace of what looked like coyness sent Rowan's stomach tumbling. "And, for the record, it was the beginning of my second year, and the attending actually left the room for half the case. If you're going to talk about me, at least get the facts straight." She smiled again and gently patted Rowan on the back, breezing past them into the lounge.

Rowan might have been mortified, but Makayla could hardly contain her giddiness. "Was it just me, or was she flirting with you?"

"What? That's ridiculous."

"I'm pretty sure she was. You aren't—"

"No!" Rowan snapped at her. "I mean, no. I'm straight. I have a boyfriend back home. We're probably going to get engaged soon."

Makayla shrugged. "Well, either way, I'd use this to your advantage, Duncan. Think about all the surgeries you could get in on."

Was Makayla seriously suggesting that Rowan flirt with her to scrub in on cases? She'd heard of surgeons going to some low places to operate, but pretending she was a lesbian? Jesus. She had a conscience. "I'm good, thanks. I'll just get in the old-fashioned way. You know, hard work?"

"Yeah…good luck with that." Makayla crossed the room and sat on the sofa, immediately chatting up one of the tall, handsome third-years they'd seen earlier, leaving Rowan alone.

"Duncan." Galen suddenly hailed her from one of the nearby computers. "Come get your OR schedule."

"Here?"

"No. I have to print it in my office. It's just around the corner."

Rowan swallowed hard and followed her out the door and down the hall. Her chief made her nervous. Of course she did. She was the chief. Instilling anxiety was in her job description. The problem was, no one made Rowan nervous. At least not in the way that caused her to constantly wipe her palms against her scrub pants.

❖

"Shut the door."

Rowan's heart seemed to be pushing its way out of her sternum, beating so hard it was almost painful, but Galen seemed to remain as cool and confident as ever.

"Sure, Dr. Burgess."

"Seriously. Galen. My father is Dr. Burgess." As Rowan laughed nervously, Galen took a seat in the expensive-looking leather office chair she'd probably had shipped from Italy. "No, but really. My father. Dr. Henry Burgess? He's the chief of surgery here."

Stupid. Rowan silently scolded herself for forgetting such a crucial piece of the hospital hierarchy. Of course she knew that Galen's father was the department head. Henry Burgess was a legend at Boston City.

"Right. I thought you were being…Never mind…"

"Sit." Galen's commands were sharp and free of suggestion, but somehow, Rowan found them more than a little endearing. Her face warmed a bit more as she remembered Makayla's earlier accusations. Galen was not flirting with her. Wait. Was she? Even if she was, Rowan reminded herself…Brian.

"Doctor…Galen." She swallowed hard, strangely uncomfortable with the informality of the encounter. "Before we start, I just wanted to tell you how incredibly embarrassed I am about earlier. I promise I know my way around an abdominal cavity much better than I know my way around the halls of this place." She quietly commended herself on such a witty rationalization.

Galen smiled. It was a slow, kind smile laced with promises of all sorts of things Rowan didn't understand, framed by her big, bedroom eyes. "I've been reading up on you, Duncan." Rowan's heart once again exploded into a tiny firestorm that pulsed all the way down to her feet.

"You have?"

"I have." Galen angled her chair slightly and hitched her ankles together. "Top of your class at UT Austin. Made quite a name for yourself at Dartmouth too. Hatcher-Johnson Fellow in your second year of med school. Even published three times in the *New England Journal of Medicine* student section."

Rowan's ears suddenly burned. "Four times, actually. It was four." As soon as she heard the words leave her mouth, she immediately wanted to take them back. Fantastic. Her first real meeting with the chief, and she was not only bragging but correcting her.

For a long time, Galen sat in silence, her eyes narrowed and fierce, looking Rowan over until sweat built around the waist of her scrubs. And then, that same enchanting smile peeked through, and Rowan didn't know whether to be relieved or afraid. For a paralyzing moment, time had stopped, and she was overwhelmed with the inexplicable urge to stand up from her chair, walk over to Galen, and straddle her lap, burying her face in her neck and letting Galen's hands drift up her scrub top. The burning in her ears spread over the top of her head and down her neck, and she prayed she wasn't actually speaking these thoughts out loud. What was wrong with her? *God, maybe I am a lesbian?* She laughed internally at the thought, dismissing it as her composure quickly returned.

"Huh. I like that confidence, Duncan. I hope you turn out to be as good with your hands as you are with your head."

Galen smirked again, and this time, Rowan had no doubt in her mind she was being catcalled. It was flattering, she had to admit. And she couldn't help but notice the dampness that had grown between her legs.

❖

"So? How'd it go?" Makayla was waiting around the corner from Galen's office when Rowan left.

"Fine. It was fine." Her breathing was just a little too labored for her not to notice that something inside her was off.

"Why are you all flushed, anyway?" Before Rowan had to answer her, Makayla grabbed the piece of paper out of her hand. "Let's have a look here, shall we?" She ran a long finger down the page and squinted hard. "Lap chole, Burgess. Lap chole, Burgess. Ventral hernia, McIntire. Overnight call…Burgess." Makayla grinned uncontrollably as she looked up from the schedule.

"What?"

"What? Come on now, Rowan. You're a Dartmouth girl. An intern scrubbing in on so many of the chief's cases? Be smart."

"I don't know what you mean." There couldn't be even an ounce of truth to Makayla's theory. Galen Burgess was a surgeon—a professional. No way would she manipulate the schedule so she could flirt with an intern. And a straight intern at that. Please!

"Here. Take a look at mine." Makayla handed her a carefully folded sheet of computer paper with tiny, pristine handwriting in the margins.

"Umbilical hernia, McIntire. Lap chole, Conway. Lap chole, Patel. Ventral hernia, Burgess. Overnight call, Phillips…" Rowan continued to scan the page for signs of Galen's name anywhere, as Makayla waited with a knowing twist to her brow.

"See? I think I'm with Burgess, what, three times all month? She has you with her three times this week alone."

"I just can't believe she would fix our schedules so she could…"

"Hit on you?" Makayla chuckled wryly. "I told you she likes you. And you've heard the rumors about her as much as I have. She's a playboy. Surgery is the only thing she likes more than women, and if she can have them both? Well, you get it."

Rowan grabbed her schedule back from Makayla's tight grip. "You're wrong."

She'd been in her residency for only six hours, and already she was making waves. Makayla was a gossip. That was becoming clear quickly. But there was something about her that Rowan liked anyway. Back in Texas, she didn't have many friends left. The area she came from didn't exactly tend to breed overachievers like herself.

Most of the people she'd gone to high school with were living at home, working blue-collar jobs and having babies. Nothing was wrong with that, she told herself. But it just wasn't her. She'd met a few girls in Dartmouth she'd become close with, but they were all in their own residencies now, scattered across the country. None of them had much time for anything else. Really, Brian was all she had.

But Makayla seemed to have her heart in the right place, even if her mouth was a little loose at times. And Rowan got the distinct sense that Makayla was genuinely looking out for her.

Rowan sat in the on-call lounge for the next several hours. All the other interns had gone home for the day, knowing they'd be starting at four am the next morning and basically every other morning after that for the next five years. But Rowan stayed, pretending to be practicing her one-handed knot ties while quietly deciding whether she should confront Galen.

"Oh, sorry. I didn't know anyone else was in here." Rowan turned, startled to see a good-looking man with a mop of wavy brown hair and a surgical mask hanging from his neck.

"No problem. Please, come in."

The man, who really still looked like more of a boy, smiled kindly and moved to open his locker. "I'm Teddy, by the way. I'm a second-year."

"Rowan Duncan. I'm—"

"An intern?" He took out a sandwich and began aggressively shoving it into his mouth.

"How did you guess? Do I smell or something?"

Teddy laughed. "It's a small program. Everyone knows everyone here. I just haven't seen you around." He finished the last piece of his sandwich faster than Rowan had ever seen anyone eat and took a seat on the couch next to her. "So where are you from, Duncan?"

"Texas." She liked Teddy instantly. Something about him was warm and easy—a stark contrast from most of the others she'd met at Boston City so far.

"Really? Whereabouts?"

"Arlington. Just outside. An even smaller town called Euless. I know, I know. It's Conservativeville, USA." She rolled her eyes, always feeling the need to defend her hometown to everyone in the Northeast.

"I was going to say you don't have an accent." Teddy laughed again, and Rowan was more comfortable than she'd been since she woke up that morning.

"No. No, I don't. Not everyone from Texas sounds like an episode of *Howdy Doody*, you know."

"That's too bad, really. I was hoping I'd get to see you lasso someone in the OR soon."

"I didn't say I don't know how to work a rope." She grinned at him. "Listen, Teddy. You said everyone here knows each other pretty well, right?"

"Too well, actually."

"I know this may be way out of line, since I'm the new kid, and if it is, just stuff some gauze in my mouth or something…

"Ask me whatever you want. Off the record. Besides, I was the new kid all of five minutes ago. I get it."

"The chief…You know her well, too?" Rowan felt her heart rate take off for the millionth time that day. Jesus, if this kept up she'd need to take a beta blocker or something.

"Galen? She's my best friend around these parts. And I'm pretty sure I'm hers. Or, maybe not her *best* friend, but like, definitely a really good friend and…Well, anyway, that's beside the point. What's your question?"

"There's a lot of talk about her. You know, people say that she…They say she has a…" Rowan selected her words carefully. "A history with a lot of people here. Sexually…" So much for careful.

This time Teddy's laugh was booming and sounded almost uncontrollable. "You mean does Galen sleep around?"

"More or less, yes. That's what I'm asking." The room was suddenly hotter than a Texas summer.

"Let me put it this way. The only thing Galen loves almost as much as surgery is women. And if she can combine the two? Well…You get it."

Rowan was nearly certain Makayla had read some kind of secret residency handbook she had yet to see. Maybe she was right about Galen after all.

"Thanks. Well, I've got to get going. It was nice to meet you, Teddy." She jumped up from the couch abruptly, grabbed her bag, and headed for the door.

"Hey, wait. Why do you ask? Are you interested?"

She kept her back to him, terrified her face would give her away. "In Galen? No. I have a boyfriend. I'm straight."

"I see."

For whatever reason, she'd found herself justifying her sexuality more in one day than she'd had to in her entire life.

CHAPTER THREE

B efore she could change her mind, Rowan turned the corner to Galen's office, knowing she'd likely still be working well into the night. If she was going to make it as a surgeon, it wouldn't be because some hotshot wanted to get in her pants. She figured she'd avoided this type of situation when she learned her chief was a woman. Apparently not.

The door to Galen's office was cracked, and Rowan knocked assertively, trying to stop the shaking in her knees.

"Come in." Galen was facedown in a pile of paper charts, cup of coffee in one hand, the other thoughtfully twirling a rogue piece of hair. For a frightening moment, Rowan's mind shut down, and she had no idea what she was doing there.

"Galen?" After Rowan spoke, Galen looked up and smiled as the cogs in Rowan's head slowly started turning again. "Can I talk to you for a minute?"

"Of course. Come in. Do you want coffee?" She gestured to a brand-new cappuccino maker on the corner of her enormous desk. It was almost ten pm.

"No. Thank you, though. I wanted to talk to you about my schedule."

Galen frowned, and she closed the chart she'd been reading. "I see. Is something wrong with it?"

"No. Well, yes. Dr. Burgess, I've worked extremely hard in my life to get here. My family has next to no money. I waited tables through med school, and I'm in more debt than I care to even acknowledge. But I got here because I earned it." She took a deep breath, hardly able to believe she was about say this. "I don't want preferential treatment because you're…Because you want to…Because you like me."

A look of surprise that Rowan found extremely uncharacteristic of what she already knew of Galen registered on her face, and she was quiet for a long time. Galen took a lengthy sip of her coffee, opened a document on her computer, and sighed. Finally, a small smile appeared. "You think I made your schedule so I could flirt with you?"

"Well, didn't you?" Galen didn't answer. She just looked at Rowan with her eyes like the warm waters of the Pacific. "Besides, I'm straight. I have a boyfriend. Brian. He's still in Texas, but we're probably going to get married and…" She felt sillier by the second.

"Thank you. For the rest of your autobiography, I mean." Galen's smile grew. "But I didn't make your schedule."

"You didn't?" *Someone come kill me now. Please?*

"My father makes the schedules for the interns."

"Oh, my God." Rowan was sure her surgical career had just ended before it even had a chance to begin.

"Frankly, Duncan, I'm a little offended." Galen's tone was unwavering, but the small grin never left her lips.

"I'm so incredibly, unbelievably sorry, Dr. Burgess. Please. If there's any way you can forget I said anything—"

"Relax. This program is a rumor mill. And I highly doubt you came up with this insane theory all on your own."

"Thank you." Rowan realized she'd been holding her breath.

"I'm a lot of things, Duncan. I'm tough. I'm abrasive at times. And more often than not, I'm a little too much like my father, I think. I'm also gay. I don't hide that fact from anyone. But one thing I'm not is the kind of shitbag that would use their position of power to get someone into bed. I don't exchange surgeries for sex. If you want to get in on my cases, you have to earn the privilege."

"I understand."

"And," Galen's smile widened, and her eyes flashed a sultry shade of blue that Rowan had never seen anywhere else before, "if you want to have sex with me, well, you have to earn that too."

"I…" Rowan was absolutely sure she felt the blood drain from her head and settle into the bottom of her feet.

"My father picks the intern cases based on your residency interview, your application, your USMLE scores, and about a million other little things even I don't know about. But I can promise you that not one of them is whether I'd want to fuck you. And definitely not whether I, what did you say, I like you?"

"Again, Dr. Burgess, I am so sorry."

"Galen. Not Dr. Burgess. Please. Every time I hear that I think of that cranky old curmudgeon who reluctantly helped bring me into this world."

Rowan nodded resolutely. "Right. Galen."

"Don't be sorry. You're hardly the first intern who thought I was trying to woo her. But being a lesbian doesn't mean I'm ready to jump into bed with anything that doesn't have a dick."

"Of course it doesn't." For whatever reason, Rowan found the comment oddly hurtful.

"You're from Texas, right, Duncan?"

"That's right. Outside of—"

"Arlington. I remember now. So I'll write this off as some small-town, Southern naîveté, as well as a downright misunderstanding, and send you away with a word of caution. Don't believe everything you hear around this place. For a bunch of surgeons, these people seem to have nothing better to do than talk about each other." Galen looked back down at her desk, and it became very clear to Rowan that the conversation was over.

"I appreciate that. Thank you, Galen. It won't happen again." She got up and left, more humiliated than she could ever remember feeling in her twenty-six years.

❖

Not many things rattled Galen. She often found herself standing in an OR for eleven hours straight, with the discipline to not even use the bathroom until she was done, and still, she remained unfazed. But Rowan Duncan had crawled under her skin just now. Even Galen couldn't defend some of the things she'd done when it came to women and sex. She'd slept with straight women, married women, subordinates. At times, the bar hadn't been particularly high. But she'd never dreamed of compromising her life as a surgeon, not for the sake of anyone. And, more than that, she would never degrade herself, or anyone else, by abusing her newfound position as chief. The fact that Rowan had known her for all of a day and was already accusing her of trying to sleep with her was maddening and, even more surprisingly, hurtful.

She glanced at the clock on her cell phone, sighed, and hit Teddy's number on speed dial.

Teddy answered immediately. "Boss. What's shaking?"

"Stop calling me that."

"Sorry, Chief."

"Where are you right now?" Galen knew he was on call that night. It was getting on toward midnight, and she had a seven am thyroidectomy, but she needed a friend. She needed someone who could remind her she wasn't that person Rowan apparently thought she was.

"I'm in The Pit, why? Do you need something?"

Galen hated the ER, better known to the surgical residents as The Pit. Something about it felt dirty and chaotic—the exact opposite of how she liked her OR. But she was desperate for a surgery, or anything to get her head right again. "What do you have down there?"

"Not much. I got called for a car crash, but it looks like just a femur fracture on one of them. Ortho's coming down in a little bit. Oh, and a forty-year-old drunk guy fell off his roof trying to clean his gutters. It looks like he has a small liver lac, but I don't think it needs to go to the OR right now."

"Thanks." Galen's disappointment was almost overwhelming for a moment. But she quickly tucked it aside, stuffing a fist into the pocket of her white coat. "Keep me posted. I'll be in the on-call room. If he ends up needing that lac repaired, page me. I want in."

"You got it, Boss."

Galen cleared her throat.

"Sorry."

"Shut up." She laughed. "Hey, Ted?"

"Yeah?"

"Do you think I'm a creep?"

"What? No! Why would you even—" Galen could hear Teddy's pager chirping in the background. "Sorry, B...Galen. The floor is calling me. Looks like one of my post-ops is bleeding from his incision. Gotta run." Her phone beeped three times, and the line was dead.

❖

Rowan should have anticipated that sleep wouldn't come freely that night. By the time she got back to her new apartment in Brighton, showered, and climbed under the covers, she was wide-awake. She wasn't sure whether it was because she had her first surgery as a physician in only a few short hours or the jarring and downright humiliating conversation with her chief that had her on edge, but whatever the cause, it wasn't good. It was earlier in Texas, and she'd briefly contemplated calling Brian. He was usually the person she wanted to reach out to when she'd had a bad day. But the thought of his monotone, often lifeless voice on the other end rambling on about how his company was no longer providing free Keurig cups for the coffeemaker irrationally irritated her, and she quickly decided against it.

After a dinner of cheese and crackers, which she ate in bed, she read the chapter on thyroidectomies in her copy of *Current Surgical Theory*, not making it past the section on basic pathophysiology before drifting off with the book sprawled across her chest. Rowan was shocked to find she woke to her alarm blaring its grating tune from her cell phone next to the bed. Four am. She hadn't needed an alarm in decades. But that wasn't what startled her to a state of full alertness. Before she'd even opened her eyes, she noted the warmth in her belly and the tension between her legs. She reached a hand up under her T-shirt and gently stroked one of her nipples, already hard and ready.

As her other hand drifted down under the band of her shorts, she stopped. The dream she'd had only a short hour or so ago came flooding back, flushing her skin with a juxtaposition of embarrassment and arousal.

Galen sat behind her office door, cracked just enough for Rowan to see inside. She typed furiously on a computer keyboard, looking disheveled and tired but sexy as hell. Without a word, Rowan entered. She wore nothing but a lacy red bra and matching panties. Galen looked up from her computer, her eyes on fire with a want Rowan had never seen on anyone before. She angled her chair toward Rowan, who slowly walked toward her, straddling her so her cheek pressed against Galen's.

As she replayed every vivid detail of the dream, the pulse between her legs beat harder, until she could almost feel her clit pressed hard against Galen's stomach. She allowed her hand to wander back down inside her shorts, stroking softly until the tempo built into a fury of need.

Rowan's alarm once again blared to life, dousing the flames that had built inside her.

"Fucking snooze button," she groaned.

After the sobering ring tone once again ceased, the reality of her arousal sank in. Why did a dream about Galen have her so worked up? Why was she having dreams about a woman anyway? She chalked it up to being away from Brian, her sex life nonexistent since she left Texas. But that didn't sit right with her either. Not when she and Brian hardly had sex anymore. Not when she could have easily left sex with him off the table completely.

Stress. This is all just stress. She got out of bed, collected her clothes, and walked into the shower, the cold water doing absolutely nothing to ease the need still painfully present.

CHAPTER FOUR

It wasn't unusual for Galen to spend the night at the hospital when she wasn't on call. Becoming the best—becoming a Burgess—meant putting in hours you didn't have and doing work you didn't need to do. It meant hanging around for surgeries when your shift was technically over. It meant reading up on those surgeries both before and after so you could do them better the next time. It meant three am trips to the simulation lab to operate on computer screens when the hospital was quiet and everyone else was asleep.

Last night was no exception. Once Rowan had left her office, Galen had been irritated and more than a little turned on. People didn't usually stand up to her. She was a fifth-year resident and the spawn of the great Henry Burgess, God of Surgery. And now, she was chief resident. Maybe that was why she seemed to sleep with women who thought she was untouchable—mostly new nurses who didn't know any better. Then she could keep her control. She liked to be challenged at work, but not in her personal life.

She wasn't angry at Rowan for confronting her. After all, if she really believed that Galen had manipulated her schedule just to get in her pants, Galen wouldn't blame her for slapping her across the face. She was angry that her reputation was catching up with her and that within twenty-four hours, someone like Rowan Duncan would think Galen was the kind of asshole who would do something like that. Maybe it was time to cut the shit? Or, at the very least, try to be a little quieter about who she took to bed…

By midnight, no patients were waiting in the ER to be operated on, but Galen was still restless. Teddy was busy, and she couldn't seem to sit still long enough to read up on the newest techniques in laproscopic hernia repairs. The pinging from her nearby cell phone had been a welcome reprieve from her own thoughts.

I'm on a break. Can I come up?

The message came through to her iPhone from "Jen SN." SN stood for scrub nurse because Galen didn't know Jen's last name, or care to, really. And she needed to make sure she didn't get her mixed up with Jen Red Hair, Jen Coffee Shop, or Jen Paramedic. She sighed, picked up the phone, and typed a reply.

Sure.

She tried not to put too much thought into what she was getting out of these meaningless flings. But if she'd allowed herself to put her minimal psychiatric training from medical school to use, she might say she was compensating for a lack of attention and affirmation from her father. No. That was creepy Freud psychobabble.

Galen liked sex. She liked to get off, and even more than that, she liked to get beautiful women off. She loved it. She loved the way they writhed under her touch, the way they said her name, the way their muscles twitched when she did something just right. Sex gave her power. It gave her control. It made her feel needed and important—something she'd struggled to feel most of her life. It rarely went beyond that. She had no connection behind the lust.

Still, what the hell was wrong with lust? A few minutes later, a quiet knock had sounded on Galen's office door, and Jen SN entered without a word. Within seconds, she'd stripped off her scrubs, climbed into Galen's lap, and latched her mouth onto

Galen's neck. They hadn't talked, unless it was to tell Galen to go harder, or faster, or lower. This was exactly how Galen liked sex— quick, easy, and uncomplicated. She'd watched the last shudder of Jen's orgasm echo through her, and they both moved to put their clothes back on. That was it. Jen kissed her on the cheek, said a coy "thank you," and left.

❖

A strong cup of coffee would help Rowan shake this funk she was in. She stopped at the hospital cafeteria after her morning rounds, filled the tallest cup she could find, and topped it off with five or six sugars. Everything in the South was sweet, and the mere thought of black coffee turned her stomach. The heat in her belly that had been there since her unsolicited dream this morning had finally cooled, and she felt like she had the mental reserves to assist in her first surgery this morning. A healthy degree of terror and humility that was expected of her as a new doctor who'd just been handed a knife replaced her arousal.

"Well, good morning."

Rowan turned from the coffee station, still reviewing her thyroid landmarks as she tossed her sugar packets into the trash. Galen stood just close enough to bring every second of her dream flooding back to her.

"Good morning." She immediately felt her face warm and knew patchy hives were forming around her exposed neck.

"Total thyroid at seven am, OR 2. You ready, Duncan?" Galen smiled, and Rowan felt at least four more hives erupting.

"Looking forward to it." Her voice was scratchy, and she was having trouble swallowing over the potato-sized lump in her throat.

"You feeling all right?" Galen reached out and gently ran a finger over Rowan's neck, leaving her skin burning under her touch.

"Huh?"

"You're kind of flushed..." Galen didn't wait for an answer. She grinned knowingly and turned to go. "See you in a few."

❖

Rowan filled with panic at every step she took toward the locker room. She had no doubt that Galen knew every bit of what she'd been thinking. *God, how humiliating.* Never in her entire life had she dreamt about a woman like that. Never in her entire life had she even thought about a woman like that! She once again reminded herself that these were unusual circumstances, and she was absolutely in uncharted waters. A new residency, a new career, a new city, a whole new vat of responsibilities...*That explains it. Doesn't it?*

She moved to the nearby storage closet and took out a set of small scrubs, her phone falling to the ground as she did. For several seconds, she just stared at it before finally picking it up and hitting the first number on speed dial.

"Hi. Is everything okay?" Brian's voice on the other line sounded stifled and far away.

"Yes. Everything's fine. I just...I just miss you."

"You do?" She could nearly hear him smiling from Texas.

"Yes." It wasn't exactly a lie. Rowan did miss him, in some ways. So what if it wasn't in the same way he missed her?

"I miss you too, Ro. What are you up to?"

Rowan finally collected her scrubs and rounded the corner, kicking her heels off as she walked. "Well...I'm about to assist on my very first surgery."

"It's not your first surgery. You've done this a million times. You'll be great."

"I've done this a million times as a medical student, Bri. That's like telling Alex Rodriguez at his first major league game that he'd be fine because he was a water boy once." She groaned internally, kicking herself for forgetting just how little Brian understood of her world.

"And I still say you'll be great. Besides, A-Rod was a chump. What's the surgery?"

She knew he didn't really care. "It's a…" One of the nearby showers had shut off, and a strong, muscled figure wrapped in a less-than-conservative towel stepped out. Her heart ricocheted in her chest, and the sense of embarrassment that had become all too familiar to her during the last couple of days reappeared like an unwelcome guest.

"Hello? Ro? You still there?"

Brian's voice did little to shake her trance as Galen finally made eye contact, smiled her shy smile that was surely manufactured, and mouthed, "Sorry."

"Sorry. Hey, I've got to go, okay?"

"Um…okay, sure? Are you sure you're all right?" But Rowan had already let the phone drop to her side. "Hello? Ro? Rowan?" She laughed nervously in Galen's direction and hit the red button to end the call.

"I didn't know anyone else was in here," Galen said, picking up a corner of the towel and running it over her wet curls. The top of her strong thigh peeked out, and Rowan silently reminded herself to get it together.

"No problem."

"That the boyfriend?"

"Yeah." Rowan suddenly and foolishly wanted to prove to Galen just how solid her love life was. "He's the best. I really miss him, you know."

Galen just raised her eyebrows slightly, and Rowan swore she saw something that looked like skepticism on her face. "Huh. That's great."

"How about you? Do you, you know, miss anyone?" She couldn't believe she'd just asked her that. What an idiot! Was she twelve? Galen's love life was none of her business. And it was of absolutely no interest to her.

"Her name is Suzie." Galen flashed her mischievous smile that Rowan was sure got her into all kinds of trouble. "When I get home every night, I mean, when I actually make it home, we eat dinner together. And then we watch *Mary Tyler Moore* reruns and fall asleep on the couch."

For whatever reason, a bubble of jealousy traveled up from Rowan's stomach and settled in her throat.

"She loves to kiss me too."

"Oh. That's…How long have you and Suzie been together?"

"About eleven years now."

Everything Rowan had heard about Galen suddenly came into question. Was her whole Lothario persona just an act? Or was she some kind of serial cheater? "Really?" She tried to sound unfazed.

"Yeah. My dad got her for me when I was a teenager." Her grin grew. "We have a date tomorrow at the vet's, actually."

Rowan felt her eyes bug just for a second and then laughed. "Might this Suzie be covered in fur and enjoy playing fetch in the park?"

"As a matter of fact, yes! You want to see a picture?" Galen was already running to her bag to dig out her cell phone. "Here she is."

"She's adorable." Rowan noted the graying Goldendoodle but couldn't look away from a tan, smiling Galen kneeling next to her in the summer sun, wearing a baseball cap and tank top. They were on some kind of hike, and Rowan wondered what it would be like to spend the day outside, exploring the mountains with Galen and Suzie…

"I think so, but I'm biased. Shit, is that really the time? I have to get dressed."

Rowan found herself roaming Galen's body with her glance, suddenly too aware of her near-nakedness. "Right." She watched as Galen's towel dropped just enough to expose the crest of her breasts, forcing herself to leave.

❖

"Good morning, everyone." Galen's favorite attending, Dr. Jay Peterson, entered the OR, holding his hands just in front of his chest. "Burgey. What's shakin', kid?"

"Ready to get going, Boss." With Jay at the helm, it was going to be a good day. He often let Galen do the majority of the surgery, even leaving the room to let her finish the procedure on her own. Working with him was nothing like working with her father. She didn't live in perpetual fear of fucking up, or not fucking up but being yelled at regardless.

"Aren't you always? And you must be one of the new interns." Jay turned his attention to Rowan, who'd been standing patiently near the patient's head, careful not to ruin the sterile field.

"Yes, sir. I'm Rowan Duncan." Galen watched as Rowan started to reach out to shake his hand but quickly seemed to realize her error and brought it back close to her body.

"Don't give me that 'sir' bullshit. Who do you think I am, Henry Burgess? No offense, Galen."

Galen chuckled. Why couldn't Jay be her father instead? Jesus, life would be so much easier.

"Okay, Dr. Peterson."

"Jay. Please. If you call me Dr. Peterson, I'll kick you right out of my OR."

Galen could see the smile on his face even in spite of his mask.

"Jay. I've got it."

Galen warmed at the exchange. Rowan was likable, she had to admit. So many of the new residents were like petulant children with no social skills. They couldn't hold a conversation, never mind make a joke. Rowan was charming. She thought back to an hour earlier, in the locker room. Galen had known exactly what she was doing. She was already in the shower when she heard Rowan's voice nearby. It didn't take long for her to figure out she was on the phone, likely with this Brian doofus.

Everything Galen did with a woman was calculated, meticulous, from her words down to her shoes. It was no accident that she chose that moment to leave the shower, making sure to let her towel fall just enough to gauge the look in Rowan's eyes. The shaking in her voice, the color of her cheeks—it all served to confirm what Galen was sure she'd seen earlier in the day. Girls broke out in hives around her for two reasons—they wanted to fuck her, or they were allergic to her cologne. And Galen hadn't been wearing any cologne.

CHAPTER FIVE

In a few months, a 24-hour call shift would probably feel as welcome as a tooth extraction. But for now, Rowan was thrilled. It was only twenty minutes past seven in the morning, and she was already pulsating with the feeling that absolutely anything could happen. Besides, nighttime in a hospital is different: a sort of controlled chaos supersedes the darkness. Because fewer staff are around, first-years like Rowan had more opportunities. And it didn't hurt that her first call shift was with Galen.

Her mind once again skipped back to the morning before. Galen had been nearly naked in the locker room, and for whatever reason, Rowan had been extremely uncomfortable. She'd been around naked women before, of course—in the sauna at her gym, in her girlfriends' bedrooms at high-school sleepovers. Hell, there was even that time in college when her roommate convinced her to watch porn (admittedly not her thing). But she'd never felt so innately awkward as she did with Galen standing there, her towel barely covering her wet skin, her damp hair framing her confident smile. Oh God! Had it finally happened? Had she finally succumbed to her years of homophobic inbreeding? Was she uncomfortable around Galen because she was a lesbian?

No. That wasn't it. One of Rowan's best friends at Dartmouth was gay. They'd shared a bed on a weekend road trip. They'd hugged and had dinners. And never once was Rowan suspicious that she wanted to sleep with her just because she liked women. She certainly didn't think Galen wanted to get into her panties because she was a lesbian. So what the hell was her problem, then?

"Duncan. Heads up." The voice that had been so clearly resonating in her head all day erupted in full stereo as a small, black object the size of a deck of cards barreled toward her face.

"What?" She hardly had time to duck to keep the pager from taking off the tip of her nose.

"Your pager. You're on call with me tonight, right?" Galen grinned so quickly she almost appeared to wink. Was she winking? Was she flirting with Rowan again? *Oh God, stop it, stop it, stop it.*

"Yes. I mean, I am. With you. Tonight."

"Good. Then keep this on. I expect you to respond within five minutes."

Rowan thought it sounded like an "or else" should have been at the end of her sentence, but Galen was already gone before she could ask. It was 6:45 pm, and the hum of the hospital was starting to deteriorate with the impending evening. For the first time since she'd been there, Rowan turned to find herself alone in the hallway by the cafeteria. The buzz of a floor polisher echoed in the distance, and an elderly man waited in a wheelchair by the lobby doors. With an entire fifteen minutes left before her call shift started, she decided to pick up something to eat. After all, she could never tell when she'd have another chance. She purchased a sandwich from the cafeteria, sat at an empty table next to the window looking out onto the street, and unwrapped her dinner.

A piercing ring she didn't recognize came from under the table. It took several seconds before she realized what it was, picked the pager off her scrub pants, and groaned.

"Well, that was short-lived," she mumbled to herself. She thought about rewrapping the sandwich and putting it in her locker, but what was the point? She probably wouldn't see food for the next twenty-four hours, and besides, she wasn't particularly hungry. Her nerves were getting more than the best of her—first night on call, first night under Galen's thumb.

See patient J. Kensington in ED. 17 M, question appy.

The Emergency Department was just down the stairs from the cafeteria, in the basement. It was one of the few places she'd learned how to access since she arrived at Boston City. Rowan took one last look at her sandwich, tossed it into the trash, and jogged down the stairs.

"Hi. Dr. Duncan, from surgery, here to see Kensington?" She hoped the secretary behind the desk didn't notice the sweat forming just under her bangs.

"Room four. But someone from surgery is already in there."

Rowan's heart lurched as she raced around the corner.

"Um, four is the other way, dear," the secretary shouted.

"Right. Thanks."

Galen was already standing at the patient's bedside, her face stone as she stared at her watch.

"Dr. Burgess…I'm sorry…I…"

"Two minutes, twenty-eight seconds. Not bad." Galen's expression melted into her charming smile, and Rowan felt the hives once again pop up around her collar. "I'm playing with you, Duncan. This is Jeff. Mid-epigastric pain for two days radiating to the right lower quadrant today. Positive rebounding. Fever to 100.8. Leukocytosis of 14. CT showed thickening of the appendix with positive fat stranding."

"Hi, Jeff. I'm Dr. Duncan. I work with Dr. Burgess."

"What's all that mean? What she said?" The tall, lanky boy in the bed was pale, and his pupils were pinpoints from various doses of morphine.

"That's just big-shot talk for your appendix needs to come out." She glanced at Galen to make sure she was still smiling. She was.

"Bread and butter," Galen said once they'd stepped out of Jeff's room.

"Excuse me?"

"This is your bread and butter. A laproscopic appendectomy. It doesn't get a whole lot more basic than that. Good case for a newbie."

Rowan's excitement suddenly overtook her nerves. "I can't wait."

"That's what I like to hear. So, what do you want to do now?"

"Now?" She forced herself to slow down and think. Her answers tonight would set the precedent for how Galen saw her. They would determine whether she would trust her. "Now, I want to call the OR team and get a room prepped. I want to get him started on IV cipro and flagyl and review all his labs for pre-op. Then I want to page Dr. Morgan and let him know we'll need him at the bedside, although I'm sure you'll be doing most of the heavy lifting." She swore she saw a rare shade of pink touch Galen's cheeks.

"You were doing well there for a while."

Rowan's composure suddenly felt weakened and frail. "What did I miss?"

"How many lap appys did you assist in as a fourth-year?"

"Well, I did four extra months in general surgery at UT Austin, so I'd wager probably somewhere around twenty to thirty?"

"Great." Galen smiled. "Then you were wrong about one thing. You'll be the one doing most of the heavy lifting."

"I...really?"

"Yes, Duncan. Listen." She put a firm hand on Rowan's shoulder. "When I was an intern, Jay Peterson was the first attending I was ever on call with. I was so terrified I nearly peed my scrubs in the OR."

Rowan laughed. "I find that difficult to believe."

"It's true. I didn't eat for a solid fifteen hours before that case. And when I finally got in there, Jay put Lynyrd Skynyrd on his iPod, smiled at me, and handed me a scalpel. And you know what he said to me?"

"No...what?"

"He said 'Burgy. You're up, kid. You've got this.'"

"Then what happened?"

"Then he asked me to identify the anatomical landmarks where I needed to make my trocar sites. I did. And then he told me to cut. Just like that. Like I'd been doing it all my life."

"That's an insane amount of trust for a new intern."

"It sure is. And that's the level of trust I'm instilling in you. I learned more in that first case with him than I did most of the remainder of the year. And now, I'm a firm believer in the old *see one, do one, teach one* method. My father and a lot of the others seem to have forgotten how well that can work. You're here because you're good, Rowan, because you beat out twelve thousand other applicants who wanted to be surgeons. Now, you're going to take the scalpel."

Rowan's hands were tingling. She wasn't sure if it was from fear, or elation, or just another strange somatic effect of being in Galen's presence. Regardless, her chief did have an incredible way with words. Everything that came out of her mouth was either seductive and charming, or engaging and inspirational. Jesus. No wonder women couldn't keep their panties on around her.

Galen was pretty sure her pre-op pep talk had worked. She could tell Rowan was scared. And she was glad. Fear was healthy in the OR. It was necessary—as long as it was controlled. And Rowan seemed to have a healthy control of her terror that Galen felt would make her a meticulous surgeon. That, combined with her apparent work ethic and clear intelligence, left Galen feeling certain she could let Rowan take the reins, with her standing in close range. Responsibility as a brand-new intern wasn't exactly the same as responsibility as a fifth-year chief resident. It was more about giving the new surgeon the feeling of having a patient's life in their hands. When push came to shove, Galen would be right behind her. And, if that failed, Dr. James Morgan would be standing right behind her. She didn't anticipate Rowan needing much from either of them.

They still had some time before the surgery could begin. She left Rowan in the consult room to review Jeff Kensington's labs, his medical history, his family history. The other specialties think surgeons only cut. But there's so much more involved than that. If Rowan were to miss just one hint of someone in the Kensington family reacting poorly to anesthesia in the past, Jeff could end up with malignant hyperthermia and die on the table. Odds were it would never come to that. But Galen liked to think she was more than just good with a knife.

For whatever reason, Galen thought back to her frustrating encounter with Rowan from the night before. Maybe she hadn't ever really stopped contemplating it? Was Rowan going to think she was letting her do so much so she could fuck her? As if she'd ever put a patient's life in jeopardy just to get some. The concept pissed her off all over again, but she took a deep breath, told herself she was being irrational, and put it aside. Instead, she walked briskly off toward the OR suites, wondering why, exactly, she cared so much what Dr. Rowan Duncan thought about her.

❖

Rowan could do only so much more preparation. She'd read and reread Jeff Kensington's medical, family, and social history about twelve times. His maternal great-aunt had a small stroke at eighty-four, and he'd spent a year in France during high school. He'd smoked approximately four cigarettes a week for six months when he was seventeen. He was nervous about the surgery, but ready—not altogether different from Rowan, actually. She could rattle off his complete blood count, including manual differential, partially thanks to her eidetic memory. And almost as important, she knew exactly where she needed to make her incisions to insert the laparoscopic instruments.

Of course, not a single one of those things kept her inevitable heart palpitations and sweating under control as she made her way to the scrub sink outside OR 4 and ran her hands under the warm water. She took several deep breaths, counting to four on the way in and again on the way out, like she'd done when her nerves got the best of her in medical school. But it wasn't until Galen approached that her anxiety dissipated into the sterile air around her.

"I'd ask if you're ready, but I already know the answer." Galen's kind, supportive smile reminded Rowan of the South, and her heart rate settled down to its usual steady pace.

❖

The high coming out of the OR was like nothing Rowan had ever experienced. Her heart pounded, and she felt like laughing and crying and screaming, all while simultaneously running for miles on end without stopping. Energy seemed boundless and the world was hers. *Fuck, yes*. It was hers, and it was Galen's, and together they could...

Okay, so maybe the endorphins had gotten a bit out of hand. No "Galen and her" existed. Galen—her chief resident and her boss—was likely the biggest playboy of all time. And Rowan—lowly first-year resident from Hicksville, Texas—scratch that. Lowly *straight* first-year resident from Hicksville, Texas. She wasn't sure why the straight part was so important to her yet again, but it was. Slow, rhythmic clapping interrupted her thoughts.

"Dr. Duncan. Nicely done." Rowan wasn't sure why she was surprised to find Galen behind her. She seemed to be just short of flanking her all night. Not that Rowan minded. It was nice to have the support and all of that.

"Thank you." Rowan's instinct was to bow, or throw her arms around Galen, or something equally as inappropriate and ridiculous. But she didn't. She just smiled and continued to ride the wave of serotonin and dopamine that she imagined could only be derived from two things in life—a successful surgery, complete with the feel of your hands on someone's pulsating organs, and sex. She'd had sex before. Probably a hundred times at least with Brian. And she'd slept with one other boyfriend before him in high school. But Rowan could say with absolute certainty that no sex she'd ever had compared to being in that OR with Galen just now. Like a hormone-laden twelve-year-old boy who finds himself getting erections during church, her mind once again settled back into the dream she'd had that morning.

As she inadvertently remembered the feeling of Galen's breath on her neck and her hands running up the back of her shirt, her face once again flushed, and she began to itch profusely. *Stop being turned on. Stop being turned on. Baseball. Grandma June's knitting club. Dehisced surgical wounds...Brian...* The record scratched, and the music came to an abrupt stop. She had successfully squelched all sexual desire that had built inside her.

"Come on. I want to show you something." Galen moved close enough to place a hand gently on the small of her back, which was now hopelessly damp, and the high resurfaced.

"What? Where?"

"I'm your boss. Don't ask questions." Galen smiled, and Rowan couldn't bring herself to give a shit about anything other than how good that moment felt.

They took the elevator as far as it would go, until Galen led her out and down the hall. Darkened offices and conference rooms slowly turned to storage closets and broken medical equipment. IV poles and heart monitors that looked like something out of the eighties littered the corners, but Galen kept walking, Rowan in step next to her.

"Where are you taking me?"

"Not to try to get you naked."

"Actually, I was thinking more along the lines of kidnapping, murdering...that sort of thing."

"So I've gone from a playboy who wants to fuck you to a killer? Jesus, Duncan. You don't think particularly highly of me, do you?"

"I...Galen, I was kidding. I'm sorry."

Galen's laugh was laced with a heaviness Rowan wasn't familiar with—one that made her uneasy.

"Just through here." Galen pushed open a heavy metal door plastered with a strict warning not to enter. She thought about questioning her, but somehow, Galen didn't seem like anyone who needed second-guessing.

They walked up one flight of stairs and through another door that threatened to release a fire alarm if provoked. "Relax. It's just a sticker. I've done this a million times."

Sprawled in front of them was the city of Boston, lit up from the Charles River to the Prudential Building. Rowan had grown up in a town of just over a thousand, with more vets than physicians and three cows for every resident. This was like being dropped on an alien planet. She'd never seen anything like it, and she wondered if she'd ever go back home.

Galen was waiting for the question she knew was coming. She'd brought this adorable-as-fuck, straight first-year to the roof of the hospital, which overlooked what was arguably the best view in Boston. Not a tourist or even another hospital employee was even close. She was slick as hell. And subtlety was not her strongest trait. Galen once again reminded herself she couldn't fuck the interns. Her father would have an absolute fit if she did. Besides, it wasn't only about her father. The last thing she wanted was to find herself once again being questioned for her motives like Rowan had done the other day.

"How many girls have you brought up here?"

Galen sighed loudly, the sound dissipating into the night wind. There it was. "A few."

She'd thought about lying. It would be easy enough. Hell, she was good at it. But Rowan was too smart for that. She deserved too much more.

"I mean, I don't care. It's not like I need to be special or anything."

Galen contained a small grin. She couldn't help but like the way Rowan actually did seem to care. A lot. After a decade of seducing women, Galen had fine-tuned a couple of things—most important, how to figure out when someone wanted her. The skill saved her from rejection and sent her now well-honed flirtation skills in the right direction. And unless she was wrong for the first time in a while, Rowan wanted her. Not that it mattered. Of course she couldn't act on her urge. She was her intern. She had a boyfriend. For fuck's sake, she hadn't even been with a female before. Those were three incredibly good reasons for Galen to keep her scrubs on.

"But you are the only other surgeon." Yes. Three incredibly good reasons. Yet Galen found herself wanting the hell out of this girl. Rowan smiled shyly at her and then looked at the ground. She ran a hand through her hair, and as she did, the wind caught ahold of a scent Galen could only compare to sunshine and line-dried cotton and lavender. Something about it reminded her of childhood summer vacations and a life before medicine, a life not filled with impossible expectations. The scent transcended into a feeling—one that made her skin burn and her muscles ache to be touched.

Rowan looked up at her again, and it was clear Galen had been staring. She'd perfected the art of lying to women. Her words were clear and smooth and always believable. But her face... that face gave her away every time. And she knew Rowan could see everything she'd just felt. For a moment, she felt naked and exposed—something only her father could usually cause. But the moment didn't last. No. The back of Rowan's hand, which ever so gently brushed Galen's cheek, easily overshadowed it. That same feeling of lavender and sunshine penetrated her entire being until she was too terrified to move, afraid she might break whatever was transpiring between them. Rowan was the straight one. Rowan was the one with Brian. She would definitely have to be the one to make this happen.

Forever seemed to pass as Galen waited. By her quick estimation, there was a solid 60 percent chance that Rowan would yank her hand away, mumble something incoherently, start crying, and run back inside. But she had to see for herself. She tentatively brushed a rogue piece of hair from Rowan's face, grazing her jaw. That seemed to be all the encouragement Rowan needed. They suddenly jolted forward in time, as if they had been frozen and were finally free. Rowan placed her other hand on Galen's face, held it firmly, and pulled her to her lips with a certainty that was hard to deny. For a small-town, straight first-year, she seemed to know exactly what she was doing.

Her mouth met Galen's tentatively at first, brushing her lips against hers like a whisper. But then the whisper built into a scream, and Rowan's mouth parted, hot and wet, her tongue gliding slowly over Galen's. Galen's breath shortened, and a small moan slipped from Rowan, the warmth between Galen's legs doubling. Kissing never got her this heated. Something visceral in her took over, and she slid a hand up under the hem of Rowan's scrub top, letting her fingers graze her smooth, soft skin. Rowan gasped and pulled away, yanking the top back down and rushing to tame the hairs that had strayed from wandering hands.

"Ohmygod…I'm so sorry. That should so not have happened. You're…I'm…fuck. I'm just sorry." She stood so quickly she had to steady herself and took off toward the door.

Galen didn't chase her. She'd seen this coming from three states away. In all her years of seducing women, Galen had also learned that this was par for the straight-girl course. Still, she'd never quite been kissed like *that* before.

CHAPTER SIX

She'd done some stupid things before. No question about that. At a party in high school, Rowan once smoked half a pack of Virginia Slims in a matter of hours, mostly because that's what she'd seen her grandmother do, and she assumed that was how you smoked them—consecutively. She'd spent the remainder of the evening bent over a trash can surrounded by her peers' intractable laughter. During medical school, she'd taken Aderall from a friend who promised she'd be able to study for three days straight. Instead, she once again found herself reacquainted with the trash can, this time with accompanying heart palpitations and cold sweats so debilitating she failed her first and only pharmacology exam. No, Rowan was not immune to stupidity. Even an IQ of 136 did not make her infallible. And never had that been more evident than that particular night.

What the actual hell was she thinking, kissing Galen? As if it wasn't enough that she'd just cheated on Brian, she had to do it with her boss—her very female boss. Not that Galen screamed femininity or anything…Damn it. She was getting off course again. Rowan was essentially in hiding, thinking that one of the empty exam rooms in the deserted surgery clinic might offer some reprieve from her utter humiliation. She lay on her back on one of the cots, the stiff paper that offered a sanitary covering for patients crinkling as she shuffled anxiously around. The lights around her were dimmed to near darkness, with a couple of lone EXIT signs the only thing to risk blowing her cover. It was now three fifteen am, and her head was far too hazy to even begin to process what had just happened.

Just like she approached everything in her life, Rowan dissected the one enormous problem into smaller, more digestible pieces, attempting to examine all the parts before forming a single unifying diagnosis.

She told herself to start at the top—the biggest of the pieces. Nothing mattered more to Rowan than her career. And at the helm of that career right now was Dr. Galen Burgess. The same Galen Burgess she had just essentially seduced fifteen minutes earlier. Seduced? No. That wasn't quite right. She'd kissed Galen. But it was hardly as if Galen had pushed her away. If she was remembering the moment correctly, which, she had to be honest, was about a fifty-fifty chance, given the utter shock she still found herself in, then Galen had more than welcomed her advances.

As she stretched her arms behind her head and closed her eyes, she could almost feel those soft, warm lips as they touched hers with just enough pressure to ignite a heat in her that warmed her entire body. Galen gave just enough, sliding her tongue against Rowan's, letting them dance for only a second, and then pulling back, leaving Rowan physically hurting for more. Galen was her boss. And what had transpired was completely, unequivocally inappropriate. But goddamn it, could she kiss...

"You could potentially hide from me for the rest of the night, but hiding for the next five-and-a-half years might prove a little more difficult."

She shot up bolt-straight, like being awoken from a nightmare, at the sound of Galen's voice. Boston City Hospital had 487 beds. How could she have possibly found the one Rowan was occupying?

"How'd you know?"

"I didn't. I just thought if I was trying to escape from my boss, who I'd just kissed, I might come here." Galen sat down beside her on the hard bed.

"I'm so sorry, Galen."

"Your accent. Where did that come from?"

Rowan involuntarily locked eyes with the wall in front of her. Great, one more thing to be embarrassed about. She'd spent years ridding her speech of her dreaded Texan drawl. She was convinced it made her sound dumb and uneducated. By her junior year of high school, hardly any trace of it was left, except when she was nervous. Had she just seen the first of the return of her accent, which would likely emerge every time Galen was around?

"Can I possibly beg you to pretend I didn't just do that?"

"You think you're the first intern to put the moves on me?" Galen couldn't be serious…could she?

"I…"

"Okay, so you are. But you don't need to beg me to let it go. Shit happens. Especially around here. I like you. You're a good surgeon. No harm done." Galen patted Rowan softly on the shoulder and stood up, leaving Rowan now totally embarrassed. "Oh, and Duncan?" Galen turned back as she reached the exam-room door. "I have to say…that was one hell of a kiss."

❖

The hospital was finally asleep. It was somewhere near four thirty am, although Galen wasn't sure exactly. She wore a watch like it was a part of her own skin, but she'd forgotten it at home that day. Something had her all out of sorts lately. She sat in her desk chair and perched her feet up on her desk. She couldn't believe it had been five years since she started her residency. Six, technically. In hopes of pissing off her father, while still feeding her need for a near-constant dumping of cortisol and adrenaline, Galen had tried her hand at emergency medicine. She'd spent one year in the EM residency program at Boston City before succumbing to her hatred of chaos, mess, and drug seekers, and switching to a surgical residency.

Much to her chagrin, surgery was in her blood. Her father was a surgeon. His father was a surgeon. She had two older sisters who'd gone off to get married and live sensible suburban lives— one a physics professor at MIT and one a yoga instructor with four kids of her own. It was no secret that Henry Burgess was more than a little disappointed that he seemed to be unable to produce any male offspring. Apparently, it didn't occur to him until 1980, when Galen was born, that women could also be surgeons. And, although there would never be a Dr. Henry Burgess II, he could groom Galen to be somewhere close to it. Galen wasn't even the smartest of her siblings. But she was tenacious. And she wasn't sure how much of that quality she had been born with, and how much of it she had manufactured.

Regardless of how she got there, Galen often found herself here, in her office chair at four thirty am, reflecting on how glad she was that she had. Surgery was where she belonged.

"Get any sleep last night?" Teddy didn't bother knocking, and Galen wondered when he had become that kind of friend.

"The usual. Rounds so early?"

"My roommate has some chick over. I finally gave up on listening to them bang sometime after four am. I have no idea how he can hang that long! But if he keeps this girl around, I'm going to be putting an air mattress in here and moving in."

"My office? Dream on. Do you know how valuable this little piece of real estate is?"

"Not firsthand, no. But I hear they accept payment only in blood, sweat, and/or tears. Checks made payable to Dr. Henry Burgess, Chief of General Surgery."

Galen laughed. "Bingo."

"How was the night, anyway?" Teddy asked.

"It was…well, it sure wasn't boring." She smiled, the smallest, most unprofessional part of her wishing she could kiss her little fledgling maybe just once more.

❖

Makayla must have spotted Rowan across the cafeteria retrieving her five thirty am bucket of coffee. She'd gone home and slept a measly nine hours, got up, prepped three days' worth of salad and peanut-butter sandwiches, and began reading up on her next scheduled case. So much of her was dreading going back to the hospital and seeing Galen. But so much more of her was looking around every corner, hoping she'd run into her.

"Hey! How did it go?" She liked Makayla. Rowan had already decided that. But she really wasn't great at interacting with anything with a pulse before her first cup of coffee.

"What?"

"Um, your call shift? Obvi." Did she really just say obvi? Rowan wondered just how much younger Makayla was than the rest of her intern class.

"It was fine." She dumped five sugar packets into the dark pool, followed by a stream of cream that turned the coffee the color of eggnog.

"I heard it was more than fine."

Rowan stopped short, gripping the lid of the paper cup. "What do you mean?"

"Don't be humble, Texas. I heard you basically ran point on an appy."

She sighed so loudly she figured half the cafeteria had noticed. "Oh, right. I mean, yeah. Kind of. Galen let me place the trocar sites, and once I was in, she showed me how to manipulate the camera and the graspers at the same time. And then I put in the staples."

"So you basically did everything." She couldn't tell whether Makayla was happy for her or fighting back a wave of jealousy. Probably somewhere in between.

"Not everything, no. She made the cut."

"So cool. How many other surgical residencies do you know where first-years get to do all that? I have a friend at Penn. They barely trust her with the camera. It takes an act of God for someone to hand her a knife."

Rowan had to admit, it was a pretty phenomenal experience—one that had been tremendously overshadowed by the also-kind-of-phenomenal kiss she'd shared with her boss. "Yeah. Anyway, we should go. Can't be late for rounds."

❖

"Who's following Mr. Jeffries?" Galen had led her pack of five bleary-eyed first-years down the hall of the fifth floor and stopped in front of room 513, where an elderly man sat upright in his hospital bed working a crossword puzzle.

"I am." Makayla stepped forward.

"Right. Go for it."

"Mr. Jeffries. Eighty-two years old. Came in yesterday with diffuse abdominal pain and nausea times three days. CT revealed small bowel obstruction—"

"Where?" Galen asked.

Makayla's face blanked, and her color seemed to drain onto the tile floor. "I…"

"It's not enough to know that it's an SBO, Makayla. You have to know where it is."

"I'm sorry. I can't remember." Galen hadn't realized Makayla had the ability to be so humble.

"The obstruction is proximal. Just distal to the duodenal junction. And why would we have suspected that Mr. Jeffries' bowel obstruction was proximal and not distal?"

"Because of the location of his pain," Jordan Phillips, one of Galen's least-favorite and newest showboaters, blurted out.

"His pain was diffuse, Jordan. Think before you start vomiting up answers." She hated being a hard-ass. Especially in front of Rowan. But it had been done to her, and to every other surgeon who became successful. It was a rite of passage. It was necessary. "No one? Come on, guys. This is basic knowledge. Surgery 101."

"We could have suspected it's a proximal obstruction because he was vomiting profusely." Rowan stayed toward the back of the group, but her eyes met Galen's unapologetically.

"And why is that, Duncan?"

"Gastric content and fecal matter back up proximally from the duodenum to the pyloric sphincter, causing nausea and vomiting, rarely helped by medication."

"What is the most likely cause of Mr. Jeffries' SBO then?"

"Adhesions, probably. He had an open cholecystectomy thirty years ago and probably has some pretty wild scar tissue in there."

Galen felt herself smile. "Treatment?"

This time, Rowan took a step forward. "Nasogastric tube to relieve the pressure in hopes of reversing the volvulus and avoiding surgery."

"Excellent. And what are the indications for surgery?"

Rowan was silent now, the tension quickly muddying the air around all of them. "I...I can't remember." She slinked back behind the very tall Makayla, whose color had finally returned.

"You're off the hook, Rowan. I've harassed you enough for this morning." Galen knew how the interrogation was supposed to go. It was a long-standing term known as "pimping." The attending surgeon, or senior resident, asked questions about the procedure, disease, or patient, each question getting more difficult. The goal was to fail. In fact, the one doing the pimping was not supposed to stop until the victim on the other end was unable to successfully answer the question. The tactic was designed to humble and belittle, until the recipient wanted to run off and cry, or bury their nose in every medical textbook they could get their hands on. Galen wasn't entirely convinced the process did anything to benefit the education of young surgeons. But it was the way things had always been done. So it was the way she would do it too.

However, if Galen had been following the true spirit of pimping, she would never have "let Rowan off the hook." Was she being soft because she wasn't her father or because of that moment on the rooftop she'd spent with this particular pimpee?

❖

Rowan was waiting for Galen outside of OR 4. "Perforation, bowel ischemia, or failure of the obstruction to resolve with bowel decompression."

"I'm sorry?"

"Perf, ischemia, or no resolution with an NG tube."

Galen pulled her surgical mask off and tossed it into the trash. Her short waves clung around her ears where her scrub cap had been, and a fine shine had settled over her forehead. She looked as if she had just been out for a run, and Rowan found it oddly sexy. She'd allowed herself to process why she'd been willing to kiss the woman in charge of her. Over the last several days, she'd chalked up the mishap to impulse, adrenaline, and a little hero worship. She could live with that. But she hadn't allowed herself to delve into Galen's pronouns. Never in her entire life had she found herself attracted to a female—not that she was in any way admitting to being attracted to Galen.

"Still not following you, Duncan." Galen patted her face with a towel and rotated her right wrist in small circles, wincing. "I swear, if I keep up these hours, I'm going to have carpal tunnel by the time I'm forty."

"This morning, on rounds—"

"Walk with me to the lounge."

Rowan struggled to keep pace with Galen's long stride. It was quick but somehow never appeared hurried. She followed her around the corner into the surgeons' lounge, where Galen cracked a bottle of water and chugged half of it.

"Now, want to tell me what you're talking about?" she finally said, once she'd settled into a nearby chair and stretched her legs out in front of her.

"This morning, you asked me what the surgical indications were for an SBO. I told you I didn't know. I lied." Rowan wasn't sure why she'd lied. She'd never played dumb before. She'd spent her life being the smart kid—getting picked on for reading at recess instead of playing kickball, and writing term papers for her friends in college. But this morning was different. Of course she knew the surgical indications for a small bowel obstruction. She'd studied them two dozen times. She was embarrassed and afraid to look like a showoff to Galen. And, maybe most of all, she was terrified everyone would somehow know what she'd done.

"And how do I know you didn't just run back to Dr. Google or ask someone?"

"Because! I wouldn't!" Rowan suddenly regretted proving her point. What difference did it really make if Galen knew she had all the answers?

Galen grinned. "I'm teasing you." She took another sip of water. "Why didn't you speak up this morning?"

"I don't know."

"Yes, you do. You were afraid people would think you were kissing my ass, weren't you? And if they thought that, they might wonder how far you would go."

"What?" Rowan scoffed at the idea she had just decided was absolutely true. "Like anyone would think I'd—"

"Be hot for teacher?" She smiled again and ran a hand through her hair, resting it on her neck.

"Please. I'm not the one who was soft-pimping this morning."

"Soft-pimping? Did you just make that up? Because that sounds like something retired rappers do."

"What I mean is, you were tossing me loppers. I learned those things in my second year at Dartmouth."

Galen sat more upright and shifted uneasily in her chair. "Tell that to your colleagues. They apparently missed that day of class."

"Fine, so let's say those weren't necessarily gimmes." Rowan took a step closer to Galen and put her hands on her hips. "You let me off the hook. Never in the history of pimping has anyone been let off the hook. That is soft-pimping."

"Okay. So it was soft. But it wasn't because of what happened the other night."

"It wasn't?" Rowan couldn't deny the pulse of disappointment that beat through her.

"Of course not. I'm new to this too. And I may be a Burgess by name, but the similarities stop there. Well, aside from my exceptional good looks and gifted hands." Galen winked at her, and Rowan's insides fought a battle between disgust and arousal.

"Y'all are exactly alike." Rowan heard the thick drawl from her own mouth as if it belonged to someone else and cast her gaze to the floor, once again wanting to escape the encounter before she could further humiliate herself

"You know, Duncan…I like the accent. You shouldn't fight it so hard. It's kind of sexy."

Rowan looked at her again, the sultry blue of Galen's eyes now ignited with the same want she'd seen immediately after they'd kissed. "I have to go."

And, once again, Galen let her.

CHAPTER SEVEN

Galen had to find Teddy. She had to find a better way to deal with the situation with Rowan. The situation, that is, being that Galen really, really, really wanted to fuck her. A million girls lived and/or worked in Boston. And she'd be lying if she said she hadn't slept with a handful of them. But girls like Rowan didn't come around every day. She was gorgeous. Stunning long, straight, brown hair that she usually kept up in a bun but every so often would let down and shake out, reminding Galen of one of those shampoo commercials from the '90s. Her body was tight, proof that she was a regular runner, but curvy exactly where it needed to be. On most days, she wore scrubs, which still weren't enough to cover her tiny waist that sat just above those thick hips that begged to be grabbed as she pulled Rowan against her.

But what was really driving Galen crazy was that smile. It was one of those rare smiles that just made everything in the world suddenly good again. Her eyes squinted and brightened simultaneously, which made Galen want to do all kinds of inconceivable things to her. Even when Rowan wasn't around, she found herself in a near-constant state of fantasy, dreaming about pinning Rowan up against a wall and scratching her nails down her sides and leaving tiny bite marks along the soft skin of her neck. She didn't just want to fuck Rowan. Galen wanted to dominate her. She wanted to leave her completely changed from when she'd found her. She wanted to corrupt all the innocence left inside her. She wanted to elicit that sweet Texas drawl, pleading for more—more of Galen.

She couldn't think about anything else. And she wasn't quite sure how to handle it anymore.

"Teddy, I need you. Come to my office." Judging by Teddy's expression, Galen had alarmed Teddy when she found him in the lounge. Without a question, he followed her.

"What is it, G?" He sat down in her chair, but Galen continued to pace the room.

"I have a problem."

"Enough lead-up already! What's going on?"

"I'm desperately attracted to one of the interns."

Teddy stared at her for a second, then erupted in a barrage of laughter.

"What's so funny?" Galen pleaded, irritated by his nonchalance.

"That's it? You want to sleep with a first-year?" Teddy's laughter grew until it reverberated off the walls of Galen's office.

"Forget it."

"Wait." Teddy crossed his arms over his chest. "You already did it, didn't you? Who was it? Who'd you take to bed? Oh, I know. Makayla Danvers. No. No, Stacy Kiebler. That girl has 'sleep her way to the top' written all over her."

"Ted, stop slut-shaming. And you're wrong on all accounts. I didn't sleep with anyone. And it definitely wasn't Danvers or Kiebler. Come on."

"Excuse me. I didn't know you had such high standards all of a sudden."

"Shut up, will you? I didn't sleep with anyone. But I might have, sort of, already kissed someone…"

"Who then?"

"You've named two out of the three girls in the program already. Do the math."

"Not Jordan, right? Oh God, G, don't tell me you're switching teams here! And please tell me it isn't Jordan. That guy's a total douche. Besides, I always assumed if you were going to, ya know, with a dude, it'd be me. But—"

"Are you kidding me right now?" Galen slapped Teddy against the side of his massive head. He gave it one good shake and appeared to have settled back into reality. "Rowan Duncan, you dumbass. I kissed Duncan. Actually, she kissed me. And I'm really offended that you went to Jordan before thinking that Rowan would ever be interested in me."

"I didn't mean it like that. Really. It's just, Rowan is this nice Southern girl, and she has this boyfriend—"

"Brian. I'm familiar." Galen shuddered a little at the surprising bite of jealousy in her voice.

"Besides, I thought she was kind of like, well, really straight. Even by Galen Burgess standards."

"Jesus Christ, do I even want to know?"

"It's a compliment! You walk into a room, and girls throw their panties. Sometimes even the straight ones aren't so straight after a night with you. I've seen girls who've never so much as looked at a pair of boobs wake up from a night with you a full-blown les, totally in love, ready to lick—"

"TEDDY!" Galen wagged a finger. "This is why you can't get a date! First of all, no lesbian just 'looks at a pair of boobs' and is suddenly gay. You're way oversimplifying human sexuality, which is probably your first mistake. Second, it's more than just sex. Most girls don't just want a good orgasm, although I find that doesn't hurt. Girls want to feel wanted, and sexy, and desirable. Oh, and please don't ever say anything about licking things ever again. I know you're a gentleman, buddy, but we need to work on your delivery."

"Sorry. I'm just a little bummed. I sort of had a little, tiny crush-type thing on Rowan. But it's not a big deal. Jesus, you'd think your best friend being a girl, you wouldn't have to worry about so much competition, am I right?" He laughed.

"If I'd known I…Look, I'm obviously not going to sleep with her. I just need to figure out how to stop wanting to so damn badly.

There's got to be a way, right? Something I can do to get her out of my head?"

"Does she know?" Teddy's eyes held a faint sadness that Galen regretted instantly.

"No. And she's not going to. This can never happen. She's my subordinate. Not only would Henry Burgess kill me, but I'd completely undermine any position of authority I've built here so far. I can't afford anymore marks on my permanent record."

"So fuck someone else. You'll at least get rid of some of the sexual tension, and who knows. Maybe you can shift that energy onto them and away from Rowan."

Sometimes, Teddy was much smarter than he looked.

Jen SN knocked on Galen's office door at ten fifteen that night. The door was barely cracked, and when Galen heard Jen knock, she pushed it open with her foot and grabbed Jen by the hand, not bothering to get up out of her chair. Without speaking, she pulled Jen onto her lap until she was straddling her, her large breasts pushing against Galen's throat. Jen could get a little loud, and it was still early enough. With the milky skin of Jen's neck still between Galen's teeth, she reached around Jen's back and hit the space bar on her laptop, a low, trebly melody now wafting from the speakers.

"I'm glad you called." Jen's breath came in near gasps as Galen guided her upright off her lap and pushed her onto the desk, sending stray papers with notes about tracheostomies and Vancomycin dosing flying through the air, seeming to make way for Jen's tight ass you could balance a dinner plate on. Galen tugged off Jen's scrub pants, which slid easily over her narrow hips and thin legs. She continued to kiss her hard, making sure to own her mouth as she did. Although, truth be told, Galen generally tried to avoid kissing Jen—or most women, actually. Kissing was intimate. Fucking was primal. It sure was a waste though, since

Galen could essentially make a girl cum just by running her tongue across her lips. Still, tonight, she was willing to try kissing. Hell, she was willing to try anything to squelch the seemingly endless need to have her hands all over Rowan instead.

As Galen let her mouth drift down Jen's thighs, her mind once again shifted back to her newest subordinate. Rowan's body was the antithesis of Jen's. If Jen was tall and lean, with long, thin legs that seemed to go forever and narrow, almost boyish hips, Rowan was all curves. And not in the way Galen typically thought of curves, either. Her shoulders were slim, and her breasts were the perfect accompaniment to her petite frame. Her waist was small, with a stomach flat from pounding so many miles on the pavement. But below the waist, she was all curves and valleys and what Galen could only imagine was flesh as soft as crushed velvet and as sweet as strawberries. Rowan had jokingly once told her she was "built like a farm girl." Galen wasn't sure what that meant, but she was really fucking into it.

"What's wrong?" Jen weaved her fingers through tufts of Galen's hair, coaxing her head closer to the spot between her thighs.

"Huh?" Galen emerged momentarily, a sense of panic flooding her arousal. *Stop thinking about Duncan, damn it!* "Nothing. I'm fantastic."

Jen didn't seem concerned enough to ask any more questions, and Galen went back to nipping at the crevasse where Jen's legs began. She grabbed Jen's thighs with both hands, holding her with a ferocity and command that made Jen groan through clenched teeth. "Goddamn it, Galen. Will you just fuck me already?"

Galen grinned, in spite of the fact her mouth was very nearly occupied. "Ask me again." She loved to be begged. It got her off like nothing else. Her need for control in every aspect of her life definitely did not exclude the bedroom.

"Please. I'm begging you to fuck me. I need you."

Galen dipped her tongue into the void of Jen's belly button and slid one finger inside her, reveling in the feeling of Jen's muscles clenching desperately around her.

"Fuck me, Dr. Burgess. God, yes."

Galen hadn't always been a fan of her title. She'd certainly gotten used to it over the last six years. But it wasn't until that moment, hearing it from Jen's pleading lips, that she loved it. She slid another finger inside her. And for the first time in a week, the balance of utter control settled back over her.

❖

Avoiding Galen had actually been easier than Rowan thought. The gods of scheduling had been kind to her, and she'd spent that week of her residency largely in clinic, and operating with some of the less-senior residents, or with Dr. Peterson. She'd seen Galen in passing—in the lounge, the cafeteria, the locker rooms. But she hadn't gone looking for her. And Galen hadn't seemed to either. That night, though, she had to confront her.

The next morning, they were scheduled together to do a breast biopsy and a reversal of an augmentation gone wrong many years ago. A plastic surgeon or, at the very least, a specialized breast surgeon usually performed this type of operation, but Rowan had developed a particular interest in women's health, and Galen just so happened to be the resident doing her plastics rotation that week. So much for the gods of scheduling shining on her. She walked toward Galen's office sometime around eleven pm, knowing she would be there. Galen would never go home before midnight. Never. It was no wonder Galen had to have people look after Suzie so often.

As she approached, she noted the door to the office was mostly closed, just ajar enough to allow a small splinter of light, letting her know someone was probably inside. It was odd, she thought. Galen's door was always open. The one time she found it shut, Galen was taking a very rare nap inside and was probably afraid the sight would undermine her position as the diehard who didn't need sleep. Maybe she was napping again?

Music was coming from inside. Rowan stood at the door and listened—Fitz and the Tantrums. Nice choice. She heard another sound though—something a little quieter, but definitely not made by Fitz or any of the Tantrums. It was the low-pitched, guttural moans of a woman clearly deeply engrossed in whatever was going on in there. Galen? No. Reluctantly, Rowan admitted to herself she'd wondered more than once what Galen sounded like when she was making love. And this definitely was not it.

"Jesus…" The owner of the voice was doing anything but praying. Rowan stood frozen, involuntarily squinting as if it would somehow help her listen harder. "Fuck, Galen. Do not stop. Ever. Jesus, fuck…"

"OKAY!" Rowan hadn't realized she'd nearly shouted the word as she spun around on her heels and rushed to cover her ears. The sickening sensation of her entire gut dropping to the floor nearly knocked her over. All at once, she wanted to vomit and open the door and punch whoever was crying out for Galen like that. Rowan wasn't a violent person, in any way. She refused to kill even spiders, instead placing them in a drinking glass and carefully releasing them back into the patch of dying grass outside her apartment. But something visceral had just happened inside her. And it made her want to take out whatever woman was in Galen's office right now.

Alarmed by her own completely overblown reaction, Rowan took off down the hall and as far away from Galen's corner of the hospital as she could get.

❖

"All ready for this?" The next morning, Galen had once again managed to stealthily encroach while Rowan sat in the surgeon's lounge reviewing her patient's chart.

"Ready? Oh, for the case. Yes."

"Here. I brought you this." Galen slid a cup of coffee in front of her, her arm resting against Rowan's just long enough to make

Rowan's face burn. "Figured you'd have been up all night reading up on breast augs and tram flaps and anything else you could get your hands on."

Or I was up all night because I couldn't stop thinking about the religious experience you were clearly giving someone in your office last night. "Thanks." She took a sip of the coffee, hoping it might help relieve some of the pressure that had been tumbling around inside her all morning. "It's sweet. And light. You remembered."

"Of course I did. What good am I if I can't remember your coffee order?" Galen winked and pulled out the chair beside her, sitting so close their shoulders were nearly touching. Did Galen have any idea she'd been privy to her little tryst last night? Would she even care? Still, she did find it sort of, a little, tiny bit charming that Galen had learned how she took her coffee.

"How was your night last night?" Rowan couldn't believe she was capable of being so blunt. Something about being around Galen made all her rules fly out every nearby window.

"Quiet."

"Really? I sort of thought otherwise..." *Oh my God! Why can't you shut up already?*

Galen looked at her quizzically, until a clear understanding painted her telling face.

"Something you want to ask me, Duncan?" She smiled her devilish, lothario smile that Rowan hated. It was starkly different from the way she'd smiled on the roof of the hospital the other night. It was the smile of a cocky, sociopathic womanizer who had nothing to lose and fed off the hearts of innocent girls. So, maybe that was a little extreme. And as much as she hated that crooked, self-satisfied grin, she was also strangely attracted to it. Galen embodied confidence and power and a complete lack-of-damns given. It was annoying. But also annoyingly sexy.

"Actually, there was one thing."

If it were at all possible, Galen seemed to slide closer to her. "Shoot."

"With the pedicled tram flap, isn't the risk of tissue ischemia from revascularization higher?" Rowan already knew the answer, of course. In spite of being all but consumed by the thought of Galen's officemate, she had managed to read everything she could find on the case. But she was enjoying the way Galen's face fell when she realized Rowan didn't intend to acknowledge just how much time she'd spent obsessing over who Galen slept with.

"Look it up." Galen stood and placed her hand on Rowan's shoulder, letting her fingers just drift to the back of Rowan's neck, sending shivers as powerful as hurricane winds down her arm. "See you in there."

CHAPTER EIGHT

OR 6, which was usually nothing short of a meat locker, was burning up like the inner circles of hell. Sweat trickled down Galen's forehead and under her surgical mask. She could taste a salty bead as it passed her lips and settled under her tongue. Her hands remained steady though, delicately sewing the subcutaneous tissue of what used to be this patient's breasts, reminding herself that Mrs. Hopkins, a fifty-two-year-old mother of three who had the misfortune of being faced with stage III metastatic breast cancer, would have to live with these scars for the rest of her life.

"Nicely done, Galen. Your sutures are strong and will hold up well. What's the single most important thing to think about cosmetically?" Dr. Sarah Levine, the attending plastic surgeon, had a calming, soft demeanor that distracted Galen temporarily from the fire pit she was operating in. Galen couldn't help but notice her stomach rattle a little bit and a wave of nausea sweep up from the bellows of her abdomen.

"Reduce the tension. If you can put in good, deep sutures, you'll reduce the tension of the superficial layer, minimizing the railroad-track appearance as much as possible. Also, is it really hot in here?"

Dr. Levine looked at Rowan, who was standing to Galen's left, and then at the scrub nurse and the surgical nurse. Everyone shook their head. "Not really, no. I'm quite comfortable actually."

Galen tried her hardest to focus on the depth of her needle and the alignment of the skin. But sweat was now pouring off her face in rivulets, threatening to fall onto Mrs. Hopkins's sterile field if the scrub nurse hadn't been nearly constantly patting her down with a dry towel. The rumbling in her intestines was now a full-blown cascade of explosives, and her vision was tunneling ever so slightly. Finally, she threw her last stitch.

"Looks like you're all set here. Nice work, Galen." Dr. Levine left the room.

"Rowan, do you mind finishing up? Just cover these with some ABD pads and Koban and see her off to the PACU." Galen offered no further explanation, and Rowan nodded compliantly.

Galen managed to make it to the bathroom just outside the OR doors before vomiting up an entire venti iced coffee.

❖

It was beyond unusual for Galen to leave a case before it was finished. She even took the simplest appendectomies to the Post-Anesthesia Care Unit, making sure to check on them again once more after they came out of their medication-induced haze. Never once had Rowan seen her walk out before dressings were placed and the patient was extubated and ready to be wheeled out. Something was definitely wrong. Rowan hoped it had nothing to do with her and then silently scolded herself for being so self-involved. Of course it had nothing to do with her. Galen probably hadn't given her a second thought since their kiss the other week.

As soon as Rowan had wheeled Mrs. Hopkins out of the OR and made sure she was settled with the nurses, she hurried to the elevators and took one to the fifth floor. Whatever was going on with Galen, Rowan wasn't altogether sure she wanted Rowan's help. But something told her she had to check on her anyway. The office door was closed for the second time this week, and for a moment, Rowan hesitated, wondering if Galen had rushed off to find herself in the company of whoever had graced her presence the other night. But she thought better of it. Galen would never leave an OR to hook up.

A low, guttural moan came from behind the office door—one altogether different from the night before. This was not someone in the throes of passion.

"Galen?" She tapped lightly on the wood molding but heard no answer, so she nudged the door open. Galen was hovering over a trash barrel. Not the throes of passion—just the throws.

"What are you doing here, Duncan?" Her voice was gruff without being angry.

"Are you all right?"

"I'm fine. You should go. I don't want you to see this."

"Shut up." Rowan moved to Galen's side, wondering if she was out of line. But the pallor of Galen's face and the dark smudges under her eyes made her look so vulnerable and helpless she didn't care.

"I'm serious. I'll be fine. I just ate some bad tuna or something."

"Will you please just be quiet for once? Stay here. I'll be right back."

Galen was either too weak or too stunned to argue, and Rowan left the office. Ten minutes later, she returned, her backpack teetering on her shoulders.

"What's all this?" Galen had managed to pick her head up off the desk just long enough to look at Rowan, who had begun unpacking the bag.

"IV fluids, Zofran, a warm blanket...You know, the basics."

"It's just a little food poisoning."

"You have a stomach flu, Galen." She touched Galen's wrist. "And you're burning up."

"I have a case in an hour. It's a rhinoplasty."

"I don't think that's going to happen."

"I have to be there. I've never done one before, and this is my only plastics rotation."

Rowan had known Galen would be a difficult patient. "At least let me start the fluids."

Galen paused, then reluctantly nodded. "Can I have one of those Zofran too?"

Rowan handed her the pill, and Galen tossed it into her mouth. "Here. Put your feet up on the desk and lie back." Galen had seemingly resigned herself to Rowan's caretaking and did as she was told. Rowan wrapped the hospital-issue blanket around her shoulders.

"Thanks, Ro." It was the first time Galen had ever called her by her oft-used nickname, and a shiver of warmth passed over her.

"Don't mention it. Little poke here, okay?" Rowan uncapped the IV catheter in her hand, and Galen chuckled.

"I think I can handle it."

Rowan advanced the needle.

"Ow!"

"Sorry." She smiled.

"Remind me we need to work on your IV skills, Dr. Duncan."

"Or maybe you just need to toughen up, Dr. Burgess."

Rowan was enjoying the friendly banter between them but couldn't help but notice the shift from boss and subordinate to colleagues, or maybe even more.

A GI bug? Galen couldn't believe it. She hadn't been sick since her intern year. And here she was, ready to hurl all over the OR. And to make matters worse, Rowan had found herself taking care of her. Couldn't it have been Teddy? Or even Makayla or one of the other interns who found her at death's door? Of all the surgeons in the hospital...

Still, Galen had to admit it was kind of nice having Rowan there. When she first arrived with her care package of antiemetics and IV fluids, Galen had been skeptical. After all, basically nothing was less sexy than seeing someone's own stomach revolt against them. Not that any of that should have mattered to Galen. But the illness had worn her reserves down, and she was tired of trying to stop being attracted to Rowan. Attraction was natural. And, as Galen had reminded herself several times over the course of the day, often couldn't be helped. So she was back to being embarrassed about Rowan catching her so weak and defenseless—a feeling that altogether contradicted the enjoyment she got out of being cared for.

"I've got to go for a little while. I need to see a couple of patients in clinic." Rowan softly rubbed Galen's back. "I'll be back though."

Galen had decided to take Rowan's advice and skip out on her afternoon rhinoplasty. Only one thing was worse than being known as the chief resident who got sick, and that was being known as the chief resident who got sick in front of a patient. Without thinking, she took Rowan's hand and squeezed it. "Hurry up, okay?" Her sudden complete loss of candor and near-desperate need to have Rowan stay unsettled her. But she chalked it up to the fever.

"Are you sure you don't just want to go home?"

"I have a million and one things to do tonight. I'll just stay here until it passes and I can get back to work." There. Now she was sounding like herself again.

"Suit yourself. I'll be back to check on you in a couple of hours."

❖

It was already seven pm by the time Rowan finished with her last clinic patient and made her way back to Galen's office. The door was still partially open, just as she'd left it, but before she could knock, the ringing of her cell phone in her lab coat pocket interrupted her. Brian was calling to Skype with her.

An intractable groan escaped her mouth, and she stared at the phone for a long time. Brian's picture had popped up, as it always did when he called—his big, goofy grin and curly hair that went in just about any direction it pleased. She expected to warm at the sight. She expected to miss him. That was normal, right? That was what people felt when they were 1,900 miles apart. But all she felt was irritated. She hadn't taken his calls in two days, only answering an occasional text to appease him, reminding him that she was extremely busy with work.

She pressed the green *accept* button, and a staticky video feed of Brian appeared on the screen.

"She's alive!" Brian's voice was familiar but didn't provide the sense of comfort she was expecting or hoping for.

"Indeed I am. I'm sorry I've been MIA. It's been crazy here."

"It's okay. I sort of expected that when I signed up for this." He smiled again, and a new feeling of guilt overwhelmed her. Brian was a decent man. He loved the hell out of her. And she was seriously neglecting him.

"No. I can do better. I should do better."

After a brief, comfortable silence, he said, "I miss you, Ro."

"I miss you too." She was still standing just outside Galen's office. "But look, I have to go. I have…patients. We'll talk soon though, okay, Bry? I promise."

"I know. I love you."

Rowan pretended not to hear him and hit the *end* button in a panic. She took a deep breath and collapsed to the floor, squatting on the ground just outside of what was likely Galen's view. What was wrong with her?

"Oh, no. Don't tell me you've got it too." Apparently, she was not as out of Galen's view as she thought.

"No. I just had something to take care of. How are you feeling?" Rowan stood and moved toward Galen, coaxing her to sit back down.

"Much, much better."

Rowan eyed her skeptically, taking in her still-colorless face and sunken eyes. "Great. So we can PO challenge you then." She slid one of the unopened packets of crackers across Galen's desk,

"No problem. I'm starving." Galen's throat contracted as she swallowed hard.

"Starving, huh? Why don't I order something then? I'm thinking Indian. Maybe some nice spinach paneer. All of that creamy, ground-up spinach and cheese…"

"Sounds—" Galen didn't get another word out before covering her mouth and turning to the trash can in the corner. Rowan came to her side and rubbed up and down Galen's back, her blue scrub top now faintly damp.

"I'm sorry. I just didn't buy the tough-guy act this time. You need to go home, Galen."

"That was really mean, you know that? I didn't think you had that in you." Galen managed a faint smile.

"I'm a Southern girl, remember? We seem sweet on the surface, but don't cross us, or we'll bite." At the appearance of Galen's coy grin, she instantly regretted her choice of words. Even at death's door she was a skirt-chaser.

"Is that a promise?"

"Just…go home, will you? It's almost eight. That's well past the time normal people leave work."

"Are you saying I'm not normal?"

Rowan erupted in laughter. "Oh dear. Yes." Tears were now welling up in her eyes. "You are so far from normal."

"Whatever. Normal's for boring people."

"Agreed. I like you being less-than-normal." Instinctively, she reached over for Galen's hand and held it for just a second. She blamed the maternal feelings that had been boiling up inside her as she approached thirty but couldn't deny how much she liked the strength and definition of Galen's large, boxy palms and dense fingers. They were the hands of someone who took control—someone with resilience and ferocity and power. An alpha. She thought of Brian, his soft, quiet passivity, and couldn't help but note the extreme dichotomy.

"Fine. I'll go home." Galen scanned the room. She was like a poker player, counting her chips, quietly assessing the risk of a gamble. What was she thinking? But like most instances with Galen, she didn't have to wonder long. "I'll go home, if you'll come with me."

The entire room flashed over, Rowan's chest suddenly burning and her heart rate quickening. "You just don't have an off switch, do you?"

"Not really, no." Galen flicked her strong brow, but her face was still the color of eggshells. "But that wasn't what I meant. This may come as a shock to you, but I'm a terrible patient."

"You don't say!" Rowan rolled her eyes. Even with severe dehydration Galen was sickeningly charming.

"I promise, I won't try anything. The other night...that was a one-time deal. I know that. I'm your chief. You're a professional. And so am I. I don't care about anything in this world more than I do being a surgeon. But more than that, you have Brian. I may be a lot of things, but I'm not one to break up a happy union."

Galen's words sent a jolt of discomfort through Rowan that landed directly in her stomach. Everything she said was noble and sincere. But for some reason, she hated it. "Thank you. I'm glad we're on the same page."

"In that case, come over. Really. I just need someone to keep me company while I down Pedialyte and watch a *House Hunters* marathon."

Rowan smiled, contemplating the request. Her phone *pinged* from the desk in front of her, and she glanced at it. Brian's name appeared on the screen.

I'll dream of you tonight and every night.

She quickly hit the lock screen, sending the phone back into darkness.

"I'll have to check with my boss," she finally answered. "She's a real hard-ass."

Galen's smile was so big it took up most of her face. "Something tells me she'll be fine with it."

CHAPTER NINE

Rowan had no idea what she expected of Galen's place, but when she got there, she wasn't surprised. The apartment was on the second floor of an old brownstone in Back Bay—the most elite part of Boston where all of the old money lived. It was only a one-bedroom but spread out an impressive thousand square feet, with cathedral ceilings and walnut molding. Everything was meticulously decorated and tidy, which Rowan figured was either because Galen had a maid or Galen spent most of her waking and sleeping hours at the hospital. She knew the Burgess family had money. A lot of money. A million-dollar apartment didn't surprise her. But the decor did. For some reason, Rowan realized she had pictured Galen's surroundings like a man cave, with antique beer signs and cheesy black-and-white photos of naked women draped on sports cars. She wasn't sure why she had this sense of Galen as a privileged, overgrown child, but she fully acknowledged she had been more than wrong.

"Galen…This place. I mean, my God." She realized she'd been gawking.

"Thanks. I've put a lot of work into it."

On the dining-room wall behind Galen hung an enormous mural of a woman from the nineteen twenties, standing on a street corner with a long cigarette and a fur coat. Her silhouette was obscured in an impressionistic blur. *Naked women on sports cars. Please.*

The sofa was a soft, buttery leather the color of bourbon, and an extremely expensive-looking Oriental rug adorned the floor. It was like a showroom at a high-end furniture store, the only signs of life being a couple of open surgical journals and a coffee cup on the mahogany coffee table.

"You picked all this out?"

"Yeah. Interior decorating is kind of a thing of mine." For the first time all day, a little color returned to Galen's cheeks.

"It's incredible."

"Please, sit down. Can I get you anything? I have coffee, whiskey…"

"I'm fine, really."

"I also have water. Lots of water. And I think you'll find a box of Triscuits in the pantry that are only marginally stale."

Rowan chuckled. "I don't need anything, Galen. I promise. Besides, you're the patient. You sit." Galen obeyed and took a seat on the couch. "Do you mind if I rummage through your kitchen?"

"Of course not. Just don't judge me too hard." Galen pulled a blanket off the arm of the sofa and wrapped up in it. "Hey, Ro?"

"Yeah?"

"Thank you."

❖

As Galen had warned, Rowan really did find only a little in Galen's kitchen. It was clear just how seldom she was home. Nonetheless, Rowan had returned to the living room ten minutes later with a cup of hot tea, some chicken broth, and a thousand milligrams of Tylenol. She found Galen still on the couch, minus her usual scrubs, her legs stretched out across the chaise, her feet covered by the throw blanket. She wore a thin, fraying HARVARD MEDICINE T-shirt and a pair of basketball shorts that hung off her straight hips. Rowan had seen her in scrubs in the OR nearly every day for the last two months, but she'd somehow managed to never notice Galen's arms. They were large—much larger than she expected for someone with Galen's build. Her biceps were muscled, with a fine line marking her deltoids. They looked strong, like her hands. And all at once, Rowan found herself simultaneously turned on and completely freaked out.

She hardly knew Galen, and here she was, in her apartment while Galen lay on the couch at her most vulnerable, in her pajamas, managing to look helpless yet incredibly sexy. The scene was incredibly intimate yet seemed absolutely normal. Rowan was disturbed beyond belief.

"I managed to find a few things," she finally said, setting the tray down on the table in front of Galen.

"You're a real lifesaver, you know that? I don't know how I'd survive this without you."

Rowan took a seat next to her but purposely left a foot or two of space between them, "I didn't realize you had such a flair for the dramatic."

"Oh, I do. I started a fire in hopes of enticing you to stay a while longer. There aren't many working fireplaces in Boston, you know."

"We had four in my house growing up," Rowan said, teasing her. "I'm unimpressed."

"You will be. Just wait."

When Galen opened her eyes again, the television had kicked into sleep mode, and the last burning embers of the fire glowed a faint orange. She sat up, rubbing the bleariness from her eyes. Her fever had broken, and her stomach was no longer threatening to eject itself from her body. Rowan lay stretched out beside her, her head just a few inches from Galen's lap. Waking up to find a woman had spent the night usually sent her into a fit of panic. But Rowan's soft breathing cloaked her in a comfort she had rarely experienced in her life.

It reminded her of when she'd had chicken pox as a child. Her mother had stayed up with her all night watching *Winnie the Pooh* while Galen scratched and squirmed through the illness. When she awoke, her mother was sleeping next to her on the couch. Galen's father made her feel strong and capable and important. But he never made her feel safe. He never made her feel cared for. And her mother was usually so busy trying to please her father, she didn't have many opportunities to either. So she allowed herself just a moment to revel in the security of the scene around her.

Galen had seriously contemplated waking Rowan. But it was two forty-five am, and she couldn't find much merit in that. After all, they both had to be back at the hospital in a few hours. Instead, she covered Rowan in one of the extra blankets and curled back up on the couch beside her, fighting the urge to run her fingers through Rowan's stray hairs that splayed across the pillow.

It was still dark when Rowan opened her eyes, which wasn't altogether unusual, except that she had absolutely no idea where she was. A hand was gently rocking her awake, which only added to her disorientation.

"Hey, I'm sorry…but we should get to work…"

Holy shit, she was at Galen's house. Holy fucking shit, she'd slept there?

"I…how?" The fog started to clear, and the evening came back to her. The last thing she remembered was watching this obnoxious couple on the television arguing about hardwood versus laminate.

"You fell asleep. We both did, actually. I would have woken you up, but you looked so comfortable."

"I appreciate that." And Rowan supposed she did, although she was utterly unnerved waking up next to Galen. She could only imagine what she looked like—her makeup smeared all over her face and her hair snarled. Oh, God. Did she snore? What if she snored? She shook her head, silently kicking herself for sounding like a teenage girl.

"You can use the shower first if you want. I'll get you some of my scrubs. They might be a little big, but they'll work."

Rowan felt herself blush fiercely as she remembered ogling Galen's arms earlier that evening. "Thanks."

Several minutes later, Rowan stepped out of the beautiful marble shower, her head finally clearing.

"Here. Double espresso." Galen was standing in the kitchen in a light blue, striped, button-down shirt that brought out the Caribbean-ocean hues of her eyes and a pair of dark slacks and boots. She handed Rowan a tiny, red coffee cup and smiled.

"Thank you."

"I usually make one before I leave in the morning. They go down much quicker than coffee."

"You've really perfected the art of caffeinating. No scrubs today?" Rowan hoped she'd managed to make her voice sound casual enough. But Galen looked good. Damn good.

"Today is the first of the month, which means I get to speak at grand rounds." She groaned and rolled her eyes.

"I find it hard to believe you're dreading entertaining a room full of people."

"Normally, you're right. But grand rounds means my father will be there. Which means I can fully anticipate anything I say being torn to shreds for a solid hour afterward."

"Your dad seems like a real jerk." Rowan instantly wanted to retract her words. She and Galen were not friends. She was in no position to make personal remarks about her family. "I'm sorry. I shouldn't have said that."

"You're not wrong. Henry Burgess is a varsity-level asshole. I finally learned how to deal with him being my father, but I guess I still haven't quite adjusted to him being my boss."

"Why did you decide to do your residency at Boston City anyway? You could have gone anywhere." Rowan realized she was probing, but she couldn't help herself.

"That one's easy. I'm a Burgess. It's what we do."

Rowan figured she understood that concept all too well.

❖

"When a high-energy projectile, like a bullet, travels through the relatively liquid human body, it forms a cavity in its wake." Galen stood in front of the group of forty-plus surgeons, her white coat now covering her broad, stalky frame. She wasn't tall, but she was strong. Rowan couldn't help but notice just how perfectly Galen's outward appearance coincided with who she was inside. "And, although we still primarily see blunt trauma, with gun violence spiraling out of control in this country, we need to make sure we are on the front lines of the treatment options for penetrating injuries like this."

When Galen spoke, the room was still. Every eye focused on her, and electricity sparked the air. Rowan supposed she was the living definition of charisma. It was probably why women seemed to line up for a chance to be near her. She moved with an untouchable confidence, and every word she spoke sounded like gospel, even if it wasn't. It was a gift. And Rowan didn't succumb to it any less than everyone else did. She smiled, proud she'd arrived with Galen at work that morning. But embarrassment quickly replaced the pride. Galen was not a celebrity. And Rowan was most certainly not a fan girl.

❖

Rounds had gone well. Galen had done what she deemed to be a sufficient job discussing hemostasis techniques in penetrating trauma. People seemed engaged enough, although she was certain her father would beg to differ.

"Galen." As sure as the sun coming up, Henry Burgess was waiting for her outside the doors of the auditorium. Galen bit the inside of her cheek, a nervous tic she'd developed as a child whenever her father used her name.

"Sir."

Her father's face looked pale and worried. Something was very wrong. "It's your mom…"

Galen's heart sank to her feet. "What happened?"

"The ambulance brought her in about an hour ago. She's not doing well."

She shook her head, trying to make sense of the words. "What? I don't understand—"

"They think it may be a leaking aortic aneurysm." Even in the height of tragedy her father's tone sounded callous and cold.

"What? Is she okay? Why are you here? You should be with her! Why didn't you come get me? Why didn't she call us? Why—"

"Dr. Burgess. Galen. Stop. Take a breath. She's okay." Her father touched Galen's elbow in an awkward attempt at comfort, but the anxiety continued to bubble up inside her until she was either going to run or cry. And crying wasn't really an option.

"She's not okay. She's alone. You should have stayed with her. You should have told me right away. You should have—"

"Come on. We're going right now."

❖

Margaret Burgess lay on the hospital gurney, two nurses, an emergency-medicine resident, and an attending physician at her bedside. She looked at least ten years older than the last time Galen had seen her, which was only two months earlier. It shouldn't have been that long. Not when her mother lived only a few blocks away. Tears threatened their way to the surface, and she wished she'd decided to run instead.

"Mom…."

"Hi, baby." Her mother smiled weakly. "You look thin. Are you eating enough?"

Galen laughed as her eyes throbbed from holding back the tears. She couldn't let her mom see her scared. She had to be the strong one again. "Typical. Always worrying about everyone else." She sat on the corner of the bed and rubbed her mom's frail leg.

"I'm fine. Don't worry about me."

"How long have you been having pain, Mom?"

"A couple of days now."

"Why didn't you tell anyone?"

"It was nothing. Just a little backache. But today, when I passed out—"

"Jesus, Mom! Why didn't you call me? Or Dad?"

"I didn't want to bother you two. I know how busy you are. Especially your father."

Galen turned and scowled at the man standing uncomfortably in the doorway. Henry Burgess was, in all senses of the word, a stranger. Galen had never really known him. "That's ridiculous. You have a leaking triple-A. You could die!"

"That's just fancy medical jargon. I told you, I'm okay."

She moved closer to her mother and placed both her hands around her face. "No. You aren't okay. Listen to me. Your aorta is leaking. It's like a fire hose filled with blood, sitting right in your belly, that's slowly squirting all your blood volume into your gut. You need surgery. Right now."

"Galen Henrietta Burgess, don't you patronize me. I may not have gone to medical school, but I'm no dummy."

"I'm sorry." Galen bowed her head. She hated her middle name. She hated just how connected she had to be to that asshole who had contributed to half her genetics. "Mom. You need an operation. Will you agree to that? If you don't, you're going to die. And you can't do that to me." The dam in her eyes suddenly broke, and enormous, hot tears spilled onto the sheet covering her mother's chest. "I need you."

"Don't cry, baby."

Galen sat up straight, sniffed once with finality, and wiped her eyes. She would not give her father the satisfaction of seeing her break down—not when he looked so stoic and heartless. This was his wife. This was the woman he'd been married to the last thirty-eight years. This was why Galen didn't get close to anyone. "Dad. When is she going to the OR?"

"In just a few minutes. We're almost ready for her."

"Did you just say 'we'?" Galen's fear and sadness turned to a rage so blinding the room flashed white.

"Yes. I'll be doing the operation."

"Like hell you will," she shouted.

"Excuse me? You better watch your tone right now, Doctor. Remember who you're speaking to."

"Remember? Oh, I remember. A frigid, empty shell of a man who would rather be a surgeon than a husband, even when his wife is about to die!"

No one in the room dared to take a breath. Never in her life had she spoken to her father that way. And she couldn't bring herself to give a single fuck. All she cared about was her mother—the one person who'd ever shown her love and affection, even when she was busy catering to her husband. "Galen, honey. I'm going to be fine. Your dad is the best in town. You know that. I'm in very good hands."

"He should be holding your hand when you wake up, not checking your incision sites."

"Mrs. Burgess?" Two anesthesiologists showed up in the doorway, surgical masks hanging from their chins. "It's time to go."

"I'm ready. Let's just get this over with, huh?"

The men unlocked the gurney and wheeled it away.

"Mom. I love you."

CHAPTER TEN

It had been over six hours since Rowan last saw Galen at grand rounds, and her absence was palpable. A day hadn't gone by without Rowan running into her in the lounge, on a case, or seeking Galen out in her office. Had Galen gone home sick again? Somehow she doubted that. Maybe the reprimand from her father was too much for her and she'd gone into hiding? No. Rowan doubted that too. Maybe Galen was avoiding her? Maybe their night together was too much for her, and she was trying to get some distance. She groaned out loud, annoyed at herself for always thinking Galen's emotions were somehow tied to her own.

If she were being an adult, she would have just texted Galen. But what would she have said, anyway? "Hi, just wondering where you are?" Sure, that would work fine, if she wanted to sound like a stalker. Instead, she took to actual stalking and searched anywhere and everywhere she thought Galen might be in between her cases.

She'd checked the OR schedule first, finding that Galen's name had been taken off. That was odd. It would take a near tragedy to keep Galen out of the OR. The next logical place was her office. But she wasn't there either. She'd checked—on five different occasions. And each time, the door was shut. On three occasions, she'd taken out her phone, ready to call her. But when she realized she had nothing to ask her, she'd hung up.

By six thirty pm, Rowan had finished her last case in the OR and could no longer deny the monologue coming from her stomach. She tore down the stairs toward the cafeteria, nearly kicking the person sitting on one of the steps of the second floor directly in the back as she went.

"I'm sorry, I…" But something made her slow her pace. The person sitting on the stairs was crying. She knew that head of hair, and those strong hands that held that head that looked to be carrying ten tons of sadness.

"You have a real habit of finding me in these shitty-ass situations, Duncan." Galen looked up at her and smiled, but Rowan had never expected the melancholy behind her expression. It made her heart ache. She sat down beside Galen, instinctively putting her arm around her waist.

"What's wrong?"

"Nothing. Really."

Clearly, Galen was not interested in talking about whatever it was. And that should have been enough for Rowan. But, as she often found herself doing when it came to Galen, she pushed harder. "I have a feeling it takes more than 'nothing' to make Dr. Galen Burgess cry."

Galen scoffed and dabbed her eyes. "Cry? I'm not crying."

"Mhm. We can go with that, then. God forbid anyone should know that the big, bad James Dean of surgeons has feelings."

"Did you just call me James Dean?" Galen's sadness faded a little, and her smile grew.

"I should have known you'd take that as a compliment."

She was quiet for a long time, and Rowan just sat with her, clenching Galen's side as if to hold her up.

"My mom's sick."

"What? Oh my God, Galen. Sick, like sick how?"

The color slowly faded from Galen's face again, and her red eyes sparkled wet. "It's a triple-A. It's leaking. She's been in surgery now for almost five hours."

"Is she going to be okay?" Rowan held her a little tighter.

"I don't know. I really don't know…"

"I'm so sorry…I'm so, so sorry…"

Galen let her head collapse onto Rowan's shoulder, and Rowan closed her arms around her, encircling her, trying to take away the hurt. This was far worse than seeing her sick. Galen was the strongest person Rowan had ever met. She always thought it would take an army to break her. Apparently, she had met that army.

❖

It was another three and a half hours before Galen got the call that her mother had made it out of surgery. And Rowan had waited with her in the stairwell the entire time.

"I have to go. She's waking up." Galen stood quickly, the blood that had pooled in her feet leaving her feeling woozy. She couldn't remember when she'd last eaten.

"Do you want me to come with you?"

"No. Thank you. You should go home. Thank you for everything you did for me tonight, Ro. And last night. Jesus Christ, you really have to stop saving me all the time."

"Hey. Someone has to save the hero, right?"

Galen sat down beside her again and took Rowan's face in her hands. She'd spent her life feeling disconnected from the rest of the world. Her work was largely based on taking care of people while they slept. Her father had been treating her like his resident for her entire life. And her mother had never had the strength to speak up for herself, living in the overpowering shadow of her husband and daughter. She'd spent her life ensuring a safe amount of space between herself and anyone around her. It was why she kept her relationships to nothing more than a quick one-night stand. It was why her best friend was a sweet but goofy man-child named Teddy, whose primary topics of conversation were fantasy football and *Call of Duty*. She didn't know how to let anyone get close. But all she wanted to do in that moment was to be close to Rowan.

For a long time, Galen held her there, looking into the eyes that were all at once kind but strong and safe. She wanted to kiss her. She wanted to kiss her again so badly that every cell in her body hurt. Rowan was reprieve in the midst of chaos. And for a minute, Galen didn't give a shit about rules, or titles, or Texan boyfriends. All she wanted was Rowan.

But the harsh trill of Rowan's cell phone shattered the moment. A look flashed across her face that Galen couldn't quite make out—something that straddled the line between disappointment and relief. She didn't answer the call, but that didn't stop Galen from seeing Brian's name flashing across the screen. The moment was gone. And so was Galen's desire to let anyone in.

Rowan figured she might as well return Brian's call while she sat in the waiting area of the Surgical Intensive Care Unit. She'd walked through this waiting room three dozen times since she'd been at Boston City. Often, she was the one to come out and tell an anxious family member that their loved one had made it through surgery. Or, in some cases, not. Usually those instances were reserved for senior residents and attendings to deal with. Rowan was mostly sent to deliver good news. She'd entered this waiting room over and over again. But she'd never sat alone, waiting for someone to tell her everything would be okay. It was close to midnight, and she wasn't sure what she was still doing there. The lighting was dim—an attempt to provide comfort to the three other people left sitting in the corner of the waiting room, staring at the ceiling, as if waiting to hear if their lives were about to be forever changed. A man in a faded baseball cap glanced at the clock on the wall and squeezed the hand of the woman next to him. Rowan felt selfish. Her loved one was not in surgery. She had nothing to lose that night. But Galen did.

Galen had clearly told her not to come with her to see her mother. Why would she? Rowan didn't know her mother. Hell, she barely knew Galen. It would have been wildly inappropriate. Yet there she sat, going on hour two, wondering if Galen would still need her.

"Sorry. Did I wake you up?" She did her best to keep her voice low and somber to match the mood of the room.

"Not at all." Brian had clearly been sleeping. His voice was heavy, and Rowan thought he'd underestimated how well she knew him. She smiled to herself. She'd grown up with Brian. Their fathers had been best friends, and in middle school, when Brian was the only kid at recess sitting by himself, Rowan had offered to play catch with him. It bothered her when the eighth-graders degraded her for it. But the idea of Brian being alone bothered her more. She wasn't sure whether it was her father's insistence or just her own deeply instilled sense of loyalty, but that recess began a pattern of Rowan acting as Brian's shield.

Rowan was popular enough. She was good at soccer, and smart, and had the uncanny ability to transcend all teenage cliques. This made it a little easier to continue to spend time with Brian, who, in spite of himself, remained the target of KICK ME signs and pantsings, and, worst of all, physical assault by some of the older boys. Her shallow, boy-crazy friends occasionally teased her for her study sessions and movie nights with Brian. But she didn't care. Besides, she never had to endure even a modicum of the abuse that Brian did.

Truth be told, she loved spending time with him. He was smart—a genius, actually. Brian was the only reason she survived biochemistry in high school. In fact, he was probably the reason she made it into medical school. He was funny too. Not in a laugh-out-loud, entertain-a-room kind of way. Brian had the kind of humor that was so dry and stiff, it took you at least thirty seconds to process that he'd just made a joke. And when you did, you couldn't help but laugh at his gift for subtle and quiet, finely tuned wit that most people missed.

By high school, Rowan had more than grown into her looks. Puberty had left her with curves exactly where they should have been, and a stunning smile filled with beautiful white teeth had replaced her braces. She and Brian stayed close, and that seemed to keep the beatings at bay. No one else understood their friendship. And no one understood why Rowan went with Brian to the homecoming dance in their junior year. For Rowan, it was simple. She didn't know anyone she'd rather spend her time with.

It was no secret that Brian was in love with Rowan. And, for the most part, she was able to comfortably ignore that fact. But the night of the homecoming dance, when Brian showed up on her doorstep with a cheesy corsage and a box of chocolates, Rowan thought she might be able to love him too. She did love him. Just maybe not in exactly the same way. But that was fine enough for her. That night, he tried to kiss her in the front seat of his beat-up '96 Buick. It was not the first time he'd tried. But it was the first time Rowan let him. Rowan wouldn't have described the result as sparks, or fireworks, or *Breakfast Club*-level chemistry, but she found comfort, and security, and friendship. And Rowan vowed in that moment to do whatever she had to in order to keep Brian Hemmings safe.

"I'm sorry I missed your call. Or…calls. I've just been—"

"Busy. I understand. Listen, Ro. I don't know when's the right time to ask you this because I just can't ever seem to find a right time, but…are you breaking up with me?"

"What?!" Rowan suddenly felt nauseous. She hadn't really thought about that. It wasn't even a possibility, not an option. But when Brian said the words out loud, they sounded so incredibly appealing, she wanted to vomit.

"Just be honest with me. We've always been honest with each other, right?"

She sucked in a deep breath and sighed. "I don't know, Bry. Honestly, I don't. All I have time to focus on these days is my work. I just don't have room for anything else."

"So…you do want to break up—"

"No! Yes? I'm not saying that. I'm just saying that, maybe we should take a little time. You know, like a break."

"A break." He sounded hollow and shattered.

"Just for a little bit. While I get my shit together. It's not like this is forever, okay? If we were in the same state, things would be different. But we have to work with what we have."

The other end of the line was silent so long Rowan wondered if he'd hung up. "Okay. You can take some time."

"Hey. I love you." Rowan meant that. She just didn't know in what capacity.

"I love you too."

Her phone beeped three times, and the screen went black. The three others in the waiting room were gone. They must have received some kind of news while Rowan had been talking. She hoped to God it was good news. That was really all she could take in that moment. A TV hanging from the wall played CNN on low, but otherwise, the room was eerily quiet. Rowan rubbed her temples and thought about going home.

"I had a feeling you'd still be here." Galen's voice sent a ripple of excitement and joy through her that she so badly needed.

"I just figured I'd wait. You know, in case you needed me."

Galen sat in the raggedy chair next to her but angled her body so her knees were touching Rowan's, sending a seeping warmth up Rowan's legs that settled in her belly. Even in the midst of a potentially devastating loss, Galen embodied unwavering strength. Her shirt was unbuttoned down to the third button, an enticing amount of skin peeking out from her broad chest, and her hair was disheveled so perfectly it looked like she'd spent the afternoon at the beach instead of in a hospital room.

Galen smiled at her, and her hand drifted to Rowan's thigh, squeezing it with just enough pressure to leave Rowan dizzy. She thought about their kiss. She thought about fireworks and sparks and chemistry. She found nothing comfortable about that moment—nothing easy. Rowan thought for sure Galen would kiss her again when she took her face in the stairwell. She was glad she hadn't. It would have only further complicated things. Yes, she was glad Galen hadn't kissed her again. But God, she also wished she had.

"Thank you. But this is too much. It's midnight. You should be home."

"It's not too much. And you should really stop thanking me. It's losing its effect." Rowan weaved her fingers through Galen's on the hand that still rested on her leg.

"I'm not used to people taking care of me."

"It's not so bad, you know."

Galen smiled. "I mean, I guess I could get used to it once in a while."

"How's your mom?"

"Good. The surgery went well. They repaired the entire triple-A, and she's been stable since she got out. She's still intubated, but they're going to take out the tube in the morning."

"I'm so glad, Galen. And…your dad?"

Galen's face fell a little. "He finished her surgery and stayed with her for about twenty minutes before running off to fix some kid's spleen laceration."

"I'm sorry. She's lucky to have you." Rowan could see Galen's sadness change to anger.

"She should have him too. Thirty-eight years they've been married. Thirty-fucking-eight years. I can't even fathom what it would be like to be with someone that long. You know? To brush your teeth next to the same person every night. To wake up with them every morning. And that man can't even stay at her bedside when she needs him the most."

"Is that really what's bothering you?"

Galen pulled back from Rowan quickly. "What do you mean?"

"I mean, is your dad not being there for your mother really what's bothering you? Or is it that he isn't here for you?"

"I…" The anger in Galen's eyes dissipated. "You're right. Of course I'm angry he's not with her. But he should be here with me too. And what about my sisters? They aren't as tough as I am. They don't understand what he's like the way I do. Ginger and Grace are in there with my mom, and they don't know what to do with themselves either. They need someone to tell them everything's going to be okay. We all do."

Rowan smoothed the back of Galen's wild hair. "They have someone to tell them that. They have you."

"What about me? Who do I have?"

Rowan's heart pounded at the building electricity between them. It amazed her that she could be surrounded by such heartache and still want to touch Galen so much. "You have me. How about that?"

"I could be okay with that…"

CHAPTER ELEVEN

The hospital room was cold, and the recliner Galen slept in must have been cushioned with crumpled newspaper. Her mother was still sedated, the soft hum of the ventilator doing nothing to soothe Galen's nerves. Her sisters, Grace and Ginger, had gone home to be with their own kids, and Galen was alone. She wished for a moment that her father would show up. But what she really wanted quickly replaced that wish—Rowan. The comfort she had felt knowing that Rowan was nearby seemed foreign and addictive. She'd spent her entire life learning how to shut people out. Yet somehow it had quickly become so easy to let Rowan close.

She cursed herself for sending Rowan away.

❖

Rowan couldn't sleep, not that she should have been surprised. She lay in her bed and traced the swirling patterns on her ceiling with her gaze, thinking about the sharp turn her life had just taken. She and Brian were done. Or, at least, it felt that way. Rowan thought about how much she would miss him if it really were the end. Brian had been her best friend since they were ten. More than that, he needed her. The world chewed up people like Brian and spit them out so everyone who'd made his life miserable for the last thirty-something years could stomp on the pieces. She couldn't let that happen to him. So what if that meant she might miss out on real, romantic love?

Her mind shifted to Galen and the intensity in her eyes as she had stared at her in the stairwell. Rowan was tired of pretending she wasn't attracted to Galen. Never in her life had she been attracted to a woman. But, actually, the more she thought about it, the more she realized that never in her life had she really been attracted to anyone. Brian was nice-looking, of course. And she didn't mind having sex with him or kissing him. In fact, she enjoyed cuddling with him in front of a movie or before falling asleep. But she was beginning to see that these were not exactly the same things as attraction. Attraction entailed looking at someone and feeling an undeniable urge to have your hands on them. It was thinking how amazing it would feel to lie naked next to them or have their lips on the bare skin of your neck. It was Galen.

Was she a lesbian now? Jesus Christ! Rowan sighed aloud. Somehow, that seemed like the least important and least frightening question she had to ask herself.

❖

The alarm on Rowan's cell phone jingled at five thirty am, like it did every morning. She hadn't slept for more than a couple of hours, but she happily jumped out of bed without hitting the snooze button and got into the shower. Her mood directly contradicted the events of the prior evening. Rowan was almost…giddy? What would normally be a fifteen-minute commute to the hospital took twenty-five. She'd stopped at a local doughnut shop and picked up a half-dozen doughnuts and four large coffees.

"Morning!" Makayla had spotted her walking in just ahead of her and chased her down. "Ooo, doughnuts? What's the occasion? Save me a Boston cream, okay?"

"Sorry. They're not for you guys." They stepped onto the elevator together, and Makayla hit the button for the fifth floor.

"Who are they for then?"

Rowan took an awkward step past her and pushed the button numbered eight.

"No one. Really."

"No one? And where are you headed to so early?"

"You're awful nosy, you know that?" The doors opened, and Rowan stepped out and smiled, waving to Makayla. "I'll see you at rounds."

She took the long hallway to the Surgical ICU and stopped at the front desk.

"Can you tell me what room Margaret Burgess is in?"

The young secretary with a strip of pink hair could hardly be bothered to look up from her online shopping. "812. But you can't go in there."

"Look. I know the rule is immediate family, only—"

"And are you immediate family?"

"Well, no, but...here." Rowan slid her hospital ID across the desk.

The girl shrugged and went back to browsing shoes. "Whatever. It's too early for me to care. Go ahead."

Rowan's pulse quickened as she neared room 812. She hadn't exactly been invited to see Galen's family, or Galen for that matter. And she wasn't altogether sure how her visit would go over. Galen's laughter reached her ears before she'd made it to the doorway, and she picked up her pace. When she reached the room, she stood outside, absorbing the happiness that seeped out of it. The breathing tube had been removed from Mrs. Burgess's mouth, and she was sitting up in bed, telling what appeared to be a very animated story to Galen and two other women with her same intense eyes.

"Knock, knock. Can I come in?" She smiled nervously, unsure if she would be welcomed.

Galen looked up, her clear surprise quickly turning to pleasure. "Ro. What are you doing here?"

"I thought y'all could use some coffee."

"I don't know who you are, but clearly you're some kind of angel," one of the other women said. "Come in. Please. I'm Ginger."

"Rowan. I'm a...friend of your sister."

The woman who introduced herself as Ginger glanced at Galen with a raised eyebrow. A friend of Galen? "Nice to meet you." She extended her hand to Rowan.

"I'm Grace, the middle Burgess sister." Grace, who appeared to be the subtler of the two, shook her hand.

"Nice to meet you both. I hope you like hazelnut. This place has fantastic coffee. And their doughnuts are basically worth dying for."

"You really are an angel," Ginger said.

"Ro, I want you to meet the matriarch of the Burgess clan. This is my mama." Galen gestured to the woman in the hospital bed, who had been quietly awaiting her introduction. Rowan leaned toward her and touched her shoulder gently.

"It's so nice to meet you, ma'am."

"Ma'am? Oh God, you're making me feel old. Or maybe that's this enormous scar across my chest?" Margaret's tone was filled with good nature.

"I'm sorry. I'm from Texas. Everyone there is a ma'am."

"It's very nice of you to come by. I haven't met many of Galen's friends."

Rowan glanced at Galen, who looked as red as the skin of an apple. "Well, I'm happy to meet you. And I'm so glad you're feeling better. I hope y'all enjoy the coffee." Goddamn it, her drawl was strong today. "I should get going so I don't miss rounds."

"Rounds?" Ginger said, sounding curious. "So you're a—"

"Surgical resident, yes," Galen answered, curtly. "I'll walk you out, Ro."

Rowan's insides churned with the anticipation of being alone with Galen, even for just a second. "Nice to meet y'all."

Galen followed her out the door. "That was really nice of you."

"I hope I didn't overstep. I just thought your family could use some respectable coffee. We all know that stuff in the cafeteria is garbage."

"You didn't overstep at all." Galen placed her hand on the small of Rowan's back, and Rowan wanted to lean into her until she was resting against Galen's strong chest. "It was really amazing."

"Well, you know, Southern hospitality." She smiled.

"You just keep showing up for me, Duncan." Galen moved nearer, closing the space between them. The thunder pulsated in what little air was left around them, and Rowan's vision tunneled. If Galen didn't kiss her right now, she might actually die.

"It's nothing." She laughed in order to keep herself breathing.

"It's a lot." Galen now gently held her waist with one hand, creating just enough contact to leave Rowan weak and disoriented.

"You're welcome. I should go...Rounds and all."

"I'll meet up with you guys later. Teddy's volunteered to substitute for me this morning so I can stay with Mom. But I'll be back in the afternoon. I have a lap chole at noon."

"Brian and I broke up." Rowan wasn't sure where the words came from or why she'd picked that moment to say them.

"What? Really?" The excitement in Galen's voice was hard to miss. "I mean, that's too bad. I'm sorry to hear that."

"Don't be. Distance is hard, you know?"

"I do..." Galen nodded thoughtfully. "Actually, I really don't. But I'm still sorry. If you need anything, I'm here. Okay?"

"Please. You have enough on your plate right now to worry about my relationship drama. Besides, I'm okay. Really. Brian might be another story, but I'll be fine."

"Well...good, then..."

"I guess, um, I'll see you around later?"

"Yeah. You bet."

Rowan turned and started walking down the hall, her heart echoing in her ears.

"Hey, Ro?"

She stopped and turned to look at Galen.

"Just come find me later, will you?"

❖

"And who, pray tell, was that?" Ginger was definitely the nosier of her sisters, and Galen knew she'd have something to say when she walked back into her mother's hospital room.

"One of my interns." Galen shrugged.

"So do all of 'your interns' bring your family coffee while they're visiting?"

"Shut up, Ginger," Galen snapped.

"She's really pretty, Galen. Like…wow." Grace always was her favorite.

"Thanks. I mean, I don't know what that has to do with anything," Galen said.

"Yeah, well, the color of your face right now says differently, kiddo," Ginger remarked.

"Will you guys just back off already?"

"Don't bring me into this," Grace said. "I just said she was pretty. Statement of fact."

"Enough, all of you." Margaret never seemed to have trouble speaking up around just her and her kids. "It's my turn. Galen, she's lovely. If you aren't dating her, you should be."

"Gee, thanks, Mom. Big help. Okay. I'll settle all of this right now, since apparently the Burgess family enjoys speculation more than reality. Rowan is my friend. My intern. She's helped me out a lot the last couple of days. That's all. Besides, she has a boyfriend. Or had a boyfriend, I guess."

"Had?" Ginger asked. "As in past tense?"

"I guess so. She just told me they broke up."

"You've got to get in there then! Make your move! Give her that old Burgess charm. Come on, kid. What are you waiting for?" Ginger sounded like a cheerleader.

"Seriously? It's been like, five minutes. And I'm nobody's rebound."

"The way that girl looked at you…You're no rebound, G," Grace said.

"Hate you guys." Galen waved dismissively but quietly hoped Ginger was right.

❖

Nothing broke Galen's focus at work. Especially not women. But as she stood over her afternoon patient, the next recipient of a gallbladder removal, she couldn't clear her head. Her mother was doing well. She was coming close to the twenty-four-hours mark, when the risk of surgical complications would dramatically decrease. But Galen still couldn't keep herself from worrying.

The short, ninety-minute surgery was almost over, and so far she'd managed to at least appear to have her mind in the game. It didn't help that her father was the attending on the case. Instead of being with her mother, he'd seemed to pack his OR schedule with as many elective cases as he could. Galen thought about taking the rest of the day off, but her father's aloofness pushed her into a fury that seemed to be relieved only by work. She wouldn't be his emotional buffer anymore. He would not be able to use her as a stand-in when her mother needed him.

"We're all done here," Henry Burgess said, once Galen had placed the final staple in the hepatic duct. "Go ahead and close up, Dr. Burgess."

In that moment, she couldn't have hated him more.

She finished her last stitch, made sure the patient was safely left in the PACU, and headed to the lounge. Galen was alone. The news played loudly from a TV on the wall, and magazines and journals were spread across the end tables next to two large leather couches. She pulled off her paper scrub cap and collapsed onto one of the sofas, closing her eyes and exhaling loudly. It wasn't just her mother who was hijacking her concentration. It was Rowan.

She'd spent the better part of the last two days with this woman and found herself unsettled by the fact that she actually missed her. Missing a woman was foreign in and of itself. But it was unheard of after only a few hours. She thought about Ginger and her annoying insistence that she make her move.

There was no way. Rowan was her intern. This was completely against the rules. The hospital had a strict "no fraternization" clause, but Galen had been breaking it for years. It was her father that terrified her. If he found out she was pursuing the junior residents, he'd make sure she was stripped of her title of chief resident and maybe even her entire residency. She took a fistful of her hair and tugged in frustration. Reminding herself that her monster of a father would royally screw her over if she acted on her desires was doing little to nothing to stop the fantasies.

In fact, they were only getting worse. Galen could hardly look at Rowan now without thinking about getting her clothes off. When they touched, which they seemed to be doing more often than not lately, the fantasy manifested into a physical ache that bordered on torture. She'd silently thanked God, or the universe, or whoever, that they had run across each other only in public spaces lately, at least since the night at her house. If they were alone, all bets were more than off.

CHAPTER TWELVE

Just come find me later, will you? Rowan had spent the entire day trying to figure out what Galen could have possibly meant. She replayed the words over and over, trying to make sense of them. But every time she did, her imagination took hold, and she could no longer rationalize anything. Maybe Galen wanted to talk to her about something. Or maybe she just wanted to hang out. Yeah, like "I'll see you around," Rowan told herself. But that didn't feel right either. At least, she hoped it wasn't.

She made a deal with herself. If she didn't see Galen by eight pm, she'd go do exactly what Galen had said—seek her out. That was reasonable. Wasn't it?

By five pm, her work had dwindled significantly, and she found herself in the lounge, staring at the same page in *Current Surgical Theory* she'd been on for an hour, anticipating being near Galen again. What was happening to her? Was she really becoming another Galen Burgess groupie? She groaned at the idea, absolutely disgusted by herself. "Gross," she said out loud.

"What's gross?" Rowan was so absorbed in her school-girl crush she hadn't heard Makayla come in.

"Oh, just this tumor I'm reading about."

Makayla sat down beside her eagerly. "Let me see! I love gross stuff." She pulled the book away from Rowan. "There's no picture."

"Yeah...But, I...I have a great imagination." God, was that the truth.

"This section isn't even about tumors. It's about hemorrhoids. Which, admittedly, are gross. But what is going on with you, Texas?"

"Nothing. Just tired."

"Bull. Do you know what my undergrad degree was in?" Makayla said with a smirk.

"Torture? Annoyance? Interrogation?"

"Psychology."

"Great. Well, there's not much to psychoanalyze about hemorrhoids." Rowan wanted Makayla to stop asking questions. She was a terrible liar. And she was brimming with enough feelings and thoughts and daydreams about Galen that the smallest push might spill everything out in the open. If anyone was going to crack her, it would be Makayla.

"Spill." Makayla slammed the book shut and pushed it aside, forcing Rowan to look at her.

"I don't know what you're talking about."

"Yes, you do. I know that look. That look is about a boy." Rowan didn't answer. "I'm right, aren't I?"

"No, actually."

Makayla angled her head so she was staring directly into Rowan's eyes in a way that made Rowan feel exposed and transparent. "It's not a patient. No. You aren't sad. This is...no, this is definitely infatuation I'm seeing."

"Kayla, will you stop? I have things to do."

"Not a boy. A girl! I was wrong about the gender...but so right about the lust."

"What? Now you're just blindly guessing." But Rowan's legs shook under the table.

"Rowan..." Makayla's face grew uncharacteristically serious. "I realize we don't know each other well and that I come across like kind of a gossip. But I promise, you can trust me. I mean, come on. How many other friends do you have around here, anyway?"

For some reason, Rowan was compelled to believe her. Maybe it was the Southerner in her that always made her a bit of a pushover. Or maybe she just desperately needed someone to talk to. But this was the tiny push it took for her to empty out everything she'd been thinking.

"You won't tell a soul?"

Mayakya made a fist and extended her little finger toward Rowan. "Pinkie promise." They grasped their fingers together and kissed their hands like twelve-year-olds, and something about the gesture made Rowan feel better.

"You were right." Rowan took a deep breath and forced it out again.

"About which part? The boy, or the girl?" This was a bad idea. Makayla was already far too interested.

"Girl."

"I knew it! Who? Wait…"

Rowan knew Makayla would only need one guess. "Don't…"

"Galen!?" Makayla nearly shouted her name.

"Shh! Will you keep it down?"

"Sorry…"

"It's okay. I just…no one can find out." Rowan couldn't believe she was telling anyone what had felt like the most private feelings she'd ever experienced.

"Of course. Pinkie swear, remember? But really? Galen?"

Rowan scanned the room again, in case anyone had snuck in under cover of Makayla's excitement. "I mean, nothing's happened. Yet. Aside from this one kiss."

"You kissed her? You kissed our chief? You kissed a girl? But what about Brian? I just…so many questions!"

"Will you settle down? It wasn't a big deal." But it was a big deal.

"Sure. Okay. And Henry Burgess is a nice guy. See what I did there? Opposite day."

"It was just a kiss. And it was a while ago now. Nothing has happened since."

"But you want it to." Makayla made her perfectly shaped eyebrows dance dramatically.

"Yes. Like, a lot. A lot, a lot. As in, more than I've ever wanted something to happen in my life."

"Oh my God. This is more than just a little lady-lust, isn't it? You actually like her. "

Rowan rolled her eyes. "I don't know."

"So, is this, like, a girl thing? Or is it just a Galen Burgess thing?"

"What do you mean?"

"I mean, even I'd sleep with Galen. And I love men. I mean, I really, really love men. So, is it her? Or are you gay now?" Makayla was clearly not interested in practicing what little tact she had.

"I don't know." Rowan sighed. "Does it really matter anyway?"

"No. It really doesn't. What matters is what you're going to do now."

"I have options?"

"Texas, you always have options." Makayla put her hand on Rowan's shoulder. "To act or not to act? That is the question."

"I thought you said you were a psychology major."

"Classics minor. Now, are you going to sleep with her? And if you do, can you please tell me every last detail? Believe it or not, I've never been with a woman. It's always been on my bucket list, you know? Come to think of it, if you aren't going to make a move—"

"Kayla! Back down, will you?" Rowan glanced around herself, as if looking for whoever the words had just come from. "I mean, I don't know yet, okay?"

"Jeez. Settle down. I won't steal your girl, all right?" Makayla chuckled to herself.

"Stop. Just stop."

"Okay." Makayla got closer to Rowan and rested her chin on her fist. "Now I have questions."

"Questions?"

"What about Brian?"

"We're…taking a break right now. You know, until I figure things out."

"You mean like whether or not you're a lesbian."

"Yes, like that! Ugh. I don't know what's wrong with me. Brian is the perfect guy. He's smart, and sweet, and he loves me far more than I deserve."

"But you aren't hot for him." Makayla had simplified it to one, completely accurate sentence.

"No. I'm not hot for him. And I always thought that was fine. In fact, I didn't know any differently. I was relatively content with him. Not head-over-heels or anything like that. And I never wanted to rip his clothes off. But I didn't care."

"And then?"

"And then I met Galen. And now I care. A lot." It was the first time Rowan had said the words.

Makayla's eyelashes fluttered. "What was the kiss like?"

"The kiss?" Rowan shook her head and smiled, sucked back into the moment she'd shared with Galen on the roof several weeks ago. "Life-changing."

"Go. Now."

"What?"

"Get up out of that chair, splash some cold water on your face, fix your hair that you've been fussing with all night from your sexual tension, and go find her," Makayla said.

"I can't."

"Life-changing, Texas. Nothing trumps that. Don't waste another second in here thinking about what it would be like to touch her. Go find out."

"I don't even know if she's interested."

Makayla squinted with obvious annoyance. "You're just stalling."

"It's true." Rowan needed to hear someone say it—someone to convince her this was worth the enormous risk.

"Galen is more than interested in you. Now, will you go already?"

That was all the cheering on that Rowan needed.

❖

During the entire two and a half months Rowan had been at Boston City, she didn't remember the hallway down to the OR being so long. Her heart was racing so fast she couldn't separate the beats, and she felt dissociated from her body, like she was watching someone else live her life, making choices she would never make. She'd checked the OR schedule earlier and knew Galen would be finishing a case any minute, so long as everything went according to plan. And, dear God, Rowan hoped everything would.

She peeked through the glass double doors of OR 4, where a lone custodian in a paper gown and gloves was picking up gauze and towels from the floor. When she didn't see Galen, she walked down the hall toward the downstairs surgical lounge. This was where Galen often went after her cases, before she retired to her office for the night. But the lounge was empty. Where was she? Rowan was beginning to lose her nerve.

"See you tomorrow. I'm scrubbing in on your colectomy in the morning." Rowan's confidence continued to falter at the sound of Galen's voice coming from around the corner.

"See you then, kid." Rowan recognized Jay's voice but stayed just out of view until she was certain he was gone and Galen was alone.

"Hi…" She emerged from her hiding spot and waved awkwardly at Galen but continued to move toward her, until she was standing close enough she could smell the sweat and musk coming off her skin. Rowan shuddered, and pure need replaced her inhibitions.

"Hi, yourself…"

She watched Galen scan the halls and knew they were thinking the same thing. "How was your thyroid tumor?"

Galen smiled, her eyes gleaming with suggestion. "Enormous. I have pictures if you want to see."

"I do." Rowan's hand shook as she placed it on Galen's chest. "But not right now."

"Right." She watched Galen swallow hard, her lips parting, just begging Rowan to kiss her again.

"Do you want me, Galen?"

Galen's eyes widened, and her mouth opened a little more. "I…"

Without waiting for anymore affirmation, Rowan placed her other hand around the back of Galen's neck and pulled her in, letting her lips sink into Galen's until she couldn't breathe anymore. She didn't care. This was better than air.

"Yes," Galen finally said, pulling away from Rowan's hold, her words hot and winded. "I want you. More than you know."

"Then take me."

Galen glanced around the hall again as if looking for an escape route, while she clutched Rowan around her hips. "Let's go." Without warning, Galen grabbed her hand and whisked her through an open door into one of the empty on-call rooms, turning the lock and shoving Rowan hard against the door.

Rowan heard herself moan as Galen pressed against her. The weight of her entire body set Rowan's skin on fire, causing her to claw at Galen's clothes, pulling them every which way to try to get them off. She couldn't seem to think clearly enough to figure out how to remove Galen's scrub top. Luckily, Galen took the cue and stopped her probing kiss long enough to run her expert hands under Rowan's shirt, pulling it up over her head.

"What? Why did you stop?" Galen was staring at her, frozen in place, her eyes locked on Rowan's exposed stomach and breasts covered only by a blue lace bra. Oh God. Had she worn her good underwear today? Panic set in as she desperately tried to remember what panties she'd pulled out of her drawer at four thirty that morning. *Please don't be the period underwear. Please don't be the period underwear.*

"Jesus Christ, Duncan." But Galen's tone was anything but disappointed.

"What is it?" Rowan gave her coyest grin. No one had ever made her feel sexy like this before. No one had ever made her feel truly wanted. She'd spent her life as the conservative girl-next-door from Euless, Texas. So-called pleasures of the flesh were a sin. And even with Brian, she always felt a hint of shame. Not now. Not with Galen. She stood in front of her, half naked, feeling like a vixen finally let out of her cage. She didn't even know the definition of the word shame now.

"Just. Jesus Christ." Galen shook her head, as if to refocus, and started kissing Rowan again, weaving her hand through Rowan's long hair that she'd freed from its daily ponytail and pulling hard. Her fingers moved to Rowan's bra and unclasped it in one smooth snap, which briefly reminded Rowan that Galen had done this countless other times. But she cared far less than she thought she would. Galen was there with her, not one of the OR nurses or anyone else. And she could be sure of one thing—Galen didn't experience the connection pulsating between them with many others. All her thoughts dissolved as Galen's fingers found one of her nipples, gently brushing it at first with just the tips, then squeezing, the sensation traveling from Rowan's breasts down between her legs. She wasn't sure how much longer she could wait for Galen to touch her. But Galen was in complete control. And Rowan liked it exactly that way.

Galen's mouth found its way to that same nipple, sucking it into her mouth and then dragging her teeth softly across the top. Rowan shuddered and involuntarily pushed closer, aching to alleviate the pressure that seemed to be reaching critical levels. As if reading her thoughts, Galen pulled away and took off her shirt. She was strong and solid, with those muscled arms Rowan had never expected and a set of broad shoulders and narrow hips. A tattooed hummingbird sat under her left collar bone. She'd never seen anyone more attractive in her entire life. Before she could take any more time to admire the figure in front of her, Galen grabbed her around the waist and guided her down to the twin bed placed against the wall in the tiny room.

"I know it's small. Just pretend you're in college again," Galen said, smiling as she hovered over Rowan.

"This is nothing like college." Rowan cupped her hand around the back of Galen's neck, brushing the soft, short hairs with her palm, and pulled Galen on top of her, kissing her hard again. She let her tongue venture into Galen's mouth, gliding against Galen's and then darting back out. With her hands she explored Galen's back, letting her nails trail down with more ferocity than she'd intended as Galen's fingers fluttered around the waist of her scrub pants. Galen moved toward Rowan's hips, her hands following her mouth as she tongued a trail down Rowan's stomach and around her navel. She nipped just hard enough at the sensitive skin to make Rowan convulse in a beat of need with just a hint of pain. Sex with Brian had always been soft and sweet and conventional. Rowan didn't know any other way. Apparently, she liked it just a little bit rough. Apparently, she *really* liked it.

Once Galen had her almost undressed, she scratched her short nails down the inside of Rowan's thighs and traced her tongue just under Rowan's panties until Rowan gasped so loudly anyone walking by would surely have heard. It took every ounce of control she had not to grab Galen's head and guide her where she wanted her. But she didn't. Galen knew what she was doing. She trusted her. Galen slowly pulled the panties down, and Rowan opened her eyes for just a second, breathing a sigh of relief to see that she'd had the foresight, or luck, to put on some of her better underwear this morning. With her eyes open, seeing Galen's head between her legs, with those usually cool, blue eyes now a fiery pool staring up at her, turned her on more than she'd ever imagined she could be. Galen let her tongue walk down as far as it could without actually touching Rowan, and just when Rowan thought she might actually die, Galen stopped and climbed back on top of her, kissing her mouth softly, sensually, in a way she hadn't yet.

Rowan whispered breathlessly into Galen's neck. "Galen. If you don't touch me soon, I don't know what's going to happen to me."

"You know I can't resist that sweet Southern drawl." Galen smiled, and Rowan seemed to melt into the bed underneath her. She closed her eyes again and let Galen's fingers slowly tiptoe down her belly, tensing as Galen finally touched her.

"Oh my God." Even through closed eyes, her vision seemed to dim further. "Oh. My God. Galen." Her words only seemed to encourage Galen, who skillfully built the symphony between Rowan's legs into a deafening crescendo. Rowan thought she'd cum before. But it turned out, she hadn't. At least not like this. She shouted one final time and went limp.

Galen propped herself up over Rowan, their faces just inches apart. Her eyes held a hint of the pride and cockiness Rowan imagined she displayed whenever she got a girl off like this. But what she saw was more—a sweetness, a gratitude she knew most women didn't get.

Rowan thought about what she'd told Makayla about her first kiss with Galen—*life-changing.*

In hindsight, that kiss felt like child's play.

CHAPTER THIRTEEN

Galen woke up several hours later, still naked, with Rowan cradled against her. She could have slept for days, with the comfort and the warmth of Rowan's skin in such close proximity. Fortunately, or unfortunately, the ringing of her cell phone had pulled her out of her euphoria. Her mother's name appeared on her screen, and she struggled to make sense of what was happening. The clock on the call room wall told her it was after three am. Her mother should have been asleep, recovering on the fourth floor where she'd been moved the day before, once she'd become stable enough to be transferred out of the ICU. This woman was a stubborn Polack who'd raised her twelve siblings single-handedly after her father died and her mother was forced to work full-time. She never complained about anything—even an aortic dissection. And it had nearly killed her. Whatever was making her call Galen in the middle of the night couldn't be good.

"Mom? What's wrong?"

"Hello, dear." At least her mother sounded well. And the fact that she could talk and was calling Galen herself held promise that she wasn't in imminent danger.

"Mom. It's three am. Are you okay?"

"Oh, I'm fine! I just couldn't sleep. Did you know they still come into this damn room every two hours and take my blood pressure? For Pete's sake. How is anyone supposed to heal if they won't leave you alone?"

Galen looked at a sleeping Rowan and gently moved so Rowan was no longer underneath her. She hated leaving her side. Everything about being there with her felt right. "I know. They just want to make sure you're okay." She shielded the phone from Rowan, put on her undershirt and scrub pants, and quietly slid out of the room.

"Well, will you tell them I'm fine? Because I am. And I'd like to go home now," Margaret Burgess said.

"You can't go home yet, okay?"

During the silence on the other end of the line, Margaret seemed to be weighing the concept and deciding whether to fight back. "Okay, fine. You're the doctor. Now, I really called because I want to talk to you."

"It's the middle of the night. This couldn't wait?" Galen paced outside the call room, not wanting to stray too far from Rowan.

"Oh, please, child. You don't think I know you? You haven't slept a full night since you were eleven years old. I just about had to lock you in your room to get you down. Finally, I bought you that damn Walkman, and you'd listen to books on tape until you'd pass out for a few hours. I imagine nothing's changed. Now you just have an excuse to be up all night."

Her mother wasn't completely wrong.

"As a matter of fact, I was asleep." Galen smiled to herself, still bathed in the exhilarating feeling of Rowan's lips on hers, the way she moaned when she touched her, the softness of her skin and the curves of her hips.

"I guess you're awake now! So can you come up to my room? I assume you're still at the hospital. I don't know why you pay that ridiculous mortgage on that gorgeous apartment if you're never in it. You really are your father's daughter."

"I'll be right there." Galen hung up the phone. She thought about waking Rowan but didn't want to interrupt what looked like a rare moment of peace for her. God, she was even more beautiful when she was asleep. Something about the way her eyelashes fluttered and her lips parted while she breathed slowly framed

Rowan's air of innocence and Southern, good-girl charm. Galen knew Rowan Duncan would be a challenge and that she'd wanted her like she couldn't remember wanting anyone before. But she hadn't counted on being completely, uncharacteristically smitten.

Galen arrived at room 402 a few minutes later. "What's bothering you, Mom?" She found herself assessing her mother, checking her skin color, her breathing patterns, her heart rhythm on the monitor next to her. Everything was normal. But it wasn't like her mother to summon her in the middle of the night just to talk.

"Sit."

Galen did as she was told. "You're freaking me out."

"I've had a lot of time to think. They don't let me do a whole hell of a lot else. Tell me about this girl, Galen."

Galen's breath caught a little. "What girl?"

"What girl? Don't play dumb with me, child. I thought we'd already discussed this. Just because I don't have a fancy degree—"

"—doesn't mean you aren't as smart as I am."

"Smarter. Because whose loins do you think you came from?" Margaret was clearly amused with herself.

"Ew. Mom. Don't say 'loins' again. Please. And fine, you're smarter."

"This girl."

Galen sighed, ready for a barrage of questions. "I assume you're talking about Rowan."

"No. I'm talking about Kate Middleton, the Duchess of Cambridge. Of course I'm talking about Rowan."

Galen laughed. She'd certainly inherited a lot of her baggage from her father but was immensely grateful for the wit, humor, and warmth her mother had passed on to her. "Don't tell me you called me to your hospital room in the middle of the night to interrogate me about my intern."

"Your intern? Is that what you call her? You realize you sound like a misogynist, don't you? I raised you better than that, Galen Henrietta Burgess. You don't own that girl. You don't own anyone. Your big-shot title doesn't give you that right."

"I'm sorry. She's not *my* intern. She's just an intern."

"No." Margaret shook her finger at her daughter. "She's not just an intern. I saw something the other morning. Do you know what that was?"

"No, Mom. What was it?" Galen rolled her eyes dramatically.

"I saw my baby completely and totally enamored with someone for the first time in her life. Now, what kind of mother would I be if I didn't make sure you didn't do what you always do and give up any and all happiness in your personal life in exchange for your career?"

"I do not do that."

"Honey. You may have your father's handsome face, but you also have his stubbornness. And his tenacity. It's what makes you both great surgeons and well, frankly, terrible romantic partners." Galen hated that her mother always seemed to be right.

"Okay, so let's say you're not so far off."

"I'm not. You really care about her, don't you." It wasn't a question.

"Yeah. I do." Galen saw no point in arguing. What she was feeling was painted all over her face like a road sign.

"Then go for it. Make it happen. Do not let this one slip through your fingers because you're too busy holding a scalpel."

"Nice. Are you going to post that one on Pinterest now, Mom? Really, very poetic."

"Listen, Galen. You're an adult now. I can't tell you what to do. But I'd be remiss if I didn't try to encourage you to go after her. Be happy."

"She's my...she's *an* intern. That means she's my subordinate. I could lose my job. Rowan could be kicked out of the program. Dad would—"

"Do you know how your father and I met?" Margaret's face grew stern and serious.

"Of course I do. You were a secretary at Harvard when he was going to medical school. You screwed up his schedule, and he came into your office in typical Dad fashion and chewed you a new one. And you lived happily ever after."

Margaret laughed. "Yes. That's the story we always told you kids."

"What do you mean?"

"That's not really what happened." She sat up straight in the hospital bed and folded her hands in her lap. "I never told you this because I didn't want you to resent your father any more than you already do."

"What are you talking about?" Galen slid farther forward in her chair and stared at her mother intently.

"I did meet your father at Harvard. That part was the truth. But I wasn't the secretary. I was a surgeon."

Galen felt the entirety of what she'd ever known or thought about the woman in front of her cease to exist. "What?"

"I was a first-year resident. Your father was just a fourth-year medical student. I planned to go into OB GYN. I wanted to do minimally invasive hysterectomies and oophorectomies. Back then, these were major procedures. Women would come in to the hospital for a week just to deal with something as small as an ovarian cyst."

"What happened?" Galen felt the weight of her mouth hanging open in disbelief. After all these years, everything she'd known about her mother was a lie.

"What do you think happened? I met your father. I fell in love. A few months later, I was pregnant with your sister. That was the seventies, baby. A man's career always came first. Your father wanted me to stay home and raise you kids, and so I did. He went on to be, well, you know who he is. And I got to bring up three amazing, talented, beautiful girls."

"That's bullshit."

"Excuse me?"

"That's bullshit!" But Galen wasn't angry at her mother for lying to her. "How could Dad allow that? You had dreams! You had a career! He was still in medical school. You'd already started residency. Why couldn't he have given up his life to take care of us?"

"That's just not how things worked back then. I know it doesn't make much sense now. But the world would have balked at a man giving up a potentially lucrative surgical career so his wife could be a physician."

"But why? Why didn't you tell me any of this until now?" Galen tried to keep her voice down to avoid disturbing the nearby sleeping patients.

"You have enough to contend with when it comes to your father. I didn't want you to hold this against him. It was as much my choice as it was his. And I have no regrets. I've had a great life so far. So please. Do not resent him. He became a huge success, and you are becoming one too. And I know you both thank me for that. Besides, that's not why I'm telling you this story."

"I'm sorry, Mom. You're going to have to give me a minute to process what you've said. All of these years I thought—"

"That I was just a secretary? That I wasn't as smart as you or your sisters, or your dad?"

"No! But what about all that talk about my 'fancy degree'? You had one all along!"

Margaret winked at her. "Sure did, honey. Now, will you let me get to my point, please? I told you this because I'm hoping you'll see some parallels. Technically, your father was my subordinate. As a medical student, he scrubbed in on my surgeries. That's how we met actually, over an OR table. It certainly didn't look good when it came out that we were together. In fact, I almost lost my position. But I didn't. I fought for it. And do you know why?"

"Why?" Galen was beginning to see her mother's point.

"Because we were in love." Margaret looked into the distance for just a moment, seeming to stare at a memory buried deep in her soul. "Believe it or not, your father used to look at me the way you looked at Rowan the other day. And that made all the risk worth it."

"So you're saying you want me to turn out exactly like Dad?"

"No. I want you to be your wonderful, charming, kindhearted self that hasn't been hardened by the world or your career yet. I know he's not the man you'd want to aspire to be right now. But I promise, he used to be. And you can make better choices. You can have love and your career, Galen. You just have to try a little harder than he did. You can be better than Henry."

Hot, warm tears built behind Galen's eyelashes. Her mother was always warm and nurturing, but she couldn't remember ever having this kind of raw, devastatingly real moment with her. "Thanks, Mom." She stood and kissed Margaret on the forehead. "Now get some rest, okay?"

❖

Rowan woke up of her own volition, alone, in the on-call room in the basement of the hospital. Dread filled her stomach, and she suddenly felt like crying. She'd spent so much time thinking about how she'd feel if she slept with Galen that she never took the time to think about the consequences of falling for a player. And that's exactly what Galen was. Of course Galen was gone. Of course she'd fled the minute she got what she wanted—her conquest of the straight girl from Texas who'd somehow managed to leave her safe, secure relationship to explore a treacherous rendezvous with Galen. Just as Rowan began to kick herself for being so incredibly daft, the door to the call room opened quietly.

"I'm sorry. I had to run out for a second." Galen moved to the bed and crawled in next to her, taking Rowan in her arms again.

"Everything okay?" Rowan tried to hide the fact she'd been at near-meltdown level only seconds earlier. Maybe she'd had Galen wrong after all.

"My mom called. She just wanted to talk."

Rowan buried her head in Galen's chest, sinking into her scent that left Rowan turned on all over again. Galen stroked the skin on her upper arm, and Rowan had forgotten completely that she'd ever been mad at Galen for leaving. "Is that normal for her?"

"Not at all, no. Which is why I went down there. She's fine though. I think this hospital stay is messing with her. She gave me this whole talk about not letting my career become my whole life and not letting love pass me by, or whatever. It was weird."

"Interesting." Rowan wondered for a moment if this talk had anything to do with her presence in Galen's mother's hospital room the other morning. She wished that were true, hoping Galen would be so wrapped up in her that her entire world would be thrown off kilter. Because God knew Rowan's was.

"So, how are you feeling?"

"What do you mean?"

"You know. About last night?"

Rowan rolled on top of Galen, keeping her lips just out of reach. "If this is your sad way of fishing for compliments about your crazy skills in bed, it's not happening. And, even more so, if this is the 'are you freaking out about your sexuality' talk, then spare me that too. No part of me is freaking out. Everything about last night was amazing."

"Is that right?" Galen grinned and kissed her, the warmth and the need Rowan had felt the night before seeping back in.

"Yes." Rowan pulled away from the kiss. "And no way in hell am I stroking that finely tuned ego of yours anymore by telling you what a savage you are between the sheets."

"You don't need to. Your little grunts and groans said it all."

"Ugh." Rowan shoved her palms against Galen's chest and sat up. "You're a pig. Did you know that?"

"You know underneath all of this gusto is just an insecure little kid waiting to get out, right?"

A grave silence fell between them, until Rowan broke it with a string of furious laughter. "Yeah! Okay."

"I'm going to have my hands full with you, aren't I, Duncan?"

Rowan smiled and moved closer to her, brushing the tip of her index finger along Galen's bottom lip and trying hard not to tremble when Galen sucked it into her mouth and gently bit down. "I sure hope so, Dr. Burgess. I sure hope so."

❖

Once Rowan had gone to shower and start her day at the hospital, Galen headed home. She needed to feed the dog, change clothes, and get a couple of hours' sleep. She also needed a little space from Rowan. Galen had heard stories about girls falling in love after one romp in bed and knew about the supposed biological urge women have to nest after sex. But she'd never believed it. Not until now, at least.

After she'd left Rowan's side early that morning, she felt like every cheesy love song she'd ever scoffed at on the radio. She constantly replayed that night over and over again, starting with the way Rowan had grabbed her around the back of her neck when she kissed her in the hallway, like she had to have her right then and there or she'd explode, to the way Rowan felt when she held her as they talked about Galen's family. With every replay, she felt the same Ferris wheel turning in her stomach. It was addicting. Galen had never done drugs, but she imagined this was what it was like.

By the time she got home, she was wide awake. Sleep would probably be impossible, so she strapped on her running shoes and went out into the early fall air, the crisp breeze distracting her. Three miles later, she was still thinking about Rowan. And by mile four, she gave up and went back to her apartment. After a long, hot shower, which probably should have been cold, she made a pot of coffee and poured some into a travel mug. For a few seconds, she stared at the mug, then pulled a second from the cupboard and filled it. She added cream until it was nearly white and followed with several heaping spoonfuls of sugar. Both mugs teetering in her hand, she called a car and headed back to the hospital. When she arrived, she left the coffee in her office and went off to the surgeons' lounge, where she knew Rowan would be studying for her next case.

"Rowan, can I see you in my office a second?" Galen tried her best to keep her voice even, but she realized it had just come out sounding stern.

"Ohhh. Someone's in trouble." Teddy, who was sitting across the room in an oversized chair stuffing his face with a pastry, had chimed in. Makayla and one of the other junior residents sat next to Rowan. For the blatant loudmouth she was, Makayla was unsettlingly quiet.

Without a word, Rowan stood and left the room, following silently until they reached her office and shut the door.

"What are you doing?" Rowan asked, sounding anxious.

"Relax." Galen smiled and handed her the coffee. "I brought you some coffee. French press. Way better than that cafeteria trash."

Rowan's defense melted, and she pushed the door shut the remaining few inches, wrapped her arms around Galen's neck, and kissed her until Galen had to lean against her desk for strength. "Thank you," Rowan said, once she finally pulled back.

"That was...unexpected." Galen kissed her again, more quickly this time, but kept her firm hold on Rowan's hips.

"What? Just because I don't want Teddy and Blabbermouth in there knowing about us doesn't mean this isn't happening."

"So...this is happening, then?" Galen's heart raced, and all those cheesy love songs rolled along on repeat in her brain.

"Yes, Galen." Rowan stroked Galen's cheek with the backs of her fingers. "This is happening. So you better figure out how to deal with it."

"I think I can manage. Honestly, Ro, I can't stop thinking about you. It's annoying, actually." She laughed.

"I know the feeling. But what *do* we do about it?"

"Today? I just want to feel exactly what I'm feeling. Tomorrow, we can figure everything else out."

Rowan's eyes lit up, and she pulled Galen closer. Tomorrow, they would figure out the details. But this moment? This was all theirs.

CHAPTER FOURTEEN

It was a small risk to assume Galen wanted to see her later that evening. But Rowan went to Galen's office after her last case of that day anyway.

"Can I come in?"

Galen sat hunched over some paper charts, a tiny cup of espresso in hand. She brightened immediately when she looked up. "Always."

"How many of those have you had today, anyway?" Rowan said, teasing her.

"This is my sixth. What are you, nagging me already?" Galen smiled. "Besides, it's slightly safer than whiskey, and I won't lose my job for operating under the influence of caffeine. You want one?"

"Do you even have to ask?"

Galen's eyes were coy and mischievous, and Rowan had already figured out what that look meant. She gestured with one finger for Rowan to come closer. No part of Rowan wanted to protest, so she took a couple of steps nearer until she was standing over her.

"Hi…" Rowan said.

"Hi, yourself."

Rowan almost didn't recognize herself as she spread her legs and straddled Galen's lap, kissing her neck as Galen's hands found their way to her hair. She wasn't sure when she'd become so bold, so liberated. But she was thrilled. "You don't mind me dropping in like this?"

"Mind? Are you kidding? I'm ecstatic." Galen weaved her arms around Rowan's waist and pulled herself into her until she was resting her head on Rowan's chest. "Actually, I kind of missed you today."

"Is that so?"

"Yes. Again, I find that fact so incredibly annoying."

"I missed you too." Rowan kissed her cheek. "How was the day?"

"Pretty standard. That lady with the ascending cholangitis is doing fine now. Her LFTs are down, and so is her white count."

"You know, it's really sexy when you talk about medicine."

Galen's cheeks colored a little, and she bit her lower lip in a suppressed grin. "You think so, huh?"

"Oh, yes." Still fully in Galen's lap, Rowan took Galen's face in her hands and kissed her with the same need she'd had the night before. "Wait." She pulled away abruptly. "Are we becoming those people I hate?"

Galen looked confused. "Which people are those?"

"You know! *Those* people. The gross ones who gush about each other constantly and can't stop making out. The ones I want to punch."

"What? No way. We are so not like that…Okay. Maybe we're a little like that. But at least it's not in front of anyone, right? Besides, I like being gross with you." She kissed Rowan again, feeling some of Rowan's panic and discomfort ease.

"I like being gross with you too. And I suppose, as long as no one's around to see it, it's fine. Right?"

"Absolutely."

"Good. When do you think you'll be done tonight?" Rowan didn't want to sound too presumptuous, but she hoped she could manage to see Galen again. She realized fully that she was acting like a crazy person. She'd just spent the previous night with her.

And the following morning. It would be insanity to spend another night with her. But it was all she wanted.

"You know what?" Galen straightened, and her eyebrows jumped a little. "I'm done right now. I mean, I'm never really done. I have four cases tomorrow I could always read up on and fifteen post-ops I should check on. And a million other things on my to-do list. But you know what I want to do more than anything right now?"

"What's that, Dr. Burgess?"

"I want to take you on a proper date."

"I've heard your idea of a proper date consists of a quick fuck on this desk right here. Not that I'd necessarily mind that."

"Oh my God! Did you just swear?" Galen pressed her hand against her chest dramatically.

"I'm not quite the good girl you think I am, you know." Rowan ground her hips into Galen's and teased Galen's neck with her tongue until Galen's breathing was fast and heavy and her eyes were glassing over.

"I think I'm starting to believe that."

"Good. Now, about this date. What did you have in mind?" Rowan smiled, pleased at the power she seemed to have over Galen. It was both exciting and comforting to know that someone she wanted so badly could want her so much in return.

"Dinner. And then maybe I'll take you up on your version of my dates." Galen winked.

"Maybe?" Rowan kissed her, her lips just a whisper against Galen's at first, until the kiss built into a tug-of-war of resilience and sheer will, both of them taking exactly what they needed without fully submitting.

"Okay, yes. Yes, you can have me if you want. Anywhere, anytime," Galen finally said, laughing joyfully.

"That's better. And I'd love to have dinner. But I need to go home and clean up first."

"Great. How about Porto?"

"Honestly, my experience of the Boston-area cuisine has been limited to the sushi place down the street from my apartment and the cafeteria chicken fingers." Rowan briefly worried that her humble Texas upbringing couldn't match wits with the money and sophistication of the Burgess legacy. But then Galen took her hand and ran her thumb gently over the top, easing any fear Rowan might have been harboring. Their backgrounds were different, that was true. But their paths had led them to the same place. And Rowan, always the fatalist, was finding it hard to believe that was a coincidence.

"You'll love it. It's Jody Adams's place. She's a family friend, so I'm sure I can get us a table."

"Are you showing off for me? Because your money and power largely unimpress me."

Galen pretended to look hurt. "Guess I'll just have to rely on my good looks and intelligence to win you over."

"Pick me up in an hour." Rowan kissed her chin, physically forcing herself to untangle herself from Galen.

What the hell do people wear on dates, anyway? Galen felt completely clueless as she flipped through her enormous walk-in closet. It was filled end to end with designer shirts and suits and shoes, but she couldn't figure out what to wear. Not only had it been years since she'd been on a date that didn't consist of a quickie in her office (Rowan hadn't been wrong), but she rarely had to wear real clothes anymore. She spent the majority of her life in scrubs, and when she wasn't in those, she was likely at home in sweatpants. Neither of those seemed like a palatable option for a date with Rowan—not when she wanted things to be perfect.

"No. No. No, no no." Galen tossed aside shirt after shirt before finally stopping at one that still had the tags on it—a navy, plaid Tom Ford she'd bought for a conference and never worn. She tried it on, buttoned the buttons one by one in the mirror, and smoothed her hands down her sides. "Yes." She smiled, pleased with what she saw but unable to keep from noticing just how much she looked like her father. He may be a dick, she told herself, but at least he's not bad-looking. After years of having girls fall all over themselves in her presence, Galen knew she was attractive. She also knew looks only counted for so much.

From the top of her closet she pulled out her best pair of dark jeans and put them on, tucking in her shirt and securing it with a belt. She topped off the outfit with a fitted black jacket and a pair of boots, and sprayed a little hairspray in her usually unruly hair. A bottle of expensive cologne that her sister had given her for Christmas several years ago sat nearly untouched on her nightstand. After a few generous spritzes, she took one last look in the mirror, decided she would do, walked to her building's parking garage, and got into her car.

❖

It had been forever since Rowan had been on a "proper date." Unless, of course, she was counting Thursday night dinners at Zaxby's with Brian, which she wasn't. She couldn't remember the last time she'd had to find something to wear that wasn't scrubs or yoga pants. Whatever it was, it needed to be good. It needed to wow. She realized, alarmed, that Galen had never seen her in actual clothes before, and her anxiety tripled. She found her best dress that she'd worn three times, to two different weddings and again the previous New Year's Eve, and decided it was her best bet. It still looked good. And she had a feeling if the way Galen looked at her earlier was any indication, she'd be just fine.

An hour and ten minutes after she'd arrived home, Rowan received a text from Galen saying she was out front. A tsunami of nausea unlike anything Rowan had ever experienced threatened to knock her over, and she wanted to vomit. Were these nerves? Had to be. The feeling was too similar to her first days in the OR. Still, she'd never felt like running to the toilet because of a date. This was so incredibly different than everything she'd ever known.

A new BMW idled in front of her apartment building, and Rowan knew it had to be Galen. The cold October air bit at her cheeks, and she was glad she'd managed to find a warm coat before the notorious New England weather unleashed its annual wrath. Galen emerged from the driver's side and moved to open the door for her.

"This is what people do on a date, right?" Galen said, teasing her.

"You're doing great so far." Rowan would have been lying if she said she didn't notice the wafting of Galen's cologne and the shape of her body under her long, tailored wool jacket. She had been raised on fairy tales—Cinderella, Snow White, all of them. But Rowan always thought Prince Charming was bullshit. Yet there she was. Instead of a carriage was a BMW. Rowan's glass slippers were just Macy's specials. And she sure as hell wouldn't be home by midnight. But there she was.

A special favor called into Jody Adams at Porto landed Galen the best table in the restaurant, complete with a bottle of a rich red wine waiting for them.

"Show-off," Rowan said, when Galen dropped her name to the hostess.

"I don't know what you're talking about."

Rowan wove her arm through Galen's. "It's perfect," she mumbled. But she was sure Galen had heard her.

Dinner was everything Galen had promised. And after she'd eaten the best meal she could ever remember having, Rowan finished her third glass of wine and leaned forward contentedly on her hands. "Thank you."

"You're very welcome. But the night isn't over yet."

"Oh, it's not?" Rowan kicked off one of her heels and slid her foot under the table, rubbing Galen's leg slowly.

"I mean, I hope not. Come home with me."

"That's very forward of you, Dr. Burgess. But I'm going to go ahead and say, 'Check please.'"

Galen immediately flagged down the server, argued briefly when Rowan tried to pay, and signed the bill, nearly yanking Rowan by the hand out of the restaurant.

During the entire ride back to Galen's apartment, Rowan couldn't stay off her. She was like a teenager, her hormones completely soliciting the actions of her hands and her body. She stroked her palm up Galen's thigh, and at every red light she leaned over to kiss her ears, her face, whatever she could get ahold of. Galen didn't seem to mind. In fact, Rowan was sure she felt her driving faster the closer they got to home. "You're killing me, you know that, Duncan?"

"What do you mean?" Rowan batted her eyelashes as innocently as she could.

"I mean, if we don't get back to my place in about two seconds, I'm going to have to take you right here in the front seat of my car."

Rowan would have had Galen in the car, or anywhere else, really. But she was pleased when they arrived at Galen's building a few excruciating minutes later.

Neither of them spoke. Both were too determined to get inside and up the two flights of stairs to Galen's apartment. When Galen finally opened the door, a huge, furry beast that Rowan immediately recognized as the infamous Suzie bounded around the corner and jumped on them.

"Down, girl," Galen commanded her. "Heel." The massive dog panted wildly but did as she was told, sitting obediently at Galen's feet. "Good girl. Now, Suzie, I'd like you to meet Rowan. Ro, meet my leading lady, Suzie."

Rowan crouched and rubbed Suzie's head with both hands. "Hello there, Suzie. It's so nice to finally meet you."

"She was at my sister's last time you were here. She takes care of her a lot when I get busy at work. I just have to take her outside really quickly, okay? I promise, it'll be just a minute."

"Take all the time you need," Rowan said, placing her hands on Galen's hips and kissing her slowly. "But also, hurry back."

While Galen took care of Suzie, Rowan wandered around the apartment. She picked up a handblown vase off one of the side tables that probably cost more than her college tuition, but put it down when she noticed a framed photo sitting in the corner near the television. It was old, but it clearly showed Galen, standing with her two sisters, her mother, and Dr. Burgess Senior. Galen wore a cap and gown adorned with sashes and pins that undoubtedly represented numerous honors she'd earned. Everyone in the photograph was smiling, happy. Rowan stared at it for a long time. She'd been with Brian for years. Marrying him was expected, the logical next step. But she'd never really been able to picture what a life with him would look like. As she grew lost in the photo in front of her, she could so easily see a life with Galen—a house, two successful surgical careers, a couple of kids, holidays with the Burgess sisters. All of it. The prospect terrified Rowan. Too soon, she told herself. Too much, too soon. But the vision was so clearly there she could almost see it in its own picture frame, right in front of her.

"That was the last time my father told me he was proud of me." Galen and Suzie had snuck in so quietly Rowan hadn't noticed. Either that, or Rowan had been so consumed by her white-picket-fence fantasy that she hadn't heard them.

"It's a great picture of all of you."

"That was my graduation from Yale. Undergrad, obviously. 4.0 GPA. Salutatorian. The works. My acceptance to Harvard was in the bag, and Henry Burgess looked at me and said, 'You did well, Galen.' Last time I ever heard that. First time, too, actually." Galen's face fell a little, and Rowan turned from the photo and made her way toward her.

"You know what I think?" She placed both of her palms on Galen's strong chest and smiled. "You are the smartest, most talented, most tenacious and charming human being I've ever met, including your father. His perceived disapproval is only a reflection on him, not on you."

Galen kissed her with what felt like an undertone of gratitude, and once again images of a future overwhelmed her. "You are amazing. Did you know that?"

"No. But you can tell me any time you like." Galen took Rowan in her arms more forcefully, holding her around the waist in a way that made Rowan feel both wanted and needed. She realized in that moment that the two things were not one and the same. Not at all. "Will you please take me to bed now?"

Her question was met by another kiss, until Galen broke free and led her down the hall to her bedroom.

"God, you're gorgeous." Galen watched as Rowan slowly, deliberately slid her hands up her stomach and underneath her shirt, grazing her breasts with her fingertips as she did. Galen was swallowing nervously. Much to her surprise, never once had Rowan worried that she was too inexperienced for Galen when it came to sex, or just being with women in general. It all felt so easy. Besides, she didn't think of Galen as "female" or "male." She was just this person—this incredible, brilliant, sexy person—that Rowan was already falling helplessly in love with.

❖

Galen had never been one for sleepovers. She could count on one hand the number of girls she'd actually spent the night with, and it was usually only when she couldn't find a reasonable escape route. Yet, for the second morning in a row, she woke up next to Rowan, this time in her own bed. The mere idea of it all should have frightened her into running full speed out the door. But it didn't.

It was still dark when the alarm clock on her cell phone went off, but Galen had already been up for several minutes. For a moment, it was just another morning, just another five am, another day grinding her life away in the OR. But a warm body next to her reminded her that this was not just another morning. Rowan was still asleep, wearing only Galen's old Yale T-shirt and her panties.

Galen remembered the night before, in the call room. She could get far too used to waking up to that sleeping face every morning.

The unpleasant buzzing of the alarm finally roused Rowan, who opened her eyes and immediately smiled at Galen. Galen knew that expression. She'd seen it on girls before.

"What's that look?" Galen asked her, closing what little space was left between them and curling her arm over Rowan's body.

"What look?"

"*That* look. That's your smitten face, isn't it?"

Rowan sneered at her, but a smile hid underneath. "I don't have a smitten look. You must be mistaken."

"Liar. And do you know how I can recognize it?"

"All of the bazillion girls you've made fall in love with you over the years?" Rowan flicked her eyebrows sarcastically.

"No. I'm trying to have a moment here. Will you shut up and let me?"

"Okay, fine. How can you recognize this look I supposedly gave you, Galen?"

"Because it's the same one I've given you over the last couple of days."

Rowan blushed and looked up at the ceiling. "You are annoyingly charming. Did you know that?"

"That's the goal."

CHAPTER FIFTEEN

Where are you? We need to talk.

Galen sat in her office, sending her third unanswered text to Teddy, the panic engulfing her like flames.

"Where the hell are you, Teddy?" She tapped nervously on her desk, staring at her phone, willing it to ring. This was not the panic she was expecting. It was not the panic she was used to. Galen had fully expected the usual fear of commitment and claustrophobia she experienced when someone got too close. But this wasn't that. She was horrified, that was true. But she wasn't afraid of Rowan falling in love with her. Galen was afraid Rowan wouldn't.

She had absolutely no idea what was happening to her. And she desperately needed someone to talk to about it.

"What is it? What's wrong?" Teddy was at her office a few minutes later, his tall, thin frame looming in the doorway like a welcomed hug.

"Damn it. Am I glad to see you."

Teddy came in and sat on the desk in front of Galen, paying no mind to the papers and empty espresso cups he sent flying everywhere. "What's going on?"

"I'm having a crisis," Galen said, glancing at the door to make sure no other prying ears were nearby.

"What kind of crisis?"

"Promise you won't tell anyone. Like, anyone, Ted."

"Jeez. Okay. I promise." Teddy gestured impatiently.

"Rowan and I…well, you know." Galen couldn't even say the words, and she wasn't sure why.

"Had sex?" Teddy looked largely unimpressed.

"Yes, that."

"Uh, yeah, of course you did. Am I supposed to be shocked or something?"

"What do you mean?"

"I mean, you've never exactly been one to deprive yourself of something you wanted. And you wanted Rowan. Of course you slept with her. So what's the big deal?"

Galen found herself slightly annoyed with Teddy's nonchalance that was in direct juxtaposition to her inner turmoil. "You know I'm her boss. We'd both be screwed if it ever got out."

"Then don't sleep with her again. I'm not going to tell anyone. And Rowan seems like the private type. I wouldn't worry about it, G. Just keep it in your pants."

"Thanks, bud. That's helpful." Her frustration boiled hotter.

"What? Is there more to it than that?" Teddy suddenly appeared drastically more interested in the topic at hand. "There is, isn't there? You wouldn't have called me into your office at ten just to tell me you stuck it to one of the interns. You and I both know you've done far worse things in this hospital."

"There's more, yes. I think I'm falling for her, Teddy."

Teddy stared at her silently, the disbelief on his ruddy face far from subtle. "You're serious."

Galen groaned and crossed her arms, angling her chair away from him. "Obviously. And I don't know what to do about it. I'm completely messed up. All I want to do is be around her, constantly. You know she actually slept over last night?"

"You're kidding." Teddy's skepticism appeared genuine.

"No. And I even liked it. A lot."

"Damn. What are you going to do?"

"I don't know! If my dad finds out, I'm done. Sleeping with the nurses is one thing, but an intern? He'll hang me."

"But you aren't just sleeping with Rowan. You care about her. You want to be with her. Right?"

Galen thought about it, but she had made that decision days ago. "Yes. I want to be with her."

"Then maybe Dr. Burgess will understand?"

Galen sighed in exasperation. "Have you met my father?"

"Just do one thing for me, okay?"

"What's that?"

"Don't throw this away because of him. Don't let that guy dictate every part of your life anymore. The child of Henry Burgess the First or not, you're a rock star, G. You don't need his blessing to be happy."

Talking to Makayla about her relationship with Galen probably wasn't the best idea Rowan had ever had. But the truth was already out there, and anyway, Makayla was no dummy. She'd figure it out on her own even if Rowan didn't come to her. Besides, she needed someone to talk to. Her mother wasn't an option. She had yet to decide how to broach the topic of her newfound queerdom, if that were even a term, with her, and dealing with the fire-and-brimstone talk was really the last thing on Rowan's to-do list. She had her friends from Dartmouth, but no doubt they were all dealing with their own baggage. And it might be nice to talk this over with someone who knew Galen. Maybe she wasn't giving Makayla enough credit. Maybe she could keep her secret.

"How about grabbing a drink tonight?" Rowan had tracked Makayla down outside one of the ORs later that morning.

"Really? You want to go out? You want to do, like, normal-people things?"

"Ugh. Yes, I want to do normal-people things. With you."

Makayla smiled. "Sounds fun. Count me in. Meet you in the lounge around eight?"

"Great." Coffee wouldn't cut it for this conversation. Rowan needed wine. And lots of it.

❖

"I'm ready and fabulous," Makayla shouted, standing in the doorway of the surgeons' lounge, holding her hands dramatically over her head. She wore a pair of tall, strappy heels that looked impossible to walk in and a sequined shirt cut far too low for the falling temperatures outside.

"You really are a gay man trapped in a woman's body," Rowan quipped.

"Totally. Come on. Let's blow this place. I'm over it."

A short walk later, Rowan found herself seated at the bar of one of the local pubs down the street from the hospital.

"What are you drinking? I'm buying," Rowan said. Maybe if she got Makayla drunk enough, she could talk to her without her remembering anything.

"In that case, a cosmo, please." Makayla pouted her full, red lips at the tall, lumberjack bartender. "He's cute," she mumbled to Rowan through clenched teeth.

"Are you ever not on the prowl?"

"Hey. You never know when I may meet the future Mr. Doctor Makayla Danvers."

"You are absolutely ridiculous." The lumberjack brought over their cosmos, and Rowan extended her glass for a toast. "To new friends. Thank you for coming out with me tonight."

They clinked their drinks together. "To new friends," Makayla answered. "Now," she took a torturously long sip, "spill it."

Rowan's heart rate took off. "What?"

"We already went over this, Texas. You're a smart girl. So am I. Don't belittle me by playing dumb. You. Galen. You promised me details. And I will accept no substitute."

In a strange sort of way, Rowan was relieved she didn't have to do much to broach the subject. Truth be told, she'd been ready to explode for the last fourteen hours. It would be nice to be able to say Galen's name aloud without it being followed by "after you clamp the hepatic duct, do you want to irrigate the common bile duct or cut the surrounding tissue?"

"I see there will be no beating around the bush with you," Rowan said.

"Is that your idea of a lesbian joke? Do you make jokes now?"

"Remind me again why we're doing this?"

"Because. You need a friend. And here I am." Makayla waved emphatically.

"You're right. And thank you. Thank you for being here for me."

"You're welcome. But we had a deal. Now tell me. Everything."

Rowan picked up her glass, chugged enough of her cosmo to make her shudder in distaste, and took a deep breath. "The last time you and I talked, you told me to go get her. Right?"

"Oh God, I love this so much." Makayla nearly bounced out of her seat with excitement.

"I went down to the OR, and we talked about her thyroid tumor for about two seconds, and then, I just kind of kissed her again."

"You kissed her again? I had no idea you were so aggressive, Texas. Nicely done."

"Whatever. She was sending some pretty strong signals, okay? Anyway, we ended up in one of the on-call rooms."

Makayla shook her head repeatedly. "No. Hell no. You think you're going to get away with that PG level of vagueness? What happened when you got to the on-call room?"

Rowan finished the rest of her drink in one more gulp and raised her hand to signal to the lumberjack she wanted another—many others, actually. "We kissed. A lot. And then clothes came off. She touched me…" The alcohol was beginning to kick in now, and Rowan's anxiety and shyness were turning into giddiness. "It was incredible, Kayla. I mean, I've had sex before, or, at least, I thought I had. But this was otherworldly. The things she can do with her hands, with her mouth…I didn't even know people were capable of them. I think I came four times."

"Shut up." Makayla's eyes bulged. "Galen Burgess lives up to the hype then."

"Exceeds it." Rowan grinned, and at the mention of Galen, all she wanted was to be naked in her bed again.

"Jesus, Texas. What happens now? I mean, has it happened since?"

Rowan looked at the floor, her cheeks burning from some combination of the drinks and the topic at hand. "Yes."

"How many times? This is serious! Galen rarely has doubleheaders like this!"

"Let's see…The other night was the call room. And the next morning, she went home and made coffee for me, and we made out in her office when she came back. Then, later that night, she took me out to dinner at Porto—"

"Hold up. Stop. Right there." Makayla held her hand up directly in Rowan's face. "She took you to dinner?"

"Yeah?" Rowan failed to see what the issue was.

"Galen doesn't do dates. At least not from what I've heard. And I've heard a lot. She fucks girls in her office, call rooms, whatever, but she does *not* do dinner. I was right. This is serious."

"Stop it."

"Uh-huh. If I'm wrong, then tell me what you did after dinner."

"We went back to her place, and I spent the night. So what?"

"I'm sorry." Makayla shook her head again, this time in clear disbelief. "I'm just having a hard time processing how you're a semi-functional human right now. You spent not one, but two nights with Galen, one of which was at her place?"

"That's right." Rowan took another drink, enjoying the warmth settling in her belly.

"Oh my God. What's that face? You're making a face right now, Texas."

"Why does everyone keep saying that?" She groaned but couldn't stop herself from smiling like the idiot she felt she was.

"You're falling in love with her!"

"I am not!"

"Wow, that happened fast. I mean, I heard Galen has some sort of magic fingers or some shit like that, but damn. She sleeps with you twice, and the sweet little straight girl from Texas is in love? Amazing. People should study that woman."

"Why am I strongly regretting my decision to tell you any of this?" But Rowan was still grinning.

"Galen is dangerous, Rowan." Makayla's face had grown serious.

"How do you know so much about her love life anyway?"

"I may have scouted out a couple of the nurses she was with to get the inside scoop."

"Who are you, Woodward and Bernstein? Why would you do that?" But Rowan had to admit she was flattered that Makayla cared enough to want to protect her.

"You're my friend. And I don't have a whole lot of those, if you can believe it. I don't want to see you get hurt like those other girls did."

Rowan let her head collapse into her hands, the disappointment she would have normally felt magnified tenfold by the second cosmo she'd just finished. "Am I being the world's biggest moron right now?"

"Honey, no!" Makayla rubbed Rowan's shoulder. "Here's what I know. Galen is a player. And she is an enormous liability." Rowan lifted her head and scowled. "However...I also know that her spending this much time with you, letting you sleep in her bed, encouraging it even, is not her norm. If I learned one thing from talking to the others, it's that Galen doesn't take girls home. And I also highly doubt she looks at them the way she looked at you the other morning when she came into the lounge trying to find you."

"You...you really mean that?" Rowan's spirits rose and soared into the sky.

"You're damn right I do. Does Dr. Makayla Danvers ever say things she doesn't mean?"

"Does Dr. Makayla Danvers always refer to herself by doctor, and in the third person?"

"When the mood calls for it."

Rowan laughed hard and hugged Makayla with all her strength. She wasn't a hugger—not by any means. But in that moment, she was grateful beyond words for the new friendship she was fortifying.

"Easy, Texas. I don't want you falling for me next," Makayla said, teasing her.

"Way to ruin it, Kayla. Way to ruin it."

"I'm happy for you. I really am. But what are you going to do about work? I mean, if you guys do this, what's going to happen to your jobs?" Rowan had been avoiding that question for days.

"I don't know. I guess I've been sort of waiting on Galen to figure that one out. She's so strong and decisive. Besides, it's her father who's going to be the issue."

"Listen." Makayla slid her barstool closer to Rowan and folded her hands intently in front of her. "I didn't want to say this before I had all the facts, but I did a little sleuthing. It turns out that the hospital revoked its 'no fraternization' clause back in the early nineties, after one of the CEOs married his assistant. Technically, you and Galen are free to date."

"Tell me this. Are there any lengths to which you won't go to entertain yourself?"

"Not that I've found yet, no. As for Dr. Burgess Senior, well, the guy's a blowhard. He's going to flip his shit no matter what, so you and Galen have to find a way to get past it."

"He's the chief of surgery. He runs my entire life! Not to mention he's the father of my potential girlfriend." Putting the word out into the universe was strangely freeing and exciting. Could Galen be her girlfriend? Is that what they were working toward? She wasn't sure. But the prospect was amazing.

"I'm not going to say a word to anyone. You know that, or you wouldn't be here with me right now. Also, I think we're getting a little ahead of ourselves, aren't we? You and Galen have only slept together twice."

"But I thought you said—"

"I'm just playing devil's advocate. Don't worry about the Henry Burgess piece yet. You and Galen figure yourselves out first, and then you'll get to that when you do."

For a loudmouth, Dr. Makayla Danvers sure was wiser than she seemed at first glance. The room was starting to shift a little, and Rowan recognized that she might be a bit drunk. For a Southern girl, she didn't hold her alcohol well. Her phone buzzed in front of her.

"Who's that?" Makayla asked.

"Nothing. It was no one." Rowan quickly picked up the phone and flipped it over.

"Nice try. It's her, isn't it? I don't even know why I'm asking. I saw her name, stupid. What did she say? Don't leave me in suspense."

After everything they'd shared that night, it felt a little futile to hide anything else. Rowan turned over the phone again, unlocked it, and slid it in front of Makayla without saying anything.

What are you doing right now? I can't stop thinking about you. Come fix that for me?

Rowan's face burned again. "Shut up."

"Holy shit, Texas. Forget any of my uncertainty before. Your disgustingly-cute-but-also-obnoxious infatuation is one hundred percent mutual."

"You think so?"

"Yes! Now, answer her! Tell her you're coming over."

"But…"

Makayla waved dismissively. "Don't worry about me. I'm fine. You and I can hang out anytime. I'm always here for you. But right now, you need to go to that woman and lock this shit down."

"I…Thank you!" Rowan hugged her again. "I don't care if you think this means I want to kiss you," she said, squeezing Makayla tighter.

"I love you, too, Texas."

Rowan picked up her phone and answered the text.

What did you have in mind?

She didn't take her eyes off the screen in the forty-two seconds it took to get a reply.

Come over. I need to hold you again.

"Look at this," Rowan said, smiling from her entire face and handing the phone back to Makayla.

"Wait. Play it cool. Here, try this." Makayla began to type but turned the screen to Rowan before sending the message.

It is kind of late...but I suppose I can. Be there in half an hour?

"Almost..." Rowan added a smiley face to the end of the text. "There. Now send it."

Both girls sat frozen until the phone lit up again several seconds later.

Can't wait.

With that, they squealed like schoolchildren, as Rowan quietly told herself life couldn't possibly get any better.

CHAPTER SIXTEEN

Galen knew she was coming on strong by reaching out to Rowan again. After all, it had been less than a day since she'd seen her, and just a little longer than that since they'd shared Galen's bed. But she couldn't bring herself to care. Talking to Teddy had proved surprisingly helpful, and she had a renewed sense of hope that she could be in her first real, healthy relationship. Was that what was happening—a relationship? Galen hadn't had one of those in over a decade. The mere mention of the word usually made her want to vomit. But not with Rowan. This was different. Everything was different.

Galen paced nervously around her apartment. She picked up her phone and checked the time stamp from Rowan's last message. Rowan should have been here by now. What was taking so long, anyway?

As she went to her bar cart to pour herself a couple of fingers of bourbon, her doorbell rang. Galen raced down the stairs and found Rowan outside, bundled in her wool coat and scarf like it was the middle of winter.

"If you think this is cold, wait until January," Galen said, teasing her. "We're going to have to thicken that Texas skin of yours."

"Are you going to let me in or leave me here to freeze to death?"

"I mean, you do look awfully cute out there…But I really want to kiss you, so yeah, get in here." Galen ushered her inside, and the second the door was closed behind her, Rowan threw her arms around Galen's neck and kissed her endlessly. For the shy, quiet girl who couldn't find the elevators on her first day, Rowan was certainly shedding much of her inhibition. And the change left Galen's legs shaking.

"I'm glad you texted me," Rowan said, continuing to play with the strands of hair on the back of Galen's head.

"Me too." Galen led them back up to her apartment and took her coat. "What were you doing anyway? Home studying up on your next lap chole, I bet."

"For your information, I was actually out with Makayla."

Galen thought she'd picked up hints of vermouth on Rowan's breath. "Wait. Are you drunk?"

"What? No! Maybe a little tipsy. But definitely not drunk."

Galen laughed and pulled Rowan against her, reveling in the smell of her hair and the softness of her skin. "Hold on." She took a step back and held Rowan at arm's length. "Does Makayla know?"

"I…" Rowan looked panicked, her eyes darting around the room seemingly searching for the right answers. "Yes! I'm sorry, Galen. She figured it out on her own, long before anything happened."

The house was silent. Galen kept her face stern, but she never let go of Rowan. When she couldn't feign anger anymore, Galen let her face soften and form a sly grin. "Are you saying you've had the hots for me for a while now? Because that's what I just heard."

Rowan tilted her chin and raised an eyebrow to her. "You would hear that, wouldn't you? But really, you aren't mad?"

"Of course I'm not mad, baby." Galen held Rowan closer again until her head was resting on Galen's chest. She was hoping Rowan hadn't heard what she'd just said.

"Did you just 'baby' me?"

"I…No, I said 'maybe.' 'I'm not mad, maybe.'" She sounded ridiculous, but it was too late to own her words.

"Are you sure? For someone as articulate as you are, that's really not even a sentence. I'm pretty sure you called me 'baby.'"

"What are the odds you'll let this one go?" But Galen wasn't sure she wanted Rowan to. She liked the way the pet name sounded.

"I'd say slim to none."

Galen laughed. "In that case, let's sit down. While we're on this topic, there's something I should tell you too." Galen realized her words sounded far more ominous than she intended and instantly regretted them. Rowan followed her to the couch and sat beside her. Their shoulders touched, but Rowan refused to look at her. "No, it's nothing like that, Ro. I'm not ending this or anything. No way in hell. I just wanted to tell you that, well…Teddy knows too."

"Teddy?!" Rowan threw her hands up in the air and turned to Galen.

"I'm sorry! I had to talk to someone. Besides, he's way less of a risk than Makayla Fucking Danvers."

"You're absolutely right." Much to Galen's surprise, Rowan took her face in her hands and kissed her tenderly. "And I don't mind that you told Teddy."

"You don't?"

"No. I actually think it's really sweet that you're so hung up on me you needed to tell someone." Rowan wove her arms around Galen's waist and chuckled.

"Very funny." She thought long and hard about what she wanted to say next. "But you aren't wrong, Ro."

Rowan's expression turned from teasing to tentative. "I'm not?"

"I am so hung up on you. I haven't stopped thinking about you for a minute since we left that call room the other day. If I'm being honest, I haven't stopped since you kissed me on the roof that night. I don't know what Makayla told you tonight, but I have a feeling a line or two in there was about what a player I am and how you should be careful."

"That might have come up once or twice."

"That might have been true." Galen took both of Rowan's hands and gazed as far into her eyes as she could. She needed her to hear this. She needed her to really, truly hear it. "I don't want anything like what I used to want. I don't want meaningless flings in the hospital with girls I don't think about again. I don't want to hide behind my knife anymore just because my father taught me to. I know it hasn't been long, but goddamn it, Rowan, you have sent me for one hell of a loop. I want things I've never wanted before. And I want them with you."

Rowan was quiet for so long, Galen had to wonder if she'd actually said anything at all. "What things do you want now, Galen?"

"I want…" Galen's heart was beating so loudly now she couldn't hear anything else. "I want you. I want just you. I want to do this, all the way. I want you to have all of me—not just the parts that are easy for me to give."

"Dr. Burgess…" Rowan smiled, and her eyes brightened to a warm, chestnut brown Galen had never seen before. "Are you asking me to be your girlfriend?"

"That's exactly what I'm asking. I know it's fast. And I know you have Brian to think about, and your life back in Texas, and we have our careers, and everything with my dad but—"

Rowan gave Galen a hard kiss, gripping the sides of Galen's head like she was afraid to ever let go. "If you think my answer to that question is anything other than yes, then you aren't the brilliant doctor I've given you credit for being."

"Really?" Galen's heart soared to the ceiling, and her legs melted into puddles on the floor. Not even her first surgery compared to this kind of happiness. This was everything.

"Yes! I know I sound like just another Galen Burgess groupie, but I'm crazy about you. Of course I want to do this with you. I don't care about the logistics. We can figure them out as we go."

"You are anything but a groupie. You're everything I didn't know to want, Ro."

Rowan laid her legs over Galen's lap and leaned back on the couch. "But I wouldn't be me if I didn't insist on a few ground rules."

"Agreed."

"For starters, no one else can know except Makayla and Teddy. We both have our people. But it's too risky for anyone else to find out."

"And I suppose that means we should be careful where we make out?"

"Subtlety isn't one of your strongest qualities, Galen. We'll have to work on it." Rowan laughed.

"I resent that remark."

"No, you don't. You can't be good at everything, you know."

Galen looked at her, overcome by the magnitude of what she was feeling. "Turns out I wasn't very good at keeping myself from falling in love with you."

❖

When Rowan walked into the lounge the next morning, all three young physicians in the room fell eerily silent, in the way that people do when you've been the inappropriate topic of conversation. Makayla, Teddy, and Carly, one of the senior residents who Rowan hadn't gotten to know particularly well, stopped their chatter and looked up simultaneously.

"What's going on in here?" Rowan asked, cautiously. But she was afraid she already knew the answer.

"Nothing. Just talking about…" Teddy sounded indecisive.

"Perirectal abscesses!" Carly chimed in several seconds too late.

"Oh, yeah. Hate those perirectal abscesses," Makayla added. "I had one in the ED last week the size of a grapefruit. Went all the way up to the sigmoid colon. Nasty."

Rowan had to admit, Makayla was a much better liar than Teddy and Carly. She was concerned for a minute that actual smoke might have been seeping from her ears. How could Makayla tell Carly? It hadn't even been twenty-four hours, yet she'd already been talking about her? Rowan had thought Makayla was her friend. Rowan had given her a chance to prove her wrong, and she hadn't.

Because things couldn't actually get any worse, Galen entered the room shortly thereafter, stepping into the thick tension building around them. "Hi, guys. What's everyone up to?" She didn't wait for a reply. "Rowan, can I see you in my office when you get a second? I want to go over…your charts. Yeah, we need to discuss some discrepancies in your charting."

Heat consumed Rowan's face until her entire head felt like it was on fire and her brain might melt from the inside out. "Sure. I'll be right there."

Galen nodded once and left the room.

"Charting? Is that what they're calling it?" Carly muttered under her breath, followed by a quiet chuckle that wasn't lost on Rowan.

"Thanks, Kayla." Rowan glared at them and turned, storming out of the room.

"Rowan, wait." Makayla was right behind her, but it wasn't until they were clear in the hallway that Rowan stopped to look at her.

"How could you?"

"It wasn't me, I swear," Makayla protested.

"Then who? Teddy?"

"Obviously! He told me he and Carly were having dinner last night, and he just let it slip. Don't be mad at him. It was an accident. You know Teddy. He'd never hurt anyone. Especially not Galen."

Rowan contemplated Makayla's plea. "And why should I believe you?"

"Because I promised you could trust me. Because we're grown-ups. Besides, you can't honestly expect this isn't going to get out. This kind of thing never stays a secret for long. Eventually, the entire program will know, and you and Galen are going to have to figure out how to deal with it instead of berating me and Teddy for trying our best to keep your dirty secret."

Makayla was right. They couldn't expect to keep this quiet forever. Was that even what Rowan wanted? Didn't she want a normal relationship where she could be open with her friends and coworkers? "I'm sorry. This isn't your problem."

"And?" Makayla put her hands on her hips.

"And what?"

"And this is the part where you apologize for assuming I spilled the beans, not Teddy."

Rowan sighed. "I'm sorry I blamed you for telling Carly. You're a good friend."

"So is Teddy, you know. This is a big secret to keep, Texas. Think about that." Makayla turned to go, the swing in her step sassier than usual. Just as she reached the door to the lounge, she stopped. "And your apology is accepted."

❖

"Carly knows." Rowan shut the door to Galen's office, her panic escalating.

"What? How?" Galen stood from her chair, her face pinched and worried.

"Teddy told her."

"No way. It had to be Makayla."

"That's what I thought too. But Makayla had a very convincing story for why it wasn't. I don't think Teddy meant any harm. You know he worships you. It's just…"

Galen took a step toward Rowan and placed her hands on Rowan's hips. "What is it?"

"Makayla made a good point. She said this kind of thing always gets out. She's right. We can't expect this to stay a secret for long, Galen."

"Baby…" Galen rubbed the small of Rowan's back, soothing her anxiety until all Rowan cared about was being in Galen's arms again. "It's all going to be fine, okay? You're right. Why should I keep you a secret when you're the best thing that's ever happened to me?"

"I'll give you one good reason, and his name is Henry Burgess."

"Oh, fuck my father. I'm never going to make him happy. And this makes me happy. You make me happy. Besides, you said yourself that the hospital can't fire either of us."

"I know that's what I said, but everyone in the program knowing? That feels big. And scary. Everyone will think you're giving me the best cases or the best schedule—"

"I am giving you the best cases. But it's not because you're my girlfriend. It's because you're the best intern I have. You've earned those cases. And if those other guys are too narcissistic to see that, then that's their problem."

Rowan was out of retorts. "So we just go tell everyone, then? Maybe some kind of grand Facebook post?"

"I'm not suggesting that. I'm just saying maybe we don't try so hard to hide it. Let them figure it out for themselves." At some moments, and they were becoming closer and closer together, Rowan looked at Galen and knew exactly why she'd fallen in love with her so quickly. And this was absolutely one of them.

"Okay. I guess that sounds reasonable." Rowan kissed Galen's cheek. "Just one more thing…"

"What is it?"

"Call me 'baby' again?"

Galen laughed and touched Rowan's cheek. "Oh, you like that, do you?"

"I think I could get used to it, yeah."

❖

Thanksgiving was the next day, and Galen felt the excitement of the impending holidays even more than she usually did. Christmas was always the one time of year her parents made an effort for her and her sisters. The tree was stacked with gifts, food was plentiful, and her father never went into work. It was the one day of the year he refused to be on call. And, just to prove his sincerity, he'd ceremoniously put his pager in his dresser at midnight on Christmas Eve, all of the Burgess kids looking on eagerly. Of course, now that she was chief resident, Galen would take call on Thanksgiving herself so her residents could be home with their families. It wasn't required, but it was the right thing to do. And she did it gladly. As her father would say, "Appendixes don't give a damn that it's a holiday."

Rowan had been discreet when it came to her Thanksgiving plans that year, but Galen got the impression she didn't have many options. Makayla was going back home to Chicago, and most of the others were traveling too. Rowan told Galen she'd rather eat microwaved burritos than go back to Texas for the weekend, and a part of Galen was selfishly relieved she wouldn't be home to see Brian. As far as Galen knew, the two hadn't spoken since their "break," which apparently had turned out to be a little more permanent than Brian might have realized. Galen didn't want to tempt fate by sending Rowan back to the security of Brian's goofy polo shirts and Star Wars collectables. But she hated the idea of Rowan spending Thanksgiving alone, which was why she didn't fight as hard as she should have when Rowan insisted on working that day.

She had to do something special. Galen thought about hiring a professional chef to put together a spread that would make the Food Network weep. But Rowan wasn't quite the type to be impressed with over-the-top. This has to be thoughtful, even personal.

"Danvers. When do you leave for Chicago?" Galen found Makayla sitting alone in the quiet surgeons' lounge. It seemed like most of the other residents had already made their way home, and when she saw Makayla, an idea struck her.

"Not until nine tonight. Why?" Makayla was clearly intrigued.

"I need your help." Galen glanced around the room and shut the door.

"Galen, I'm not going to sleep with you. Rowan is my best friend."

"Oh, please. I'm not even going to entertain that remark with a response, because I know you're messing with me. But seriously. I need your help. What do you know about cooking turkeys?"

"You have come to the right place, my devilishly handsome chief. I have cooked many a turkey in my day."

"I need you to teach me."

"Uh, okay?" Galen watched as Makayla's face began to register understanding. "This is about Rowan, isn't it?"

"Yes. This is her first Thanksgiving away from home, and I hate that she's stuck here at the hospital. I tried to convince her to stay away, but she wouldn't listen, so I want to make it special for her."

"You realize she's working because she wants to be with you more than she wants to be with anyone else, right?"

Galen had suspected that was true, but it was nice to hear regardless. "I know. Which is all the more reason I want to make it worth her while. I want to cook for her. Turkey, stuffing, cranberry sauce…wait, do you cook cranberry sauce?"

Makayla laughed. "Just how little do you know about cooking?"

"So little it's not even funny."

"I don't know." Makayla looked at her watch. "That's a tall order. We only have about four hours."

"I'm a fast learner," Galen answered eagerly. "Come on. I'll give you whatever you want. Just come back to my place right now and teach me whatever you can."

"Whatever I want?" Makayla's eyes darkened, and Galen immediately regretted her phrasing.

"Except that."

She rolled her eyes at Galen. "You really do think you're God's gift, don't you?"

"I…"

"What I want is that whipple next week—the fifty-six-year-old with the pancreatic cancer that your dad is doing. I want in."

"Fine. You can scrub. But you aren't touching. First-years don't get their hands on cases that complicated. I'll figure out how to convince my father. But let's go. Time is ticking, and we have a turkey to make."

CHAPTER SEVENTEEN

Before she left for the hospital early the next morning, Galen brined the turkey, prepped the stuffing, and managed to *not* cook the cranberry sauce (although, as she'd learned, she could apparently make it from scratch). She'd convinced Rowan to stay at home the night before so she wouldn't know what she was up to, although it wasn't easy. Galen so clearly wanted to be with her every chance she got, and she could tell Rowan knew it. Rowan obviously knew something was going on. Still, Galen was sure it would be worth it.

A light snow had begun to fall as Galen walked into the hospital. Rowan was standing in front of the ER entrance waiting for her, bundled in her coat and scarf and a thick wool cap. She smiled at Galen, the glow from the neon signs and the streetlights highlighting her sweet face. Galen had never felt so lucky.

"What are you doing out here?" she called to Rowan.

"Waiting for you, obviously."

Galen approached her and wrapped her arms around Rowan's waist, layers of puffy down keeping her from getting as close as she would have liked. A snowflake fell on Rowan's tiny nose and melted almost instantly. "Is that right?" Galen kissed her.

"Isn't this great?" Rowan said, pulling away from Galen and twirling around in circles like a child, her arms thrown out.

"What?" Galen laughed. "Snow?"

"Yes! I love the first snow! It's beautiful."

"That's another thing I love about you," Galen said, pulling her close again and kissing her forehead. "You make me see everything differently than I have before."

Rowan looked at the ground and smiled shyly. "I love you."

"I love you too." Galen held her there for a while as scattered hospital employees, looking tired and disgruntled, made their way past. She thought about how happy she was they didn't have to keep their relationship a secret anymore.

It hadn't taken long for the entire surgical residency program to find out about them. Galen was pretty certain Carly had been the initial leak, since Teddy and Makayla seemed far too loyal at that point to say anything else. But within a week, three others knew. And within three weeks, everyone, including most of the attending surgeons, knew—everyone except for Henry Burgess. Galen had decided to tell him herself, mostly because the anticipation was excruciating, and the revelation was a time bomb waiting to blow up her entire life.

"Dr. Burgess, Dad, I need to tell you something." Galen had cornered her father in his office, which she never did, one afternoon toward the middle of November. "I've been seeing Rowan Duncan." Her father, who had been making a real effort to appear busy by awkwardly shuffling papers on his desk and tapping the mouse on his computer, didn't say a word. "You can say whatever you want, but I love her. And we're happy. And the hospital has no rules about this, so you can't do anything except figure out a way to deal with it. If you fire me, or especially Rowan, I will go over your head to HR."

"Fine" was all her father had said, but as Galen turned to leave, she swore she saw the smallest of smiles on his hardened face.

As it turned out, what had seemed like the end of the world hadn't been that big of a deal at all. Galen had kept her position as chief, and no one seemed to question that fact. Rowan was emerging as one of the best first-years Galen had ever seen, and she was sure that opinion was founded only partially in bias. And she'd recruited Teddy to help her make sure nepotism didn't take hold and cause her to give Rowan any special treatment. It had only been a month, and, being a surgeon, Galen was exceedingly superstitious, but so far, everything was perfect.

It didn't matter that she was at work. This was the best Thanksgiving Rowan had ever had. She'd fallen in love—really, truly fallen in love, for the first time—and suddenly, everything in her life that she didn't know was missing felt whole. She did think about calling Brian. It was the holidays, after all, and the baseline guilt she'd been harboring about hurting him was certainly heightened that day. She'd have to talk to him eventually. After all, the last thing she told him was that she needed a break. After a month of silence, most people would have taken the hint—but not Brian. He was the eternal optimist, probably sitting at home thinking any minute now Rowan would come to her senses and beg him to come back to her. She needed to tell him, but Thanksgiving probably wasn't the most considerate time to do it.

She received a text from Galen later that afternoon asking her to come to her office. The hospital had been quiet. No elective surgeries were scheduled, and only one trauma—a teenager shot by a gangbanger, with a minor leg wound—had rolled through the ER. Rowan hurried, anticipating the chance to kiss Galen again. She really was the best kisser. Of course, she seemed to be the best at just about everything else too. But Rowan didn't like anything more than kissing Galen.

The office door was mostly closed, which was still unusual unless Rowan was inside with her. She knocked once and pushed the door open the rest of the way. A makeshift table put together from several patient meal trays sat in the middle of the small room. Two large candles were lit in the center, and a tablecloth made of paper patient gowns was spread across the top. A small turkey, with patches of black char, a bowl of cranberry sauce, and what looked like partially cooked root vegetables filled the rest of the table.

"What is all this?" Rowan asked, making no effort to hide a beaming smile.

"Happy Thanksgiving, baby." Galen stood and pulled out one of the stools that was tucked under the table.

"You did all this?" Tears welled up under Rowan's eyelids.

"What gave it away? The burnt turkey or the uncooked carrots?" Galen laughed. "Turns out, I'm actually *not* good at everything."

"I'm sure it's wonderful." Rowan placed her arms around Galen and buried her face in her neck. "Thank you."

"I wanted this to be the best Thanksgiving ever. But I'm pretty sure the middle of that turkey is still frozen."

Rowan pulled away and kissed Galen's face over and over again. "You're perfect. This is perfect. And I don't care if you burn a million turkeys. This is still the most thoughtful thing anyone's ever done for me."

"You mean that?"

"Yes. This is the best Thanksgiving ever, because I found you. You hear me?"

"I know the feeling." Galen smiled warmly at her, and everything sat exactly right in Rowan's world. "That being said, I ordered Yen Chang's. It's on the way."

Rowan laughed. "Turkey was never my favorite, anyway."

Galen was on for a twenty-four-hour shift, but she'd managed to convince Rowan to leave some time after eight. Rowan wanted to spend the rest of the night with her, but fatigue had set in, and Galen had a type of persuasion that made saying no to her extremely difficult. The snow had picked up as Rowan got off the bus in front of her apartment. It was so heavy, she almost didn't notice someone sitting on her front step.

It wasn't hard to recognize Brian. His tall, lanky frame was covered only by a thin windbreaker and a baseball cap. He looked dramatically out of place. Rowan's heart fell to the ground so quickly she swore she could hear it drop.

"Brian…"

"Guess I didn't dress for the weather, huh?" He smiled his goofy, crooked smile she hadn't seen in months, and panic swelled inside her.

"What are you doing here?" Rowan kept her distance, trying to process what was happening.

"Do you think I could come in? I've been standing out here for forty-five minutes now. I'm pretty sure I have frostbite."

Rowan shook her head, trying to force her brain to focus. "Yes. Of course. Come in." She unlocked the door and led him inside to her apartment. "Let me take your coat. Go sit down." Almost instinctively, she went into her bedroom and returned with one of Brian's old sweatshirts she'd kept from Texas. "Here. Put this on."

Brian smiled again. "Thanks."

"Brian…" Rowan sat down on the opposite side of the room, still feeling disoriented and terrified. "What are you doing here?"

"What's wrong, Ro? Aren't you happy to see me?"

"I am happy to see you. But…"

"I've missed you. And I've been doing a lot of thinking over the last few weeks. You were right."

"I was?" Rowan's confusion built.

"You were. You were right to ask for time. Because I realized that I don't want to be away from you anymore. Boston is too far. I want us to be together. So I quit my job, and here I am." Brian held up his hands and grinned like this was some kind of grand gift to Rowan—like she should be thrilled.

Rowan was afraid she'd throw up, and not in the same way she thought she would the first time Galen picked her up to go out to dinner. This was bad. This was so bad. It was as if she'd been having a wonderful dream and was suddenly awake, realizing none of it had been real. She knew her mouth was flopped open, but she couldn't bring herself to close it. She couldn't bring herself to move a single muscle.

"Don't you think this is something we should have talked about first?" Rowan said, once she was finally able to speak again. "I told you we needed a break. I told you I needed time."

"I know. And you said you needed a break because the distance was too much. Now that won't be a problem ever again." Brian truly didn't get it. And Rowan blamed herself fully for not being honest with him.

"That wasn't exactly what I meant…"

"Don't you want to be together?" Brian looked so pathetic, pleading for her. It broke her heart and instantly took her back through all their years together. She'd protected and cared for him since they were kids. The world had been so cruel to him. It still would be. She couldn't break his heart—not after how hard and long he'd loved her.

"I…yes. Yes. I want to be together." Rowan felt her own heart break the second she said the words.

"Good." Brian stood from his spot across the room and came toward her, but Rowan didn't move. He put his hands on her shoulders and leaned close to kiss her, but she stayed frozen. Brian's lips were cold and unfamiliar, and Rowan wasn't sure if it was the freezing temperatures outside or the fact that all she could think about was Galen.

Brian fell asleep in Rowan's bed almost immediately, but Rowan was wide-awake. It was nearly three am, and everything in her was trying to fight the choice she'd made. She'd done the right thing. Brian was a good man. He needed her. Galen would be fine. There were a thousand other girls out there Galen could fall in love with. But not Brian. He had been there for her for so many years. She owed him this. And she had to tell Galen.

Rowan didn't want to put it off until morning. And she definitely didn't want to do this at work. She made sure Brian was still sound asleep, put on some jeans and a sweater, and took a cab to Galen's apartment.

"Ro? Is everything okay?" Galen answered the phone groggily, and Rowan's guilt expanded exponentially.

"I'm outside. We need to talk."

Galen came down the stairs a minute later, dressed in nothing but her boxer briefs and a white T-shirt, and Rowan realized this was going to be far more difficult than she'd imagined. The entire car ride over she'd practiced what she was going to say. But none of it sounded right. None of it made sense.

"What's wrong?" Galen asked, opening the door. She leaned near to kiss her, but Rowan turned away. "Okay, you're scaring me a little."

"I'm sorry to wake you up, but this couldn't wait." Rowan followed Galen up to her apartment.

"What is it, Ro? Talk to me." The look of anxiety on Galen's face was like nothing she'd ever seen on her before, and it only weakened Rowan's already threadbare resolve.

"Brian's here." If she didn't get the words out immediately, they would never come.

"What?"

"I came home tonight, and he was there." Rowan sat next to Galen on the couch but made sure not to touch her. But touching her was all she wanted to do.

"Well, what did you tell him?"

Rowan filled her lungs and looked Galen directly in the eye, careful not to let her face give away any of the anguish that was wrecking her. "I told him I would be with him, Galen."

"You...what do you mean, Rowan?"

"I mean, I'm choosing Brian." She managed to keep her voice strong and even. "He's good to me. He loves me."

"And I don't? There's no way he could love you like I do!" Galen was shouting, her words desperate and broken. Rowan had never seen her fall apart like this. She didn't know it was possible.

"I'm sorry. But I love him too."

A few tears fell from Galen's face onto her bare thigh, and Rowan couldn't breathe. She wanted to avoid hurting Brian. But she never expected she'd end up hurting Galen in the process. "So, that's it then? You've made up your mind?"

Rowan kept her eyes clear and avoided looking at Galen for more than a few seconds at a time. She'd crumble if she did. "Yes. I've made up my mind." Rowan hoped, when she said the words out loud, she'd believe them herself, but she didn't.

"I guess this is good-bye." Galen rose, stalked into the bedroom, and returned with a handful of Rowan's things, tossing them to her in a rare moment of anger and apparent spite.

"Good-bye, Galen." Rowan moved stoically to the door.

"Rowan, wait," Galen pleaded. She grabbed Rowan's hand and pulled her in close, but Rowan stayed stiff and cold. "You love me. I know you do. Don't do this. Please, don't do this."

Rowan's walls were up, and that was where they needed to stay. The same pain Galen was feeling was numb to her, sitting quietly inside her until it was safe to let it out. She felt nothing. "It's time to move on. I'm sorry."

"You're sure this is what you want?" Galen asked, a few more tears escaping down her cheek. She seemed to be barely holding it together. And it was like watching Rome fall.

"Right now, I just want to leave."

Galen appeared to compose herself, a hint of her familiar pride returning. She opened the door for Rowan, and without another word, Rowan was gone.

When Galen was twelve, she fell off her bike and broke her wrist—a comminuted, distal-radius fracture that required surgical fixation and a cast for eight weeks. Even so many years later, she so clearly remembered the pain immediately after her hands hit the pavement. At twenty-four, during her first year of medical school, she passed a kidney stone the size of a small pea. Her insides were literally being torn apart. Galen was no stranger to pain. But she never understood what a broken heart actually felt like.

This was pain. This was excruciating, unbearable pain that left her so uncomfortable she couldn't sit still. And it was utterly debilitating. For years, she'd gone from girl to girl, thinking she had the harder job of the two. She'd wait for the initial shine of new lust to wear off, and when it did, she would dismiss the person, the hint of guilt following her only for another day or two. And then she'd be fine. She wouldn't sit up at night torturing herself with what she could have done differently. She wouldn't see a photo or hear a song and suddenly feel compelled to break down in tears. After she let them go, her life would, more or less, resume its course without another thought. But Galen had never been on the other end of this particular equation before.

It had been twenty-four hours since she'd last heard from Rowan—since Rowan had looked her straight in the eye and told Galen it was time for her to move on. Her words still stung like Rowan had spoken them moments ago. She would try to shut them out, but they just kept replaying in her head. And each time they did, they gutted her even further. She hadn't expected to hear from Rowan, although she found herself constantly having to squelch the recurrent hope that said she might.

It had been twenty-four hours since Rowan left her apartment— since Galen spoke the words "I guess this is it" and shut the door behind her. She'd managed to hold herself together in front of Rowan, aside from the occasional tear she resigned herself to. But she had to let her go. This was what Rowan wanted. She'd made her choice. Galen only hoped she would come to regret it. With the living-room door shut, she looked around the apartment. It had never been so small or so dark. She felt suffocated, like the air was being plucked from her lungs—until she realized she couldn't breathe through her choking sobs. Galen wasn't at all familiar, or comfortable, with crying. On the rare occasion she did, it was about her family or something equally as substantial. But never once had it been over a girl. Yet here she was, standing alone in her living room, the tears so hot and heavy they threatened to drown her. Her abdominal wall contracted so heavily she thought she might vomit, and for a brief moment, the loss was so overwhelming, she couldn't imagine how she would survive it.

So this was heartbreak. This was what all those girls she'd broken up with had been complaining about. Galen couldn't blame them. It was fucking miserable. She'd take forty broken wrists and eighteen kidney stones over this kind of pain any day. Because she didn't know of any narcotic or treatment for this kind of pain. Nothing would take it away—nothing except time. Galen panicked. She needed a solution for everything. Everything could be fixed, right? Time wasn't good enough. She wasn't prepared to endure this kind of discomfort.

Once her breathing had slowed, she let herself glance around her apartment. It was amazing how much of Rowan was left here. They'd been together only the last six weeks, but in that time, they'd spent essentially every night together. This wasn't unusual behavior for queer people. But it was unusual behavior for Galen. She'd always needed a significant amount of space. But Rowan had stayed the night that first amazing, perfect, untouchable time, and she'd never left. Galen never wanted her to leave. Rowan had so quickly become a fixture here, on her couch, in her bed, in her kitchen. And what normally would have completely terrified Galen just felt right for the first time in her life.

And now, Rowan was gone. They had strung up the Christmas lights three days before. They had decorated the enormous tree Galen had lugged up two flights of stairs. And after they finished, they'd spent the afternoon watching old movies and cuddling. For the first time since she was a kid, she had been looking forward to Christmas—Christmas with Rowan by her side. After Rowan left, she stared at the dark tree in the corner, wondering how things could go so wrong, so quickly. Rowan had pulled the rug directly out from under her and shattered her happiness into dust. She was back to the beginning—a life without love, without feeling.

After so many years in surgery, Galen had essentially sleep-trained herself. Not once could she remember suffering from insomnia. But that night, she tossed and turned. Her bed felt far too big. Over the last several weeks, she'd gotten into the habit of sleeping all the way to the left, even when Rowan was on call overnight and couldn't stay over. Last night, after Rowan left, she'd made an effort to lie in the middle, even stacking the pillows under her head that Rowan had used only a few nights before. Everything felt too big yet too small all at once. Everything felt wrong. She was alone. Alone was something Galen had coped with many times. But she was never lonely. Not until last night, that is.

She lay awake thinking about a recent study about MRIs done on the brains of people who were in love and on people who'd just had their hearts stomped on. The MRIs of the people in love revealed a dopamine pathway that was, essentially, a constant reward center for the brain. And the MRIs of the broken-hearted? Those showed a complete blockade of that pathway. A dead end to happiness. What Galen found most disturbing was the revelation that the brain of the recently dumped was no different from the brain of someone withdrawing from cocaine. She finally felt herself drifting off to sleep, picturing that little dopamine pathway in her brain being cut short, preventing any chance at happiness from passing. Exhaustion that comes only from the kind of unbearable pain that wears you down to your bones was taking over, overriding some of the immense sadness. I'll feel better when I wake up, Galen told herself.

She was awake every two hours. The room was too hot, in spite of the fan next to her bed blowing full speed onto her face. The multiple pillows she'd stacked were lumpy and uncomfortable, but she was afraid to reposition them in case Rowan's pillow still smelt like her hair. Even at two am she didn't think she could take that. Her skin was damp, and her head throbbed. Her heart perpetually beat just a little too hard and too fast. She felt awful in every sense of the word. It was like her body was rejecting the loss as much as she was. Galen set her alarm for five thirty, but she was awake at five, her heart still pounding, feeling no better than she had the night before. As she opened her eyes, she turned to her right, for just a moment expecting to see Rowan's sleeping face she'd have to kiss in order to wake her up. When Galen found herself alone in the bed, the reality of the morning hit.

People talk about feeling like they're in a bad dream. Galen always thought that was a terrible cliché. She'd never had anyone close to her die, but she imagined that might be the only thing that could potentially compare to the terror of a nightmare. But that morning, when she woke up, she walked out to the kitchen to make her coffee, poured in the creamer, fed Suzie, and went back to bed to watch CNN like she did every day before work—like she and Rowan had begun to do every day before work.

But this time, she was stuck in that nightmare. Rowan was gone. And Galen had to fight the urge to shake her head furiously back and forth to wake herself up, like she'd done as a child when she found herself in a horrible dream. This method had always worked when she was younger. But it wouldn't do any good this time. She was already awake. This reality felt as bad as any bad dream she'd ever had. But she couldn't do anything to make it go away.

Somehow, Galen managed to will herself to get into the shower and brush her hair. She even had moments of strength between the pain, where she thought she might just be okay after all. She was resilient. She was tenacious. She was a Burgess. And Burgesses didn't let a little thing like feelings trip them up. On her way into the hospital, the radio played Christmas carols on an endless loop. But Galen had to turn it off, opting to sit in rare silence rather than bask in the joys of the season she was far from feeling. This was usually her favorite time of the year. Now she was thinking she wanted nothing to do with the happiness everyone else was experiencing.

She spent the rest of the day in the hospital, trying to keep herself as busy as possible, not allowing herself more than a second to think about the loss slowly eating away at her soul. Sometimes it worked. She even heard herself laugh once or twice. Other times, she found herself staring into nowhere, chewing on the end of her pen, thinking about the way Rowan used to feel in her arms, or her smile, or her hair. Panic would set in, because she knew what came next—the pain. The pain that sucked the life out of her. The pain that made her feel like she might never be fully whole again. Every breath felt like an accomplishment. And every minute that passed without Galen disintegrating into a ball of nothing held promise for her. But the hurt was still more than she knew how to tolerate. Maybe this was karma for all the years she'd hurt others with abandon. Galen wasn't sure she believed in karma. But she did find it incredibly cruel that once she had finally learned to love someone, she had to learn how to lose that person all at the same time.

CHAPTER EIGHTEEN

Rowan asked Makayla to cover for her for the next couple of days. She told her she had something personal going on that she would fill her in on later, and she told herself she just wanted to spend some extra time with Brian. The truth lay somewhere in between. Rowan couldn't imagine facing Galen yet. The look on her face when she'd told her they were done still haunted Rowan's sleep, and she hadn't stopped thinking about her for more than a minute.

But life would go on. It had to. Rowan had done the only plausible thing she could, and that decision soothed any pain she might have felt. For two days, Brian had been lurking around the apartment like a lost dog, and Rowan was growing irritable and claustrophobic.

"What are you going to do about a job, Brian?" she asked him while they sat eating pizza on her small sofa.

"I have a couple of leads with some startups in Cambridge." Brian had been on his computer since the morning after his arrival. Rowan thought he might have been job-hunting, but every time she caught a glimpse of his screen, he was playing some kind of game that involved shooting zombie-like creatures and yelling through his headset. It was like being back in Texas again, Rowan thought—as if someone had taken her life, picked it up, and moved it somewhere colder and darker. There was still no fire between them. There was still no part of Rowan that wanted to touch him. Life was almost instantly lackluster and unfulfilling. She supposed it had always been like this. But now, she knew better.

Later that night, when Makayla's shift was ending and Brian had been in Rowan's hair just about long enough, she texted Makayla to meet her for dinner.

Makayla was waiting for her in the entryway of one of the sushi places in Fenway. "Jesus, Texas, you look like a train wreck." She probably did look like a mess. She hadn't showered in at least a day. Her hair was unruly and thrown into a haphazard bun. Her clothes were wrinkled. She'd barely bothered to put on makeup.

"Yeah, I know."

"Tell me what the hell happened." The hostess led them to a table and they sat down.

"First, drinks," Rowan answered.

They made small talk about work until the waitress brought two glasses of prosecco. Rowan was praying Galen's name wouldn't come up yet.

"How was the whipple?" Rowan asked.

"Incredible. I mean, I didn't get to actually do anything, but I watched the entire operation. What a mess. Old Man Burgess even let me hold a retractor. Wait. How did you know I was scrubbing on a whipple today?" Makayla nodded. "Ah, right. Galen. Speaking of Galen…"

Rowan's heart pounded. "Makayla…"

"What did you do to her, Texas?"

"What?"

"The poor thing's been walking around like a beaten puppy all day. You know, like one of those Sarah McLachlan commercials? Really sad."

Rowan had a hard time imagining Galen as a helpless, dejected animal. "I didn't do anything to her."

"You two get into a fight or something? Come on, a little lesbian drama?" Makayla lightly punched her shoulder, but Rowan didn't crack a smile.

"We broke up."

Makayla's face fell, and she sat quietly for several seconds, which was probably an eternity to her. "Why?"

"Brian came back. Thanksgiving night. I went home, and he was sitting on my steps."

"So…you just took him back? And ditched Galen?" Makayla squinted, clearly befuddled.

"He loves me, Kayla. He's a good guy." Rowan thought about how many times she'd repeated those same words to herself, or to others, over the last several days. They were becoming both redundant and ridiculous.

"And Galen?"

"She'll be just fine without me."

"Is that so?" Makayla's expression of confusion turned to one of judgment.

"Of course she will."

"I'm sure she will be. Eventually. But I saw a broken human at that hospital today, and she sure isn't fine without you right now."

Rowan reluctantly and selfishly found solace in knowing Galen was hurting. Because as the initial shock of Brian's arrival and her somewhat impulsive decision to end things with Galen wore off, reality had begun to sink in, and with it came the feelings. Rowan missed her. She missed sleeping in her bed every night. She missed being held by her. She missed the way she laughed, the way she smelled. She missed the routines they'd started to build in such a short amount of time.

"I did the right thing," Rowan said. "I'm better off with Brian."

"Love isn't doing the right thing. That's the stupidest bullshit I've ever heard. Love is finding someone you're excited about. It's finding someone you want to do everything with, or sit and do nothing with. It's not complacency and idling your way through life because it's 'the right thing.' And it's not about picking the person who you think will die without you." Makayla raised an eyebrow in protest and took a sip of her drink.

"There are more important things than love."

"Like what?"

"Like loyalty. And time. Brian and I have spent so much of our lives together. Isn't that worth something?"

"Yes. It's worth something. But what you and Galen found? That's worth everything."

"I made my decision, Kayla."

"You're making a huge mistake." Why was someone as wild as Makayla always the voice of reason?

"I did what I had to do. And I'm happy." Rowan couldn't even look at her when she said the words.

"You're happy? Stop lying to me, Texas. Lie to Galen, lie to Brian, but stop lying to yourself, and stop lying to me. You aren't happy. You're guilty. You picked Brian out of guilt, and guilt alone."

"I did not!"

"Is that right? Then tell me, are you in love with him?" Makayla seemed to know exactly the right questions to ask to crack open the defenses Rowan had built around herself.

"I...I love Brian, yes."

"That's not what I asked. Are you in love with him?"

"I told you, I love him." Rowan suddenly felt trapped and wanted to run from the restaurant. But she had nowhere to go. Makayla was the only place she felt safe anymore.

"That's not the same thing."

Rowan sighed, defeated. "I know it's not."

"And are you in love with Galen?"

"Yes." She answered under her breath. Makayla saw right through her, anyway.

"I'm sorry this is happening to you." Makayla took Rowan's hand. "I really am. But you need to make this right. I'd be a bad friend if I didn't tell you that you are letting go of something you may never find again. Trust me. I've been looking for that something for a long time. It's not easy to come by. For my sake, and the sake of every other girl out there who hasn't found it yet, choose to be happy. Choose yourself."

Makayla's words were soothing and poetic, and Rowan knew just how good they sounded. But she couldn't let them change her mind. She couldn't let Brian down. "I've already made up my mind, Kayla."

"Listen to me, Texas. If you want to be with Brian, I support you. I just don't think it's what you really want. And I don't want to see you regret this someday."

❖

"You've got to pull it together, G. You're depressing me." Teddy sat on Galen's desk like always and fiddled with a Rubix's Cube.

"Oh, I'm depressing you? I'm sorry this is so hard. My breakup must be really difficult for you."

"You know what I mean." Teddy kicked her chair. "I'm not used to seeing you like this. Nothing gets you down, you know?"

"Yeah, well, shit's changed. So shut up and just be supportive." Galen was in no mood for Teddy's pep talks. She just wanted to wallow in the self-pity that felt so much easier to consume than the hurt.

"You need a good surgery. That'll pick you up. Maybe a good splenic rupture or a bowel perf will come in today."

"Teddy, are you wishing harm on other people so I can operate?" Galen had to laugh a little. He really was just trying to help.

"No! I'm just saying if it were to happen, it would probably make you feel better."

"I appreciate that."

"Look. I know it's soon to be bringing this up, but I hate to see you like this. My sister has this friend, Sunny. She got out of a crappy relationship not long ago, but she's really cool. And really cute too. Here, let me show you." Teddy excitedly pulled out his phone and began scrolling. "There she is."

Galen had to admit, the girl was cute. But sex was the last thing she could think about—not when all she wanted to do was crawl into a hole and hide until she felt human again. "I'm not sure. I don't think I'm ready to date anyone yet."

"I thought you'd say that. But the offer stands, okay? If you change your mind, let me know. I know Sunny would love you."

"Thanks. I'll keep that in mind."

When Teddy left her office, Galen tried hard to picture herself with anyone besides Rowan. The image felt foreign and wrong. It felt pointless.

❖

After Rowan's two-day hiatus from the hospital, she knew she'd have to face what she'd done. She'd have to face Galen. After all, she was her boss. Rowan shook her head as she sat alone on a bench tucked away behind one of the hospital waiting rooms. How stupid could she have been? She hadn't even considered that she and Galen would have to deal with a messy breakup and still have to work together. Would Galen take all the good cases away to spite her? Would she be nasty and bitter when they were in an OR together? Would Rowan have to explain to everyone why she'd ended things?

The questions felt endless, but time was running out, and Rowan couldn't stay hidden in the outpatient pediatrics department forever. Reluctantly, she made her way toward the surgeons' lounge on the fifth floor. She had to face her demons, and possibly her mistakes, sooner or later.

Before she could even get to the door of the lounge, Makayla intercepted her, grabbing her by the elbow and pulling her into one of the darker corners of the hallway.

"What are you doing back?"

"What do you mean?" Rowan figured it was best to just start by pretending nothing was wrong. But really, everything was wrong.

Makayla twisted her mouth and raised an eyebrow. "Are you ready for this, then?"

"I don't know what you're talking about."

"Yes, you do."

Rowan turned from her, frustrated that Makayla seemed to always be the one to call her out on her bullshit. Most of the time, she loved having a friend she was so transparent to. But not when she was trying to shield herself from reality. "I have to go. I have a case in half an hour."

"Texas, I wouldn't go in there if I were you…"

But before Rowan could heed her warning, she'd reached the entrance of the lounge and opened the door. Teddy sat on one of the sofas, his feet kicked up on a nearby chair. And beside him sat Galen. The room went as quiet as a funeral, and both of them looked up at her with an eerily similar combination of dismay and shock.

"Oh, crap," Teddy muttered loudly, as he often did when he thought he was saying things just under his breath. Galen just continued staring. She looked pale, her year-round-tan nothing more than a distant memory, and faint creases were painted under her cold eyes. Her scrub top was just a little wrinkled, and she held a large coffee instead of her usual espresso. Still, Rowan's heart broke. She'd missed her since the moment she walked out of Galen's apartment the other night—but she hadn't realized quite how much until she saw her sitting there in front of her.

"It's fine, Ted," Galen finally said, seeming to emerge from whatever trance she'd been in. "How are you, Rowan?"

Rowan couldn't answer. She was too focused on the way Galen's mouth moved when she talked, and all she wanted to do was kiss those lips again. Galen's words were calm and easy in a way that bothered Rowan more than she could justify. How was she so okay with this? She was supposed to be hurting. She was supposed to miss her. She was supposed to be lost, just like Rowan was.

"Good, thanks. How are you?" Rowan's words weren't quite as nonchalant as Galen's. But she figured Galen had spent an entire lifetime refining the art of not caring.

"I'm good. Welcome back. We missed you here." Galen offered her a cordial smile similar to the one she'd given her the day they first bumped into each other in front of the elevators, and Rowan wanted to cry. By now, Makayla had walked into the room and strategically placed herself between them. Rowan wasn't sure whether this was just in case things got ugly or because she wanted a front-row seat to the drama. She imagined it was a little of both.

"Thanks." Rowan managed to choke back the tears long enough to smile back like she had all the time in the world and leave the room, but Makayla was on her tail.

"You all right?"

"Sure. Fine. Why?" But Rowan couldn't stop a single tear from escaping. She turned away from Makayla and faced the wall, but it was too late.

"Uh-huh, because, I mean, you seem totally okay." Makayla put a hand on her shoulder.

"I'm fine. Really. It's just going to take some getting used to being around her again."

"Or, and hey, I'm just putting this out there, you could, gee, I don't know, win her back?"

Rowan wiped the tear off her cheek and straightened her shoulders. "I told you, Kayla, I made up my mind. And apparently so did Galen."

"What's that supposed to mean?"

"Didn't you see her in there? Clearly I was just another notch on the Galen Burgess bedpost. It's like she never even cared."

Makayla rolled her eyes. "Oh my God. I had no idea you were so selfish. And I really don't want to justify that comment with a response. But because you're my friend, and, let's be honest, we both know I can't help myself, I will. Galen is not fine. She's not even okay."

"She sounded it to me." Rowan sniffed, her hurt lightening a little.

"And you're basing that on what? A few words? She's faking it, Texas. Of course she's putting on a good show. But you haven't been around here for the last two days. One minute she's snapping at an intern, and the next she's sitting quietly in a corner staring at the ceiling. It's been like working for House. You know, that TV show with the super smart but totally unstable doctor? Yeah, like that, but, you know, without the drug addiction."

"Really?"

"Oh, don't look so pleased with yourself. It's not cute. And in case I haven't made it clear, even though I'm your best friend, I still think you're the world's biggest idiot for breaking up with her."

"Yeah. I got that." Rowan knew she was, in fact, selfish. But she couldn't help but smile a little. She wasn't sure when she'd become the worst human being on earth, and she wasn't sure why she was so relieved to hear Galen wasn't over her. The only thing she was sure of was that absolutely nothing made sense anymore.

CHAPTER NINETEEN

It had been a week since Brian moved in, and Rowan was starting to more or less adjust. She wouldn't say she was happy, but she was content. They'd lived together before, when her life was simpler and, admittedly, markedly less interesting. And, in many ways, it was like they were picking up where they left off. The only small, insignificant difference was the human-sized hole Rowan walked around with in the shape of Galen. Avoiding her at work had become easier once she stopped hanging out in the surgeons' lounge or near the ORs. And she certainly wasn't making any impromptu trips to Galen's office these days. Rowan spent most of her time either in the OR itself or hidden in one of the work spaces on the medical floors where Galen would never dream of going. She did have to operate with her on occasion, but so many other people were around, it was easy to keep things short and professional.

So far, work had been tolerable—pleasant, even. But Rowan knew if she were caught off guard, alone with Galen, things would be different. All it would take was one glance into that strong, perfect face, and she'd fall all over herself like always. She didn't trust herself. She still felt everything for Galen she'd been feeling for months. She was just learning how to repress it better. But Rowan wasn't sure she could say "no" to Galen yet. She wasn't sure she'd ever be able to.

Her apartment was no longer hers. Brian had taken over half the living room with his computers and video games, remote controls to God-only-knew-what spread haphazardly across the floor.

"Brian!" Rowan nearly tripped on one of the wires to Brian's Xbox as she made her way into the house that evening. A rage so uncharacteristic it left her unsettled and uncertain of who she was becoming rose up in her so fiercely she had to take a deep breath and clench her fists to keep from shouting.

"I'm in here!"

She took another big breath and exhaled, reminding herself this was the life she'd chosen, and she would just have to learn to be okay with her decision. This heartache—these feelings for Galen that were still so fresh and devastating—would pass. Through the door to the kitchen she heard pots and pans tinkering, and the scent of garlic and cumin wafted through the air.

Brian stood at the stove, a light blue apron that barely covered his knees tied around his waist, stirring something with a large, wooden spoon.

"What are you making? It smells great." Rowan instantly felt the heaviness of guilt for being irritated with him.

"Baked chicken, collards, and potatoes. Hope that's all right." He leaned down and kissed her sweetly.

"It's wonderful." She smiled at him but couldn't help but remember the catastrophic Thanksgiving dinner Galen had attempted, and her appreciation faded into a familiar, deep sadness. "Thank you."

Brian had lit candles and set the kitchen table, which they rarely did—even back home in Texas. Something was wrong. Something was very wrong. "How was your day?"

"Fine. I had a couple of surgeries in the morning and then spent the rest of the day in clinic doing…Never mind. I know you aren't really into this."

Brian came up behind Rowan and wrapped his long arms around her waist, the suffocation almost immediately noticeable to Rowan. "Of course I am," he answered.

"What about you? How was your job interview?" Rowan found herself desperately hoping the interview had been a flop, dreaming of sending Brian packing home to Texas in a horribly fantastical daydream that left her wracked with guilt.

"It was great. Here, sit down. Dinner's ready and I wanted to talk." Was he breaking up with her? Rowan could only hope. What was wrong with her? Why couldn't she either just appreciate the wonderful man she had in front of her or let him go? She sighed to herself—*because nothing is that simple.*

"Okay..." Rowan took a seat, the feeling of dread she'd had since she walked in the door only escalating with each passing moment. Brian brought over a serving dish still steaming from the oven and sat across from her.

"Before we eat, I need to tell you something." He wasn't breaking up with her. Hell. He could hardly contain his excitement. "GenTech in Cambridge offered me a job."

Was that it? Was that the big news he couldn't wait to share? Rowan was happy for him, no doubt. But she was also relieved it wasn't something directly related to her. As she had entered the kitchen that night and saw the spread on the table and the candles lit, she had a single, terrifying thought—Brian was going to propose. Rowan smiled and silently thanked all the stars in the universe she'd been wrong.

"Congratulations! That's so great!" She reached across the table and squeezed his hand.

"They're a new startup, but they have a lot of promise. They need someone to help advance their smartphone apps, and they want me. The pay is good, the hours will be decent, and the best part is, I can stay here and stop mooching off you."

"That's...wow." Rowan tried her best to look cordial, but she was crushed inside, knowing Brian now had ties to the area that went beyond her. Their web was getting woven even tighter than she wanted, especially given just how unsteady the ground beneath her had grown lately. Still, she managed to fill both their glasses with wine and raise hers halfheartedly in the air. "A toast. To your continued success."

But Brian didn't lift his glass. "There's something else."

Rowan's heart plunged and her stomach hollowed. "What else, Brian?"

She watched in horror as Brian reached into his sweater pocket and pulled out a velvet ring box, placing it on the table in front of her. *No, no, no, no, no. This can't be happening.*

"Brian…" If Rowan's face was giving away any part of the panic that was ascending inside her, Brian didn't seem to notice

"Go ahead. Open it."

Rowan hoped for a minute that there might be earrings or a lovely keychain inside the box. Tentatively, like disarming a bomb, she opened it. The inside of her chest suddenly felt squeezed so tight she didn't know if she'd find her next breath. There were no earrings. Just a rock—a big, shiny, more-than-Brian-could-ever-afford rock. She just continued to gape, her mouth like a canyon, as Brian stood up and then dropped to one knee.

"Rowan Renee Duncan, I love you. And I think you know just how much." Unfortunately, Rowan did. "Will you please marry me?"

The world stopped on its axis. Everything was so still, Rowan could almost see the air particles frozen in time in front of her. She should have been prepared for this. She should have thought about what she could ever possibly say when Brian finally asked. But she hadn't. She was too wrapped up in her own heartbreak—too wrapped up in being in love with someone else. So she said the only thing she could think of. "Yes. I'll marry you."

Time resumed, marked only by Brian's big, naive smile. Rowan tried to reciprocate even a fragment of his joy as he stood and hugged her, but all she could do was try not to cry.

"Here! Try it on!" Brian pulled the ring out of the box and yanked Rowan's left hand to him, slipping the ring on her finger. "Perfect fit."

"It's beautiful…" It was a beautiful ring. But it was also as heavy as a brick, and Rowan's entire left side suddenly felt weighed down. The burning in her lungs built to a suffocating fire until she felt like she was gasping for air. *Oh my God, what did I do? What did I do?*

❖

Eight days. Eight days had passed since Rowan told Galen she was choosing Brian. Every day was a little easier for Galen, but really, only a little. Some mornings, she awoke feeling ready to take on everything that came at her. The sunrise held promise that she'd feel better with each passing minute. Then, other mornings, Galen woke up feeling like she'd taken a giant sprint backward, her heart just as shattered as it had been that first night. She repeatedly told herself it would be three steps forward and two steps back, for whatever indeterminate amount of time it took for her to recover. Unfortunately, she didn't have a formula for this situation. She didn't have a Virchow's Triad or Wells Criteria or any other equation like in medicine that would tell her how much longer it would take before she healed. She should know, too, by the embarrassing search history on her laptop looking for someone or something to tell her how many days, months, years even she could expect to suffer. She was being ridiculous. And she hated the inner teenage girl that seemed to have possessed her lately. But Galen couldn't do anything but wait.

Today was a good day, though. Galen woke up, warm under her down comforter and expensive sheets, with Suzie curled at her feet. She made her first espresso, took her morning shower, and headed to the hospital. Maybe she was still hurting, but maybe she wouldn't hurt forever.

"Good morning, everyone." It was Thursday, which meant time for the weekly resident meeting. Galen didn't love seeing Rowan at work every day, but she'd found ways to adapt. Generally, that meant avoiding her whenever possible. She'd swapped cases around if she could so she didn't have to operate with Rowan, and when they weren't in the OR together, Galen stayed put in her office. Rowan never sought her out, though plenty of times Galen found herself wishing she would. Still, the weekly meeting would be one of those unavoidable occasions.

She tried hard not to look directly at Rowan when she spoke to the group. Doing so just caused her to stumble on her words, and, if she looked at her long enough, she couldn't help but remember just how beautiful Rowan really was and how she was no longer hers. But by sticking to data points and articles and feedback, Galen was able to survive the ordeal. And no one in the room appeared any the wiser.

"That's all for now, guys. Hit the showers." She ended all her meetings this way, and each time, Teddy cracked up. "Thanks, Ted. At least you find me amusing." Galen's gaze drifted across the room, inadvertently locking with Rowan's. She wasn't sure if she'd been staring, or if Rowan had been the one looking at her. But when their paths crossed, the rest of the room fell silent, and a soft, torturous sadness buzzed between them like a power surge. Galen wanted to look away, but she couldn't. Rowan didn't seem to be able to either. In moments like this, Galen knew nothing was over between them. Their story wasn't finished. Or, maybe, Galen was just fooling herself.

Teddy, Makayla, and Rowan lingered in the surgeons' lounge, talking about their upcoming cases and their weekend plans. Galen turned to head back to her office but stopped. Why should she have to be the one to isolate herself? Why should she uproot her daily routine just to make Rowan comfortable?

"Who's up for drinks on Friday at O'Shay's?" she asked. "Teddy?"

Teddy's face reflected surprise but quickly changed to pleasure at Galen's new reintegration to the group. "Hell, yes. I'm in. Guys?"

Makayla and Rowan looked at each other, seemingly exchanging a fully involved conversation no one else could interpret. "Yeah, sure. As long as Galen's buying."

All three looked expectantly at Rowan, and Galen's pulse clicked loudly in her head like a metronome. She had no idea what she was doing and if being Rowan's "friend" was at all possible. But she figured she'd better find out.

"I...I have plans Friday. Sorry." Rowan looked at the ground. A quiet knock on the already open door cut short the silence that followed.

Galen turned to see a tall, thin man in an unseasonably cool windbreaker and Texas Longhorns hat standing at the entryway. She knew immediately who he was.

"I hope you don't mind my dropping by..." Brian's voice was deeper than Galen had expected, with a gravelly quality that made it sound like he'd spent the previous night shouting at a rock concert. Just by looking at him, she guessed he probably hadn't.

"What are you doing here?" Rowan rushed to his side, but her words were laced with anxiety, not pleasant surprise.

"I brought you a sandwich. Figured you might be hungry." Brian smiled at Rowan like she was the only one in the room, and Galen instantly wanted to punch him. He was clearly nice. But that only served to make her want to punch him even more.

"Thank you." Rowan glanced back at the group, looking like a small animal caught in a bear trap. "Brian, this is Teddy. He's one of the other residents."

Teddy nodded politely but shot Galen a look that she knew meant he had her back if she decided to jump this tool.

"And you know Makayla." Rowan gestured to Makayla, who appeared like she was empathizing with Rowan for her horribly awkward introductions yet reveling in the drama.

"Nice to see you, Brian," Makayla answered.

"And this is, uh, Galen. Galen Burgess. My...boss." Rowan's throat rose and fell with what appeared to be a hard gulp.

"Galen. Good to finally meet you. Your name comes up a lot in my house."

Galen fought the swell of anger that built in her chest. *Your house? Up until a week ago, it was Rowan's house, you fucking ass.* "Is that right?" She reluctantly extended her hand as both she and Brian turned to Rowan.

"Galen, this is Brian. My...boyfriend." Rowan seemed to choke the words out.

"Actually, I'm her fiancé now."

No one in the room except Brian seemed to even breathe, and Galen's vision dimmed until she could see only through tiny pinholes in front of her. The only sound for miles was an almost audible crunch, which Galen swore had to be the rebreaking of an already broken heart.

"What?" Galen heard the word come out, but wasn't sure she was even the one speaking.

"Yeah...what?" Thankfully, Makayla was right behind Galen to echo her sentiment. The shock seemed to be widespread in that moment.

"Yup! It happened last night. Here, hon, show them the ring." Brian reached for Rowan's left hand and lifted it clear up into the air, but she stayed as limp as a piece of clothing line-drying in the wind. "You didn't wear it?"

Rowan's panicked expression was now anything but subtle, and she seemed to be having as much difficulty getting words out as the rest of them. "I...it's in my locker. I took it off for a case."

Rowan hadn't had a case yet that morning.

"Well...that's great news," Makayla finally said, moving stiffly toward them and hugging first Rowan and then Brian. Brian didn't know Makayla well and probably didn't notice her complete lack of the bubbly enthusiasm she usually wore like a brightly colored scarf. But Galen certainly did. Galen noticed everything in that moment—the worry and sadness on Rowan's face where happiness should have been, Brian's stupid, clueless smile, the pity emanating from Makayla and Teddy aimed directly at her. She noticed all of it. She just couldn't bring herself to speak.

"Really great," Teddy said. "Congratulations." He shook Brian's hand and kissed Rowan on the cheek. Everyone turned their attention to Galen, who stood frozen in place, their looks ranging from condolence to confusion.

"I…I have to go." Not knowing what else to do, Galen turned and rushed out of the room, straight to her office to shut the door.

CHAPTER TWENTY

S omeone tentatively rapped on Galen's door a few minutes later.

"Galen? Can I come in?" For the last eight days, Galen had hoped and prayed that every knock would be Rowan's. It never was. Now, she wanted it to be anyone else—anyone else in the world.

"Just a minute." She sniffed quickly and dabbed the tears that had found their way out of her eyes with the sleeve of her white coat. Rowan was going to see she'd been crying, and she fucking hated that. "Okay. Come in." Rowan opened the door, her eyes sad with guilt.

"Hi," Galen said.

"Hi yourself…" Rowan smiled, but all Galen could see was what must have been pity for her pathetic display of childish heartache.

"What do you want, Ro?" Galen kept her gaze fixed on the computer screen in front of her, hoping to look busy or, at the very least, to not look as broken as she felt.

"About that…"

"About what? Oh, you mean that whole you-getting-married thing. It's cool." Saying the words aloud just brought the angry, hurtful tears back to the surface.

"I'm sorry, Galen." Rowan moved to Galen's side and put a hand on her shoulder, but Galen refused to look at her.

"Don't be sorry. I'm happy for you. Really. Congratulations."

"You think I can't see right through you? Come on, now."

"I don't know what you mean," Galen said, coldly.

"Will you please look at me?" But Galen didn't move. "Fine. But you have to know this isn't at all what I thought would happen." When Galen didn't answer, Rowan continued. "I loved you. I loved us, together. I didn't plan for any of this. I swear."

"Look, if you don't mind, I have a lot of work to do." She had less than thirty seconds before she lost it again, and she really didn't want Rowan to have the pleasure of seeing that happen.

"Okay. Just please, believe that I'm sorry, okay?" Rowan let her hand linger on Galen's shoulder for a second longer, and Galen fought the shudder of warmth and need and comfort that spread through her. In one single moment, Galen managed to hate and want Rowan in equal parts.

Rowan's hand was on the door handle when Galen finally turned to her. "Is this really what you want? Is *he* really what you want?"

Galen watched Rowan struggle for answers, and she momentarily found solace in her uncertainty. Rowan didn't love Brian. She didn't look at him the way she'd looked at Galen so many times. She just didn't know why Rowan couldn't see that.

"I'll see you later, Galen."

"I want you to set me up on that date." Galen had called Teddy into her office later that afternoon rather than risk any chance of running into Rowan again.

"With Sunny? Really?"

"Yes. What's she doing tonight?"

"I mean, I'll ask," Teddy answered apprehensively. "But are you sure, G?"

"Absolutely. If you think I'll like her, I'm sure she's great. Besides, I could use a little fun these days, right?"

"I just don't know if today is the best time, you know, with Rowan getting engaged—"

"I know what happened today, Teddy. But I'm fine. Really. I'd love to meet Sunny. So, what do you say? Can you set it up?"

Teddy smiled. "I'll see what I can do."

❖

Galen didn't know if going out with Sunny was a good idea. That wasn't true. It wasn't a good idea. She wasn't ready to see anyone else, touch anyone else, or even want anyone else. Of course she wasn't. It had been only eight measly days. It took longer than that to get a package delivered. Galen did things quickly. She was a fast learner. But no one was that fast. Yet the image of Brian standing next to Rowan like that, his arm wound around her hip, smiling at her like an idiot, had been burned into her brain, and before Galen could think, she went to the only place she knew to feel better—sex.

She'd thought about calling one of the nurses she'd already slept with, or even hitting up one of the local queer nights coming up, but that somehow didn't feel good enough. Galen was looking for a quick fix, but this time, she wasn't just looking to get some. This time, she was hoping to fall in love again. She'd had a taste of what that looked like, what that felt like, and she wanted more. She wanted more, and she wanted it fast, just like she wanted everything. Patience had never been one of her more refined points, and this wasn't going to be an exception. If Rowan didn't want her, Galen would just have to move on and fall for someone new.

She said that to herself like it would be so easy.

Sunny had eagerly agreed to meet Galen that night for drinks. So Galen found her best clothes, got into her flashy car, and drove into downtown, to one of the most expensive bars in Boston. A tall, blond woman with short hair and piercing eyes Galen immediately recognized from the photos Teddy had shown her stood from her seat at the bar.

"Sunny? I'm so sorry I'm late." The woman looked briefly perturbed, but as soon as Galen smiled, her chilly expression melted like a spring snow.

"Don't worry about it. I was just getting started without you."

"It's really nice to meet you." Galen pulled out the bar stool for her, and they sat down.

"You too. Teddy told me so much about you."

"Did he? I should have known better than to let him set me up. Don't believe a word of it."

Sunny laughed. The charming, sweet laugh warmed some of Galen's melancholy. "Actually, I'm pretty sure he thinks you can walk on water, or something."

"Well, in that case, believe it all. Every last thing he said." Galen turned when the bartender approached and ordered the highest-shelf bourbon on the menu.

"He tells me you're a surgeon."

"That's right."

"And that you're his chief resident? His boss, kind of, is that right?"

Galen chuckled. "Yes, kind of."

"He also tells me you have a dog and live in a gorgeous apartment in Back Bay. You're obsessed with the Bruins. You like to run in your free time. Oh, and your dad is some kind of sadist?" Sunny smiled shyly.

"Is that all? Jesus, is there anything he didn't tell you?"

"I mean…he didn't tell me how handsome you were…"

Galen took a long gulp of her bourbon and kept her gaze fixed. The whiskey was doing little to ease her nerves. Sunny was cute. And on any other day, in any other universe, Galen would have had her home and naked by now. But something was holding her back. And it didn't take a licensed psychiatrist to figure out that thing was Rowan.

"Thanks." She took another sip and turned back toward Sunny. "So, tell me about you. What kind of work do you do?"

"I'm a nurse, actually."

Galen felt her eyes bug. "You're kidding me…"

"Yes. Totally kidding." Sunny laughed and playfully touched Galen's shoulder. "Teddy told me you tend to date nurses."

"Of course he did."

"I was just teasing. I actually have nothing to do with health care. To be honest, I don't even like having my blood pressure taken. I'm an architect."

Galen relaxed for the first time all night. "That's great. What kind of architect?"

"I don't know if you recall that new condo complex in Watertown that just popped up. I designed it."

"Really?"

"Well, about fifteen other people and I. But it's still kind of neat, right?"

"Very."

The rest of the evening was pleasant, to say the least. Sunny was charming and smart, and if things had been at all different, Galen would have absolutely taken her out again. For the three hours they sat at the bar, Galen managed to keep Rowan at the back of her mind. But it couldn't last. As much as she wanted to find someone else to fall in love with, someone to replace Rowan, it wasn't possible—at least not yet. And it wasn't fair to Sunny to let either of them think otherwise.

"I should probably get going," Galen finally said. "I have an early surgery in the morning."

Sunny's face reflected her obvious disappointment. "Yeah. I should too."

"I had a really nice time though. Come on. I'll walk you out." Galen left a hundred-dollar bill on the bar. She'd learned to carry cash, and a lot of it, so she could whisk girls out of the restaurant as soon as possible.

They walked two blocks to Sunny's car, and when they stopped, she took a step closer to Galen until their bodies were nearly touching. "So…I'd love to see you again…" Sunny said

Panic swarmed over Galen. She was hoping Sunny didn't like her. She was hoping she wouldn't have to explain herself. "I like you, Sunny."

Sunny laughed. "Here's the 'but,' though."

"I like you. But, if I'm being honest, I just got out of something, and I'm not really ready to date yet."

"I know." She smiled sympathetically at Galen.

"How did you…Never mind." Galen shook her head. "Remind me to tell Teddy he's, like, the worst wingman ever."

"It's okay, Galen. Really. But if you don't mind my asking, why did you decide to come out with me tonight anyway?"

Galen sighed. "I guess I hoped I could become ready. I do everything quickly, you know? I always have. I kind of hoped this wouldn't be any kind of exception."

"Love isn't something you can just 'do quickly.'" Sunny took Galen's hand for a moment in a gesture that left Galen more comforted than she had been in days. "You just have to let the hurt suck for a while."

"Ugh. That's exactly what I was afraid of."

"I appreciate your honesty. And I appreciate you respecting me enough not to just try to get in my pants."

"I mean I wasn't completely counting that out yet…" Galen smirked, and Sunny punched her bicep gently. "Kidding!"

"Take care of yourself, okay? And when you decide you are ready, look me up."

"I will. Thank you."

Sunny awkwardly held out her arms. "So, can we hug now or what?"

Galen laughed heartily and embraced her, feeling simultaneously proud of what she'd just done and more alone than ever.

Rowan and Brian had been engaged for three weeks, and she was already ready to jump out of her second-story window. Brian's enthusiasm for planning the wedding surprised her—and it wasn't a pleasant surprise. The night he proposed, Rowan thought she had time to figure the whole thing out. After all, he hadn't given her any time to decide whether she wanted to actually spend the rest of her life with him. The least he could do was give her a chance before she had to walk down the aisle, right?

Instead, he spent day after day online, scouting out venues, vendors, even flowers. For a guy who lived for *Call of Duty* and Mountain Dew on Friday nights, Brian had suddenly become a nightmarish version of David Tutera. Rowan couldn't escape. Every night when she came home from work, Brian was waiting with a new playlist for the reception or a caterer that specialized in Texas barbecue. Rowan wanted to scream. She couldn't breathe. She couldn't move. And she couldn't stop thinking about Galen.

And, just when things probably couldn't get any worse, they were about to.

"I have to go to the airport and pick up Mom," Brian said as they drank their morning coffee. It was a tradition they'd started when Rowan was in medical school. He would get up with her before dawn and make her French-press coffee, and they would sit at the kitchen table together in the dark and talk about their upcoming day. Rowan remembered a time when she enjoyed this. Now, all she wanted in the morning was the peace and quiet she had when Brian was still in Texas. Or, better yet, the mornings she'd spent with Galen.

"Okay." Rowan pretended to be engrossed in her surgical notes in front of her, hoping to avoid the next question.

"Are you sure you don't want to come? She's so excited to see you, Ro."

"Oh, no, I can't, really. I have a hemorrhoidectomy at seven thirty, and I still have some pre-op tests to go over."

"Hemorrhoids? Gross. Is that what we're $150,000 in debt for? So you can cut off some dude's hemorrhoids?" Brian laughed, clearly amused with himself.

Not we. Me. I'm $150,000 in debt. And it's so I can learn how to save lives, you asshole. Rowan must have rolled her eyes because Brian immediately redacted. "I was kidding. Relax."

"I have to go." Rowan stood from the table, dumped her untouched coffee in the sink, and headed for the door.

"What? No kiss good-bye?"

She knew she was being unfair to Brian, but she had to physically restrain herself from groaning. It wasn't his fault she was so irritable. What was so wrong with her that she couldn't revel in the same happiness he was feeling? Something had to give, and it was going to have to give soon. Not wanting to elicit that annoying little pout Brian gave when he didn't get his way, Rowan went to him and quickly kissed him on the lips. "Bye."

"Hey, wait. You forgot your ring." Brian rushed back into the bedroom and returned holding the piece of jewelry that told both of them, and the rest of the world, that she was going to be his forever.

"Thanks." Rowan smiled sheepishly and slipped it onto her ring finger. She hardly made it to the bus stop before taking it off again.

CHAPTER TWENTY-ONE

Work was about the only reprieve Rowan had these days, and she was more grateful than ever to be there that day. Brian's mother, who she supposed was now her future mother-in-law, was coming to town for the holiday. She liked her well enough. And, in any other circumstance, she probably wouldn't have minded spending Christmas with her. But now two people in her house would be pressuring her to set a wedding date, pick out a dress, make a guest list...And she didn't know if she could handle that. It was Christmas Eve, and all she wanted to do was cut into somebody. The elective-surgery schedule was light, so she could only hope an appendectomy or an intra-abdominal abscess would roll into the ER. At least Galen had the day off. She'd been checking the schedule diligently, every week, since the breakup because she absolutely wanted to avoid Galen, and when she couldn't, she wanted to be prepared for it.

"Ugh. I'm so bored." Makayla lay stretched out on one of the couches in the lounge, reading a copy of *Redbook* that was several issues out of date.

"Me too. I know we shouldn't complain, but God, I wish I had a knife in my hand," Rowan said.

"What is wrong with us?"

"I don't know what's wrong with you, but my soon-to-be mother-in-law is landing at Logan in a few minutes, and I basically want to do everything in my power to stay away from my apartment."

"Brian's mom is coming? Ouch."

"She's great. But Brian's been seriously on my case about setting a date for the wedding, basically since the second he proposed. And she's not going to help things. It's like he's afraid if I don't commit to a date now, I never will."

Makayla sat up and folded the magazine, staring at Rowan skeptically. "Is he wrong?"

"I…Yes? Yes, of course he's wrong. I'm going to pick a date, okay? I just haven't yet." But Rowan knew Makayla would see right through her like she always did.

"It's just us in here, Texas. You may have to lie to Brian, and his mammy, and Galen, and everyone else, but there are two people you don't have to lie to, and that's me, and you."

Rowan took a deep breath and leaned forward in her chair, resting her elbows on her knees. "So, I'm having cold feet. So what? That's normal…Isn't it?"

"Totally normal. Everyone gets cold feet."

Rowan nodded, silently reassuring herself. "Great."

"But you don't have cold feet." Makayla straightened her back like she always did when she was about to launch into one of her monologues.

"What? What are you talking about?"

"You have doubts. Big, enormous doubts. And, if I may be frank for a moment—"

"You always are."

"This goes beyond doubts. You know Brian isn't the one. You know you shouldn't be marrying him. And, worst of all, you know exactly who you *should* be with."

Rowan felt herself shutting down, not wanting to hear any of what Makayla had to say. "That's not true. I want to marry Brian."

"Oh, would you please just cut the shit, Rowan? I love you. But my good God, are you being stupid! Marrying Brian because you feel bad for him, or you think you owe him, or whatever it is, doesn't make you some kind of saint. It's downright cruel, actually. You're letting that boy think you love him. And, maybe just as bad, you're letting Galen think you don't. All the while, you're miserable. You aren't doing anyone any favors. And all you're going to end up with is a lifetime full of regret."

Rowan didn't respond. Her eyes filled quickly, and in an instant, she was spilling heavy, wet tears onto the carpet. She looked at Makayla, who seemed to be deciphering whether she'd just pushed Rowan too far. But she hadn't. Rowan needed to hear this. She needed to face the truth.

"I don't know what to do, Kayla…" The tears just kept coming as Makayla stood, turned the lock on the door to the lounge, and sat beside Rowan, cradling her while she sobbed.

The moment was shattered by the shrill of someone's beeper—no, two beepers. Both of them immediately swiped the objects from the band of their scrubs.

"Huh, that's weird. Trauma alert. I'm not on the trauma service today," Makayla said.

"Yeah, me either. I wonder what's going on."

"I don't know, but we should probably get down to the ER and find out."

❖

The first person Rowan saw when she and Makayla descended the stairs was Galen, and Rowan's heart broke ten times over like it did every time she ran into her.

"Did you get paged to the ER too?" Galen asked, her face grave and her breath short.

"Yeah. What's happening?" Makayla answered.

"Bus accident. A group of kids were on their way to go caroling at some nursing homes and got hit by a semi. I guess the truck driver was DOA, but twelve elementary-school kids were on that bus."

Rowan's heart sank. "How many are coming here?"

"At least half. The rest are going to Mass General and Beth Israel."

Galen pushed open the heavy fire door that led to the ER, and Makayla and Rowan followed in tow.

"Are they…" Makayla started to ask the question she didn't seem to want to know the answer to yet.

"I don't know. I heard that at least three are critical. Christ, I hate peds…" Galen's voice shook, and Rowan had never seen her so unsteady.

"I'm not on trauma call today, though," Makayla said.

"It doesn't matter. This is a mass casualty. And it's kids. It's all hands on deck. Do what you can. If you need me, find me. Otherwise, just trust yourself. You two are the best first-years I have. You can do this."

Rowan was instantly touched by Galen's kindness, and all she wanted to do was hug her until the nightmare scenario would be over. She hoped it wasn't as bad as Galen said.

The Emergency Room was like a war zone. It was rare for the chaos seen on television interpretations of hospitals to actually manifest in real life. But this time, it did. Rowan could only stand frozen, staring at the scene unfolding in front of her. Nurses and physicians rushed by pushing kids on gurneys, IV bags flying in the wind, as parents screamed after them.

"Hey. You okay?" Galen broke Rowan out of her terrified trance, gently putting her arm around her shoulder.

"Yeah. Sorry. Let's just go."

Galen nodded, and the three of them went off on their own, each seeking out the patients closest to death—the patients who needed them the most.

"I need a doctor here!" A robust nurse in Tweety Bird scrubs was shouting from across the department. Rowan looked to her left, and then her right, expecting at least five or six real doctors who actually knew what they were doing to emerge from the wreckage and help. But no one did.

"You. Are you a doctor?" The nurse was talking directly to Rowan.

"I…" Instinctively, Rowan glanced down at the embroidered name on her white coat—Rowan Duncan, MD. Department of Surgery. "Yes. I'm a doctor."

"Great. Then get your ass over here. This kid's crashing."

Rowan rushed to the gurney tucked away in a corner of the hallway, where a small boy about eight or nine years old lay looking pale and motionless. "What happened?"

"He was fine when he came in."

Rowan glanced at the yellow tag placed on the child's ankle. This was the triage system used in a mass-casualty situation. A yellow tag meant "walking wounded." It meant the patient could wait. Apparently, the system wasn't perfect. "Did he complain about anything when he got here?"

"Just some shoulder pain, but he was stable."

Rowan glanced at the portable monitor next to the child's bed, noting the unsettlingly low blood pressure and quick heart rate. "What's his name?"

"Jack."

"Jack?" Rowan rubbed across the boy's chest with her knuckles to try to rouse him, but he hardly opened his eyes. "I'm Dr. Duncan. But you can call me Rowan. Can you tell me what hurts?"

Jack opened his eyes again, an act that seemed to use all of his remaining strength. "My arm."

"Where, Jack?" Rowan pulled the oversized gown up to his chest, exposing his bony torso.

"Here." With a notable amount of effort, Jack was able to reach up with his right hand and grab his left shoulder.

Rowan scanned his abdomen with her eyes, noting a faint, evolving dusky discoloration that could only mean bruising. She pushed her palms first into the right, upper portion of his belly, and then the left. Jack immediately cried out in pain. "Go find Dr. Burgess. Right now. Please." Rowan noticed her hands were trembling, hovering just over the boy. The nurse nodded and went off while Rowan once again checked the vital-sign machine. His blood pressure was low and dropping by the second. *God, Galen, please get here quickly.*

She couldn't do anything—at least not without an OR. Jack was in trouble, and if they didn't act quickly, he was going to die. She searched her mind for something, anything that might buy him a little more time. Glancing at the bag of IV fluid hanging above him, she found the dial and cranked it up as fast as it would go. She then took his stretcher and tipped it backward, allowing what blood that wasn't sitting in his belly to find its way to his brain. "You're going to be okay, buddy. I promise." Rowan immediately wished she hadn't promised him anything.

"What do you have?" It took Galen what felt like several eternities to arrive, but in reality it must have been only three minutes. Her poise and confidence soothed Rowan's panic, and she was so grateful Galen was there she could have cried.

"Approximately eight-year-old boy, unrestrained on the bus. Came in complaining of left shoulder pain. He was tagged yellow. I'm guessing someone thought it was just an extremity injury. But he's tanking his pressure, he's tachycardic, and he's minimally responsive. Left upper quadrant is tender with rebounding and guarding and positive Cullen's sign. He's got a splenic lac. And he's bleeding out."

"Why the shoulder pain, Duncan?" Galen never stopped teaching.

"It was just referred pain from the blood in his belly."

Galen nodded. "And what have you done for him?"

"I cranked up his fluids full speed. That brought his pressure up to about 78 systolic, but he needs the OR."

"Anything else?"

"Yes. He needs to be intubated. But we don't have time to do it here. His airway is maintained so they can do it in the OR."

"Good work." Galen offered a small smile. "I'll call over and get him in right away. Go find the next kid you can save."

Rowan bobbed her head emphatically and took off toward the main area of the ER, leaving Galen to make sure Jack made it off to surgery.

"I'm Dr. Duncan with surgery. Who's next to be seen? How can I help?" Rowan had tracked down the charge nurse, who stood in front of the slammed patient list, looking frazzled and exhausted.

"Good. Go see the little girl in room 9. I think she's a head injury."

"Is she stable?"

"Yes." But Rowan knew that wasn't any guarantee today.

Inside room 9, she found a girl around the same age as Jack playing on an iPad with her parents flanking her bed.

"Is this Ms. Adelaide?"

The girl had a head of fiery red hair and freckles for miles. She gave Rowan a big, toothy smile complete with several empty spaces. "Yes. Who are you?"

"I'm Dr. Rowan. It's very nice to meet you. So what are you watching there?"

"I'm not watching anything. I'm doing a puzzle."

Rowan told herself that was probably a good sign, in the setting of a head injury.

"Addy isn't allowed to watch TV. Well, except for PBS." The round woman sitting to Adelaide's left, with identical hair, finally spoke up. Rowan groaned internally. A major trauma probably wasn't the time to get on your high horse about parenting skills. But she let it go. Adelaide was her patient. And, like they were so often, her parents were just going to be an inconvenience.

"Right. Well, Adelaide, can you tell me what happened today?"

"Honey, put the game down," her mother snapped.

Adelaide did as she was told and looked directly at Rowan while she explained the accident in great detail. "I was on the bus. We were going to sing for the old people for Christmas. But then, some big truck came out of nowhere and hit us right on the bus's nose! I flew forward like this!" Adelaide lunged forward, her arms splayed out, as she made a sound that reminded Rowan of lasers or light sabers.

"Honey. Stop that."

Rowan was losing patience with Adelaide's mother. The man she presumed was her father just sat there, silently scrolling through his cell phone, clearly disinterested in the situation.

"It's fine. So what happened after that?"

"My head went BOOM. Right into the wall. And then, it was black."

"You don't remember anything after that?" Rowan took a penlight out of her coat pocket and ran it across Adelaide's eyes, watching her pupils grow and constrict equally.

"Nope. I just remember the nice men in the black uniforms carrying me on the bed. And then I was in the ambulance."

"Does anything hurt you right now?"

"My head." Adelaide pointed to a large egg on the left side of her forehead that appeared to have grown larger since Rowan first entered the room.

"Has she thrown up at all? Or been acting strange?" Rowan asked the mother.

"Not at all. Why? Do you think something's wrong with her? Tell me what's wrong with her right now."

"I don't know." Rowan responded calmly.

"What are you, anyway? Like, a student or something?" The woman's face contorted with disgust.

"No. I'm a doctor. And right now, I'm the only doctor your daughter has. And I'm going to make sure she doesn't have a serious head injury. I want to send her down for a CT scan to check for bleeding."

"Bleeding?! But she just bumped her head!"

"I know that. But she lost consciousness. And that can sometimes be a sign of something more dangerous. Adelaide was involved in a serious accident, and I need to scan her head." Rowan was getting irritated having to rationalize the safety of a young girl to her own mother. The father barely looked up from his smartphone.

"John, don't you have an opinion about this? CAT scans cause cancer! I don't want her to have it," her mother said.

"We should listen to the doctor, Susan." John finally spoke, his voice as soft and tentative as his demeanor.

"Look. Mrs. O'Rourke, Mr. O'Rourke, I wouldn't be doing this if I didn't think it was worth the very small chance that the dose of radiation could be problematic. Believe me, the chance of a traumatic head injury is much higher and has much more severe consequences today."

The couple looked at each other silently for several seconds before Susan O'Rourke spoke.

"Okay. Fine. Just do it."

"Great. I'll get that ordered right away." Adelaide had gone back to playing with her iPad. "You're going to be okay, my friend. I just want to get a picture of your head, okay? Maybe you can hang it on your fridge when we're done?" Rowan said.

Adelaide smiled and nodded her head emphatically, and Rowan left the room, feeling confident in her judgment and proud of the doctor she was becoming.

CHAPTER TWENTY-TWO

Ro, I need you in here, now." Galen had popped her head out of Trauma 3 and called to Rowan. She wore a yellow, paper gown and a face shield, and her chest was covered in bright-red blood.

Without question, Rowan rushed inside. The room was just as blood-soaked as Galen, and it would have been easy to miss the tiny figure lying on the stretcher. Rowan's heart squeezed.

"What's going on?" she asked. Galen stood at the head of the bed, three nurses on either side of the stretcher.

"Blunt trauma to the chest. I think he hit the seat in front of him pretty hard. I put in two large-bore chest tubes, and his oxygen is up, but something else is going on. His pressure keeps dropping, and his heart rate is climbing." Galen was as calm as Rowan had ever seen her, even with a young boy's blood all over her.

"What do you need me to do?" Rowan asked, confused why Galen was looking for help from someone as inexperienced as she was.

"I need a second set of eyes. What are we missing here?"

Rowan threw on a paper gown and mask and moved to the head of the bed next to Galen. The boy had already been sedated and intubated. His color was good, considering how sick he was. Rowan looked at the monitors and then put her stethoscope to the boy's chest. She kept it there for a long time, just in case she was wrong. Rowan couldn't be wrong. Not about this.

"Where's the ultrasound machine?" Rowan asked.

"It's tied up. I haven't been able to get to it all afternoon. What are you thinking, Ro?"

"His pulse pressures are narrow. He's tachycardic, but there's no obvious source of bleeding. And his heart sounds are muffled."

"Pericardial tamponade…" Galen said. "Of course. Goddamn it. Why didn't I see it?"

"It's an easy miss. I wouldn't have found it if you hadn't already figured out he had the collapsed lung."

"What do you want to do, then?" Galen asked. The monitors blared. "And tell me quick, because we're running out of time."

"He needs a pericardocentesis. Let's get him to the OR," Rowan said, trying to keep her voice level.

"Right. But we don't have time. He needs this now or he's going to die."

"But…we don't have an attending available…" Rowan knew what was coming next.

"It doesn't matter. He doesn't have that long. I'll deal with the repercussions later. But right now, this kid needs us. Me and you, Dr. Duncan." Galen had a way of making everything sound like a great idea. It was part of her charm. She was able to immediately erase any doubt in your mind. And she made Rowan feel like she could do anything.

"Okay, so do it then."

The nurses in the room glanced at each other hesitantly. "Are you sure this is smart? I mean, have either of you ever done one of these before?" one of them asked.

"I have. Many times," Galen answered. Rowan wasn't sure if she actually had, but Galen certainly had everyone else convinced.

"I'll set up a tray." One of the younger nurses in the room went to the cabinet and pulled out a sterile package.

"Does anyone have any objections here before I start?" Galen asked the room. "Because we're all in this together. If anyone wants out, go now." The three nurses and Rowan all swapped nervous stares, but no one spoke. "Great. Thank you."

Rowan stood, shaking, at Galen's side.

"Have you ever done one?" Galen asked Rowan.

"I watched one, once. But it was non-emergent. In the OR. It's hardly the same."

"Place the sterile drape over his chest and slather him with betadine."

Rowan did as she was told, spreading the brown liquid over the unconscious boy's body.

"Good. Now, take the needle. You want to go just sub-xyphoid. Advance it a little bit at a time. When you see blood, you know you're in the pericardium. Don't go any further or you risk hitting the heart and causing an arrhythmia," Galen said.

A cold sweat coated Rowan's brow. "Wait. I'm not doing this. Am I?"

"See one, do one, teach one, right? Come on. You've got this. I wouldn't let you if I didn't think that. Now, go slowly. We have time."

For a moment, it was just the two of them in the room. Their familiar connection was as alive as ever, and Rowan was relieved by an overwhelming sense of trust in Galen. She wouldn't lead Rowan wrong. She would walk her through this every step of the way.

"Okay. Laurie, can you hand me the eighteen-gauge needle, please? And can you watch the monitor? Let me know if his heart does anything funny," Rowan said.

One of the nurses handed the needle to Rowan, and Rowan tried to keep her hand steady. This little boy on the table in front of her didn't need her shaking like she'd had eight cups of coffee.

"Now, slowly advance," Galen said.

Rowan tried to focus on the dulcet tones of Galen's voice as she slid the needle under the boy's sternum.

"A little farther. You're almost there." Galen sounded as confident in her as anyone ever had, and some of Rowan's fear settled.

"I've got blood," Rowan nearly shouted with joy.

"Keep pulling back on the syringe."

"Pressure is holding at 92/58," Laurie said. "And his heart rate is down to 100."

"Okay. Take the needle out now."

Rowan did as Galen said. "That's it. We did it!" she said, once the needle was safely out of the boy's chest and on the table next to her.

"You did it," Galen said, her smile filling the entire room.

"What the hell is going on in here?" Dr. Frederick, a tall, silver-haired cardiothoracic surgeon barreled into the room and stopped so quickly he seemed to skid.

"He had pericardial tamponade. His BP was unstable. I tried to find an attending, but I couldn't wait. He couldn't wait," Galen said, standing as tall and sure as ever.

"So you did an unauthorized, unsupervised pericardioscentesis? On an eight-year-old?"

"Yeah, we did," Galen said. "We had to or he was going to die."

"And where did all this blood come from?" Dr. Frederick snapped.

"He had a tension pneumothorax when he first came in. I had to put in a chest tube."

"What did you use, Burgess, a chainsaw? Jesus." Dr. Frederick shook his head and turned to walk out of the room. "Oh, and, uh, nice work, Dr. Burgess."

The smallest smile peeked on Galen's lips, and Rowan suppressed a giggle.

"Let's send this guy up to the OR, huh?" Galen said. She grabbed the foot of the bed, and Rowan followed suit, feeling like they could take on the world if they tried.

Rowan wanted to stay and see how Jack and the boy with the chest injury had done. She also wanted to make sure Adelaide's head CT was okay. But she needed to go home first. Something more important was waiting for her.

Brian was sitting on the couch with his mother, flipping through copies of some dreadful wedding magazine his mother had brought with her from Texas.

"Hello, Joanie," Rowan said, shutting the door behind her. "It's good to see you."

The obese woman in the floral dress smiled and stood to hug Rowan. "How are you, sweetheart?"

"I'm…" Rowan thought hard about the answer. "I'm great."

"You're home early, hon," Brian said. "Just in time to help Mom pick out some bridesmaids' bouquets."

"Actually, Brian, I was hoping we could talk. Joanie, would you excuse us for just a second?"

Brian furrowed his brow and looked to his mother. "It's fine, Mom. Why don't you go unpack?"

"Of course, dear. I'll just be in the other room."

"What's the matter?" Brian asked, once Joanie had left.

Rowan sat down next to him, leaving a secure foot of space between them. "This isn't going to be easy for me to say. And it's going to be even harder for you to hear. But you just have to let me get it out, okay?"

"You're making me nervous here."

Rowan stared straight ahead. "I can't marry you, Brian."

"You…what do you mean?" His voice shook with impending tears. Rowan was afraid he would cry. But she couldn't let his reaction weaken her resolve.

"I love you. I really do. You're a wonderful man who's going to make some girl very happy. I just…that girl isn't me, Brian."

"I don't understand."

"I don't either, honestly. I just know that we aren't meant to spend forever together. I can't love you the way you love me. And it wouldn't be fair to you for me to let you think otherwise."

Brian's voice rose. "Why don't you let me decide what's fair to me?"

"Marrying me would be a huge mistake. For both of us. I'm sorry." Rowan was the one who felt the tears spill out. "I'm so sorry."

"I…okay…" Any hint of anger in Brian's tone had dissipated, and he settled back into his usual passivity.

Rowan knew he wouldn't put up a fight. She didn't want him to. She pulled the ring out of her coat pocket and held it out to him. "Here."

"Did I do something?" he said.

"What? No! You didn't do anything. You've been amazing to me. I just can't be with you in the way you want." It was the best Rowan could do to explain the unexplainable.

"I'm never going to find anyone like you, Ro."

"You're right. You'll find someone better. Someone who's right for you."

"I don't want anyone else. I want you." Brian was going to pull at whatever heartstrings he could, even if he didn't argue with her.

"I'm sorry." That was all she could think to say.

"I guess I'll start getting my things together. I suppose I can go back with Mom until I figure things out." Brian kept his face flat and expressionless.

"I'm sorry, Brian." Rowan stood, kissed him on the cheek, and walked straight out the front door, never looking back.

It was nearly eight pm on Christmas Eve. Most of the staff had gone home for the night, but Galen stayed in her office, waiting on Jack, the little boy with the spleen laceration, to get to Recovery. Besides, she had nothing to rush home to. It was just going to be her, Suzie, and a bottle of Bulleit. Galen thought about staying for the night, seeing if she needed to help with any cleanup left from the accident earlier. But she didn't have any energy left. Being caught in the wake of so many injured kids had sucked the life out of her, and she was exhausted. She heard Jack had made it out of surgery, and as soon as he was settled and stable, she would leave.

Her office door was open, largely because Galen hadn't expected any visitors.

"Knock, knock."

Galen looked up at the sound of Rowan's soft voice. "What are you doing back here? I saw you leave hours ago." Galen tried to act indifferent, but she was secretly thrilled with Rowan's arrival. Even if it didn't mean anything.

"I did. But I'm back. Can I come in?"

"The door's open."

Rowan stepped inside the room and sat on the trash can in the corner. "How is Jack doing?"

"Good. He just made it out of surgery. Jay had to remove his spleen, and he lost a lot of blood, but he did great."

"And the other boy? God, you know I didn't even catch his name? How awful is that? I stuck a friggin' needle into his chest but didn't get his name."

"Marcus Hansen. He did great too. They put in a pericardial window in the OR, but he didn't have any other major injuries. He's in the ICU right now." Galen smiled at her. "You were amazing today, you know."

Rowan's cheeks turned a cherry red. "I had the best teacher…"

"What can I say?" Galen locked eyes with Rowan, trying to figure out what she was doing there. It was more than just following up on the kids.

"Today was crazy. I think I'm still in shock," Rowan said.

"Same. Can you believe we didn't lose a single kid all day? A couple are still touch-and-go, but I think they'll be just fine. We really did a great job. Especially you."

"Will you come have a drink with me?"

Galen was taken aback by the abruptness of Rowan's request. "I…right now?"

"I mean, in a couple of hours. I'd like to change, but I figure, it's Christmas Eve, right? Neither of us should be alone."

"What about Brian?" Galen involuntarily angled her chair away from Rowan, feeling apprehensive yet excited. She wanted nothing more than to be alone with Rowan, outside of the hospital, on Christmas. But she wasn't willing to get hurt again. What little progress she had made was enough that she couldn't imagine backtracking. She couldn't imagine letting Rowan do that to her again.

"He's…he's not going to be around anymore."

Galen tried to keep her heart from soaring into the air. "What do you mean?"

"I told him I couldn't marry him." Rowan kept her head down but couldn't seem to suppress a sly smile.

"Is that right?"

"Yeah, it is. So…will you have a Christmas Eve drink with me or not?"

Galen wanted to say yes so badly. But inside, she was terrified. It was just too convenient that Rowan would be at her door, asking to see her only moments after leaving Brian. Rowan was probably lonely, and Galen didn't want to be her easy one-night stand. She didn't want to fill a temporary void. She wanted to be Rowan's forever.

"I don't know. Maybe another time?" Galen felt trapped.

"Galen. It's just a drink. You're not doing anything else, right?"

Galen thought about everything she knew about Rowan. This was not a girl to call her up for some company. She was kinder than that. She wouldn't do that to Galen's heart. And Rowan wasn't blind to the fact Galen was still in love with her.

"Okay. Why not?" Galen said. Rowan beamed, and Galen hoped she wasn't making a horrible mistake. She was setting herself up to get hurt all over again. But she had to see this through.

"Great! Give me ten minutes to change, and I'll meet you back here." Rowan skipped out of the room.

Chapter Twenty-three

It was less than ten minutes before Rowan arrived back at Galen's office door. She wore a pair of tight jeans that hugged the lines of her ass and a flowing top that plunged just low enough. Galen's throat burned, and she swallowed hard. No matter what happened, she wasn't going to sleep with Rowan that night. She kept repeating the mantra to herself, hoping it would stick—although she never once believed the words. The second Rowan put a hand on her thigh, touched her face, or even looked at her in the right way, she'd be defenseless. She could only stand to hope Rowan didn't know that.

"Ready to go?" Rowan asked, standing with one hand on her curvy hips, a coy smile on her red lips.

"Sure. By the way, it's now ten pm on Christmas Eve. Where, exactly, were you planning to go?"

"Charlie's is open until two. I know it's not classy, but I like it."

Galen was familiar with Charlie's. She and Rowan had gone there on their second date. She knew it was no accident Rowan was suggesting it too. Galen told herself this was going to be even harder than she thought.

"Charlie's it is then. Come on. I'll drive."

Driving might make her feel a little more in control. On the surface, she was cold and aloof, trying to keep her heart as guarded as possible. Rowan's open, willing air gave the illusion Galen held all the cards. But that was bullshit. Rowan had walked away. She had every hand to play, whether Rowan knew it or not.

"We better walk. You know, in case we have one too many?" Rowan was right.

They walked the twenty minutes to the seedy bar that Galen always thought felt cozy and unimposing. It wasn't somewhere she took dates. But she'd taken Rowan there, because she wanted her to know her, to realize not everything had to be swanky and pretentious. Considering the holiday, a fair amount of people—mostly bearded millennials wearing flannel shirts and thick glasses they didn't need—were at the bar. The lighting was bright, and the TV played *A Christmas Carol* in black and white.

"What are you drinking?" Rowan asked, once they'd staked out two seats at the bar. Rowan always told Galen she preferred sitting at the bar, so she could be closer to her. Considering how independent Rowan usually was, Galen found it hard not to find this preference incredibly endearing.

"The usual. Bulleit on the rocks." Galen kept her voice cool, but she was facing Rowan. Her knees touched Rowan's thighs, and it was impossible to deny the electricity she felt.

"You know Bulleit is extremely homophobic?"

"What do you mean?"

"I heard that the Bulleit family just disowned their daughter for coming out as queer," Rowan said.

"Huh. Guess I better find a new brand, huh?" Galen laughed. "Starting tomorrow."

When the bartender came, Galen ordered her drink, and Rowan echoed her request. Rowan never drank hard liquor, and Galen wondered what she needed the liquid courage for.

They made small talk for several more minutes, both of them downing their drinks faster than Galen deemed normal. They laughed about nothing and shared their sentiments about the narrowly avoided catastrophe of the day. It was like nothing had changed. They were them again. The feeling that the last several weeks just disappeared left Galen anxious. She couldn't forget. She couldn't let herself, no matter how good the moment felt.

"Tell me why we're really here, Ro," Galen asked. The small talk had ebbed, and her head was starting to swim with several glasses of whiskey.

"I made a mistake, Galen."

Galen had a feeling this was going to be her answer. She just hadn't yet decided what her response would be. More than anything, she wanted to hear these words. She wanted to welcome Rowan back with her arms wide open, pick up where they left off. She wanted to believe what Rowan was telling her. But she had put up the caution tape, and it just wasn't going to be that easy.

"Go on," Galen said.

"I ended this because I thought I was doing the right thing. I thought I was being a 'good person' by choosing Brian because he needed me more."

"You don't know that he needed you more."

"Oh, come on. I was his whole life. You know that," Rowan said.

"Just because I didn't drop to my knees and beg like a loser doesn't mean I didn't love you just as much, you know. Actually, I loved you more. Besides, do you really want to be with the person who needs you? Isn't it better to be with the person who chooses you?"

"What?" Rowan furrowed her brow, clearly confused.

"I want to be with someone who wakes up every morning and chooses to love me. Someone who's with me because they want to be, not because they need to be."

"I...you're right. I don't want someone to need me. I want someone who loves me. And I want to be wildly, crazily in love with them. Because now I know I'm capable of that. I know, because I feel that way about you, Galen."

Galen's chest warmed, and her stomach tossed and twisted. "Are you saying you want me back?"

Rowan leaned toward her, but before she could reach Galen's lips, Galen turned her head.

"I don't know."

"Why not? We were great together. And you can't tell me you don't still love me too. I can see it all over your face. You're very transparent, you know." Rowan winked at her.

"Of course I still love you. But you really hurt me, Ro. I mean, really bad. I don't know if I can go through that again."

But Galen had thought about that before agreeing to meet Rowan. Letting her in was a risk. At any point, Rowan could change her mind again and hurt her. And that would kill her. But Galen had survived it once before. She would survive again. And it might just be a chance worth taking.

"I'm not going to hurt you again. I promise."

"How can you promise me that?"

"Because I'm sure of it." Rowan leaned forward again, and this time, Galen didn't stop her. Their lips connected, and Galen melted into her seat. A million pounds dropped off her and rose into the air, and everything inside her settled for the first time in a month. She reminded herself that sometimes a kiss could tell you more than words ever could.

"I'm scared, okay?" Galen said, once she'd pulled away and forced her eyes to focus again.

"I am too. I'm scared because you're the love of my life. And at any minute, I could lose you. I mean, you're Galen Burgess. Do you have any idea what kind of insurance policy you need for that level of liability?"

"Don't bring my reputation into this. It wasn't an issue before."

"And it's not now. But love is always a risk. When you feel that way, the rug could always get pulled out from under you. It's the beautiful thing about it."

Rowan was right. Regardless of the mistakes they'd made, loving someone was never without risks. But what was a life without love? Maybe Galen used to be okay with it. But the alternative now seemed lonely and empty.

"Promise me again," Galen said. Rowan couldn't actually promise her she'd never hurt her again. No one could make that promise. But Galen needed to hear it anyway.

Rowan raised her left hand in the air and extended her pinky finger. "Pinky promise."

"Pinky promise?" Galen laughed.

"Yes! This is serious stuff! Now, pinky promise me you won't hurt me either."

Galen paused, then returned the gesture, locking her little finger with Rowan's.

"Pinky promise."

Each of them kissed her own thumb, smiling. This was ridiculous. Neither of them could promise forever. But somehow, Galen couldn't imagine an easier promise to keep.

"I love you, Galen. And now I know that's more important than anything," Rowan said.

Galen ran her fingers through the wisps of hair that hung over Rowan's shoulder, studying her face. It was the face of someone who had changed her life—someone who had made her better. It was the face of someone who Galen so easily found herself giving her all to. And she knew, without a doubt, that all they really needed was one more chance to make the rest of their lives happen.

About the Author

Emily Smith is a full-time emergency room physician assistant in Boston and spends the majority of her days putting in stitches and helping people however she can. This provides great material for her books, which she loves to write in all of her spare time. She lives outside of Boston with her cat, Charlie.

Books Available from Bold Strokes Books

All of Me by Emily Smith. When chief surgical resident Galen Burgess meets her new intern, Rowan Duncan, she may finally discover that doing what you've always done will only give you what you've always had. (978-1-163555-321-5)

As the Crow Flies by Karen F. Williams. Romance seems to be blooming all around, but problems arise when a restless ghost emerges from the ether to roam the dark corners of this haunting tale. (978-1-163555-285-0)

Both Ways by Ileandra Young. SPEAR agent Danika Karson races to protect the city from a supernatural threat and must rely on the woman she's trained to despise: Rayne, an achingly beautiful vampire. (978-1-163555-298-0)

Calendar Girl by Georgia Beers. Forced to work together, Addison Fairchild and Kate Cooper discover that opposites really do attract. (978-1-163555-333-8)

Lovebirds by Lisa Moreau. Two women from different worlds collide in a small California mountain town, each with a mission that doesn't include falling in love. (978-1-163555-213-3)

Media Darling by Fiona Riley. Can Hollywood bad girl Emerson and reluctant celebrity gossip reporter Hayley work together to make each other's dreams come true? Or will Emerson's secrets ruin not one career, but two? (978-1-163555-278-2)

Stroke of Fate by Renee Roman. Can Sean Moore live up to her reputation and save Jade Rivers from the stalker determined to end Jade's career and, ultimately, her life? (978-1-163555-162-4)

The Rise of the Resistance by Jackie D. The soul of America has been lost for almost a century. A few people may be the difference between a phoenix rising to save the masses or permanent destruction. (978-1-163555-259-1)

The Sex Therapist Next Door by Meghan O'Brien. At the intersection of sex and intimacy, anything is possible. Even love. (978-1-163555-296-6)

Unexpected Lightning by Cass Sellars. Lightning strikes once more when Sydney and Parker fight a dangerous stranger who threatens the peace they both desperately want. (978-1-163555-276-8)

Unforgettable by Elle Spencer. When one night changes a lifetime... Two romance novellas from best-selling author Elle Spencer. (978-1-63555-429-8)

Against All Odds by Kris Bryant, Maggie Cummings, M. Ullrich. Peyton and Tory escaped death once, but will they survive when Bradley's determined to make his kill rate one hundred percent? (978-1-163555-193-8)

Autumn's Light by Aurora Rey. Casual hookups aren't supposed to include romantic dinners and meeting the family. Can Mat Pero see beyond the heartbreak that led her to keep her worlds so separate, and will Graham Connor be waiting if she does? (978-1-163555-272-0)

Breaking the Rules by Larkin Rose. When Virginia and Carmen are thrown together by an embarrassing mistake they find out their stubborn determination isn't so heroic after all. (978-1-163555-261-4)

Broad Awakening by Mickey Brent. In the sequel to *Underwater Vibes*, Hélène and Sylvie find ruts in their road to eternal bliss. (978-1-163555-270-6)

Broken Vows by MJ Williamz. Sister Mary Margaret must reconcile her divided heart or risk losing a love that just might be heaven sent. (978-1-163555-022-1)

Flesh and Gold by Ann Aptaker. Havana, 1952, where art thief and smuggler Cantor Gold dodges gangland bullets and mobsters' schemes while she searches Havana's steamy Red Light district for her kidnapped love. (978-1-163555-153-2)

Isle of Broken Years by Jane Fletcher. Spanish noblewoman Catalina de Valasco is in peril, even before the pirates holding her for ransom sail into seas destined to become known as the Bermuda Triangle. (978-1-163555-175-4)

Love Like This by Melissa Brayden. Hadley Cooper and Spencer Adair set out to take the fashion world by storm. If only they knew their hearts were about to be taken. (978-1-163555-018-4)

Secrets On the Clock by Nicole Disney. Jenna and Danielle love their jobs helping endangered children, but that might not be enough to stop them from breaking the rules by falling in love. (978-1-163555-292-8)

Unexpected Partners by Michelle Larkin. Dr. Chloe Maddox tries desperately to deny her attraction for Detective Dana Blake as they flee from a serial killer who's hunting them both. (978-1-163555-203-4)

A Fighting Chance by T. L. Hayes. Will Lou be able to come to terms with her past to give love a fighting chance? (978-1-163555-257-7)

Chosen by Brey Willows. When the choice is adapt or die, can love save us all? (978-1-163555-110-5)

Death Checks In by David S. Pederson. Despite Heath's promises to Alan to not get involved, Heath can't resist investigating a shopkeeper's murder in Chicago, which dashes their plans for a romantic weekend getaway. (978-1-163555-329-1)

Gnarled Hollow by Charlotte Greene. After they are invited to study a secluded nineteenth-century estate, a former English professor and a group of historians discover that they will have to fight against the unknown if they have any hope of staying alive. (978-1-163555-235-5)

Jacob's Grace by C.P. Rowlands. Captain Tag Becket wants to keep her head down and her past behind her, but her feelings for AJ's second-in-command, Grace Fields, makes keeping secrets next to impossible. (978-1-163555-187-7)

On the Fly by PJ Trebelhorn. Hockey player Courtney Abbott is content with her solitary life until visiting concert violinist Lana Caruso makes her second-guess everything she always thought she wanted. (978-1-163555-255-3)

Passionate Rivals by Radclyffe. Professional rivalry and long-simmering passions create a combustible combination when Emmett McCabe and Sydney Stevens are forced to work together, especially when past attractions won't stay buried. (978-1-163555-231-7)

Proxima Five by Missouri Vaun. When geologist Leah Warren crash-lands on a preindustrial planet and is claimed by its tyrant, Tiago, will clan warrior Keegan's love for Leah give her the strength to defeat him? (978-1-163555-122-8)

Racing Hearts by Dena Blake. When you cross a hot-tempered race car mechanic with a reckless cop, the result can only be spontaneous combustion. (978-1-163555-251-5)

Shadowboxer by Jessica L. Webb. Jordan McAddie is prepared to keep her street kids safe from a dangerous underground protest group, but she isn't prepared for her first love to walk back into her life. (978-1-163555-267-6)

The Tattered Lands by Barbara Ann Wright. As Vandra and Lilani strive to make peace, they slowly fall in love. With mistrust and murder surrounding them, only their faith in each other can keep their plan to save the world from falling apart. (978-1-163555-108-2)

Captive by Donna K. Ford. To escape a human trafficking ring, Greyson Cooper and Olivia Danner become players in a game of deceit and violence. Will their love stand a chance? (978-1-63555-215-7)

Crossing the Line by CF Frizzell. The Mob discovers a nemesis within its ranks, and in the ultimate retaliation, draws Stick McLaughlin from anonymity by threatening everything she holds dear. (978-1-63555-161-7)

Love's Verdict by Carsen Taite. Attorneys Landon Holt and Carly Pachett want the exact same thing: the only open partnership spot at their prestigious criminal defense firm. But will they compromise their careers for love? (978-1-63555-042-9)

Precipice of Doubt by Mardi Alexander & Laurie Eichler. Can Cole Jameson resist her attraction to her boss, veterinarian Jodi Bowman, or will she risk a workplace romance and her heart? (978-1-63555-128-0)

Savage Horizons by CJ Birch. Captain Jordan Kellow's feelings for Lt. Ali Ash have her past and future colliding, setting in motion a series of events that strands her crew in an unknown galaxy thousands of light years from home. (978-1-63555-250-8)

Secrets of the Last Castle by A. Rose Mathieu. When Elizabeth Campbell represents a young man accused of murdering an elderly woman, her investigation leads to an abandoned plantation that reveals many dark Southern secrets. (978-1-63555-240-9)

Take Your Time by VK Powell. A neurotic parrot brings police officer Grace Booker and temporary veterinarian Dr. Dani Wingate together in the tiny town of Pine Cone, but their unexpected attraction keeps the sparks flying. (978-1-63555-130-3)

The Last Seduction by Ronica Black. When you allow true love to elude you once and you desperately regret it, are you brave enough to grab it when it comes around again? (978-1-63555-211-9)

The Shape of You by Georgia Beers. Rebecca McCall doesn't play it safe, but when sexy Spencer Thompson joins her workout class, their non-stop sparring forces her to face her ultimate challenge—a chance at love. (978-1-63555-217-1)

Exposed by MJ Williamz. The closet is no place to live if you want to find true love. (978-1-62639-989-1)

Force of Fire: Toujours a Vous by Ali Vali. Immortals Kendal and Piper welcome their new child and celebrate the defeat of an old enemy, but another ancient evil is about to awaken deep in the jungles of Costa Rica. (978-1-63555-047-4)

Holding Their Place by Kelly A. Wacker. Together Dr. Helen Connery and ambulance driver Julia March, discover that goodness, love, and passion can be found in the most unlikely and even dangerous places during WWI. (978-1-63555-338-3)

Landing Zone by Erin Dutton. Can a career veteran finally discover a love stronger than even her pride? (978-1-63555-199-0)

Love at Last Call by M. Ullrich. Is balancing business, friendship, and love more than any willing woman can handle? (978-1-63555-197-6)

Pleasure Cruise by Yolanda Wallace. Spencer Collins and Amy Donovan have few things in common, but a Caribbean cruise offers both women an unexpected chance to face one of their greatest fears: falling in love. (978-1-63555-219-5)

Running Off Radar by MB Austin. Maji's plans to win Rose back are interrupted when work intrudes and duty calls her to help a SEAL team stop a Russian mobster from harvesting gold from the bottom of Sitka Sound. (978-1-63555-152-5)

Shadow of the Phoenix by Rebecca Harwell. In the final battle for the fate of Storm's Quarry, even Nadya's and Shay's powers may not be enough. (978-1-63555-181-5)

Take a Chance by D. Jackson Leigh. There's hardly a woman within fifty miles of Pine Cone that veterinarian Trip Beaumont can't charm, except for the irritating new cop, Jamie Grant, who keeps leaving parking tickets on her truck. (978-1-63555-118-1)

The Outcasts by Alexa Black. Spacebus driver Sue Jones is running from her past. When she crash-lands on a faraway world, the Outcast Kara might be her chance for redemption. (978-1-63555-242-3)